THE REAL PRESIDENT

To Kingsley,

With kind Regards

Noah Kaindama

12/01/16

THE REAL PRESIDENT

by

Noah Kaindama

DB
DIADEM BOOKS

THE REAL PRESIDENT
All Rights Reserved. Copyright © 2015 **Noah Kaindama**

No part of this book may be reproduced or transmitted in any form or by any means, graphic, electronic, or mechanical, including photocopying, recording, taping or by any information storage or retrieval system, without the permission in writing from the copyright holder.

The right of Noah Kaindama to be identified as the author of this work has been asserted in accordance with the Copyright, Designs and Patents Act 1988 sections 77 and 78.
Published by Diadem Books

For information, please contact:

Diadem Books
16 Lethen View
Tullibody
ALLOA
FK10 2GE
Scotland UK
www.diadembooks.com

The views expressed in this work are solely those of the author and do not necessarily reflect the views of the publisher, and the publisher hereby disclaims any responsibility for them.

This is a work of fiction. Names, characters and incidents are products of the author's imagination.
All people mentioned in this book are fictitious; any resemblance to real persons is purely coincidental.

ISBN: 978-1-326-50783-1

*To mum, my wife, my children and all my family
whose belief in me
has been of invaluable encouragement.*

PART I

Chapter One

THERE WAS FEAR, much fear in the land. You feared for your life, for your son's life and for your daughter's life. You feared for your wife, your relatives and friends. Fear in the streets, classrooms, doctors' consulting rooms and in the home. There was fear everywhere. Danger was everywhere and always lurking.

Fear had increased in the past few weeks since the death of the leader of the Mine Workers Union. He was a rising star who spoke more sense than the career politicians. He was an intelligent middle-aged man who people secretly looked to as the top challenger to the incumbent president. Sadly, he was brutally murdered in front of his house as he waited for his gate to open. He was driving in from a meeting to resolve the current government's unilateral decision to cut the miners' salary by one third. The people knew who killed him. It was the President and his ruthless and mindless supporters. This was a regular occurrence since Chimwanga became president thirty years ago. He had killed many potential leaders and of course anyone who dared criticise his regime openly. The methods varied: accidents on the road, collapsing in hotels or getting shot in front of their homes or in their houses. Others simply disappeared without any trace. It was an open secret that the killer in their midst was their own president.

There was no freedom of speech; people only whispered their concerns to trusted confidants. Even this was dangerous because many people were known to have been betrayed by friends or family. Nobody knew how big brother was watching and listening but he was. There were militias everywhere, pushing people, chopping off heads and limbs of those suspected of dissent. Stories were doing the rounds of parents disappearing after grumbling about the state of the country and the economy in the privacy of their homes. This was President Chimwanga's Lubanda.

Beyond the fear was anger, much anger. Everyone knew there was no hope of a reprieve for the Lubandans for as long as he remained president. They had been trapped for years by the first vote they cast for Chimawanga; if only they had chosen someone else who was more sensible. There was a bleeding cry for a saviour who probably would never come. They were stuck with a criminal, a viscous murderer and a monster. There was no escape. So to release their frustration they whispered under their torn blankets.

To a visitor from any better run country, Lubanda was a failed state. Lubanda under Chimwanga was politically and economically a failed state. There was no order; unemployed street boys had power to kill and to maim with impunity. Civil servants had powers to collect *tax* for each piece of work they did, not for the state but for their pockets. Minsters had powers beyond their jurisdictions; they were juries, judges and mini presidents, as long as they did it in the name and on behalf of President Chimwanga, in exchange for unreserved loyalty to him. The policemen had become national militias for the President. They too had powers, to charge anybody anything for their personal gain. The soldiers had been turned into robots; as long as Chimwanga threw a few coins at them they would crawl on their stomachs to polish his shoes. They were soldiers for Chimwanga, not Lubanda. The tragedy is that if you live in a failed state, all you know are the failed systems. They are your norms; you defend them and continue with broken systems then dutifully pass them on to the next generation. They are symptoms of a culture of failure.

The biggest political joke was in the appointments of personnel. The President had absolute powers. He appointed his children, brothers, cousins, nephews, illiterates, concubines and whoever shared blood or language with him to power, irrespective of ability or intellect. For example, his wife's brother was the Minister of Home Affairs, his nephew was the Minister of Defence and the Foreign Affairs Minister was a niece.

There were no credible systems for making policies. Any minister or civil servant with position would make a policy. There was no accountability. Since every minister or political affiliate of the president was like a war lord, policies were made on the hoof. The President would flout the law and the constitution any time he chose. This was far from any semblance of an organised country.

Economically, Lubanda was flat and non-existent. Apart from a few companies that paid tax and were often controlled by the President, there was no organised economy as the world defines it. There was more activity between people than institutions. All economic institutions were shunned either in fear of the President appropriating what did not belong to him or the institutions were corrupt and incompetent. People traded with one another in any way they felt convenient. They bartered goods, used any currency they wanted or kept the money under mattresses, in trunks and tins at home as the local currency was rendered utterly useless. In fact all major currencies had taken over from the lindi as legal tender. You could trade with the dollar, pound, yuan and God knows what else people used. Essential commodities were hard to find and price controls of everything from houses to sugar was controlled by the President whenever he felt like it. Survival of the fittest was more than a cliché – it was a real life, daily activity.

The judiciary was too much of a mockery to give it any credibility. Otherwise, the whole government machinery and system was a shambles. Public services existed only in name: hospitals became death traps and had very few trained or poorly trained staff. If you were admitted to hospital, you were likely to die of secondary diseases contracted from the hospital premises. The single dirty and torn blanket on the bed was never washed and the mattresses were infested with bedbugs that grew bold from feasting on its helpless visitors. It was better to die at home than to be admitted to the hospital. Hospital beds and nurses spread more diseases. More deaths were caused by preventable diseases.

School buildings had collapsed and teachers were teaching lessons under trees irrespective of the weather. Exams were sold like commodities, and teachers abused children at will.

Most towns had very poor sanitation. People lived in houses with blocked toilets, drank untreated dirty water and prayed to God for every breath of life.

The President behaved like he owned everything in Lubanda; the people, the houses, the land, the wives, the children and everything else. He had no concept of the difference between owning and serving. He behaved like someone only answerable to the invisible God. Or was he playing god?

So you would understand why there was a buzz in the country when it was rumoured one of the successful young businessmen had called a press conference. Few people knew about him but he was well known in business circles, especially with the subsistence framers who benefited from his chain of rural shops through which he marketed local produce. Nobody knew what he was going to say. Some speculated he was going to announce the setting up of a very big company while others thought he was joining politics though they had never heard him make a political speech. For several days, it became an active point of discussion; secretly, as most of the people wouldn't dare say it loudly for fear of the government's wrath.

The announcement seemed to come at an opportune time. The latest killing of the Union leader had annoyed all the few donors who gave Chimwanga's government money in exchange for access to the minerals. International pressure on these donors made them publicly demand that he gives people freedom of speech. Without them, the government would completely shut down within a matter of a few days. Chimwanga, who had never listened to these demands before, appeared to be listening even if it were only necessary for the political game. For the first time in many years, press conferences were grudgingly allowed, provided the people concerned had permits. However, like everything else in Lubanda, the final decision to grant permission to gather rested with the President.

Chapter Two

THE ROOM was fully packed, hot and sticky. The aroma from the different perfumes the women were wearing made the room smell like an altar of essence. All around the journalists were pushing, shoving and bumping around, jostling to find the best view for the camera. The room itself was elegantly decorated with marble tiles, a blend of local and foreign artwork and photographs: graduation photos, pictures of iconic buildings from Europe and marvellous engineering projects from around the world. The ceiling was carefully decorated in white contrasting contours with beautiful crystal chandelier glass lampshades. A large window revealed the back of the house. Lines of well measured fruit trees in the orchard and green fields backed by the bank of a stream made the place an oasis of calm and tranquillity. These luxuries were enjoyed only by the few in the land of Lubanda, and even fewer deserved them because they had not earned them.

Lubanda is what remained of what was called the Luba-Lunda Empire – a beautiful country bordering what are now called Angola, Congo and Zambia. Out of a population of seven million, many lived in abject poverty in rural areas. The beautiful countryside consisted of flat plains with umbrella canopies of semi-Savannah and equatorial trees; the many rivers flowing with clean fresh water and rich fertile soils constituted untapped wealth. The flora and fauna found here is unique to these lands. On a good hot day, the bush babies and monkeys summersaulted in the trees, while the music of the whispering birds and the distant echo of the honey hunter tingled the chords of the peace and serenity of the countryside.

In spite of all this wealth and the gold, diamond, and many precious stones embedded in the rocks below the ground, land was either given freely to unscrupulous investors or left to waste while people starved and died.

Everyone was expectant and excited. It had been rare in the past thirty years to cover an event other than the comical government functions. Often at these events an aura of fear and resentment prevailed; but on this occasion there was excitement, relaxed excitement. No policemen, no dancing and singing, just smiles.

The double door swung open, held firmly by two security men. A man in his late thirties walked in with a group of men and women flanking him on either side. He stood behind the only tall chair in the room, looked round and spoke:

"Good morning ladies and gentlemen."

"Shall we please sing the national anthem?" the man closest to him suggested.

Everyone sang enthusiastically as though each wanted to be heard by the man in a navy blue suit. The woman standing nearest to the high table did not only start the national anthem but sang it flawlessly with a smile that lightened the room.

"Thank you, please be seated. Thank you for attending the meeting at such a short notice following the change of venue. We were informed a few hours ago of the change of the venue in spite of having booked the hotel conference room three months ago."

"We understand, Sir," the audience shouted as though they had rehearsed their response.

No one appeared to listen to the rest of the introductions of the dignitaries as several glances and whispers heralded an air of anticipation. Finally, the chairman said, "Ladies and gentlemen, it is now my honour and pleasure to introduce to you Mr Moses Kabwibu Kamawu who will address you."

The room roared with whistling and clapping and quickly fell silent as Moses stood to address them. He had been quiet since he majestically walked in and appeared to be taking a memory snapshot of each person in the room.

"May I begin by welcoming you to my farm? It was not my intention to hold this press conference here since it is an important national event but I am pleased we have not been prevented from holding the meeting altogether, at least for now. You are most welcome.

"Every person in the land is aware of where we are as a nation. The economy is in shambles, unemployment is almost eighty percent, shelves in the shops are empty, innocent people are imprisoned or killed with impunity, not to mention schools without teachers, hospitals without doctors, nurses and medicines. They are indeed 'death traps' as some of you have reported. The policemen behave like party militias. Lawlessness has spread from the streets into government offices. The state of our nation is as desperate as a fish caught in a drying pond. We have retrogressed to pre-colonial days and if the slide is left to continue, we shall soon be in complete chaos. I love this nation, as I hope you do. I am here to inform the nation that I am going to stand as president in the next presidential and general elections to retrieve this country from the brink of complete collapse and anarchy. I shall offer the Lumbadan people visionary, well-informed and effective leadership."

A hushed silence descended upon the room. After a long pause, everyone broke into a round of applause; a five-minute standing ovation followed with plenty more worried faces from the local media.

"Many years ago when I was at secondary school, I visited my cousin in a once booming mining settlement town. It was a big African family with sons, daughters, nieces and nephews, in-laws and neighbours. They were living in beautiful houses with flowing water and sewage systems. They slept and ate in there. Today these houses are no longer fit for human habitation, yet thousands of people live in these conditions.

"Recently, I met a depressed family who just returned from many years abroad. They took a child to the so-called hospital; everyone who they saw asked for payment. They went to the Ministry of Lands office to get application forms for a piece of land and they were asked to pay for both the forms and the service; when they took their children to school, the head teacher asked for payment for a free admission! To get a job you have to pay, to bid for a contract you have to pay and soon to sleep and breathe in Lubanda you will have to pay. The corruption fee has even earned itself a prestigious name – *Chimwanga tax*.

"Dilapidation, neglect and abuse of power are now part of our culture. Nobody ever thinks of building decent accommodation or providing services that will keep people warm and healthy. Yet the few with access to power run themselves up and the country down. The obesity of Chimwanga's supporters, many of whom are his relatives and friends, is now accepted as the insignia of corruption.

"I have always wondered why some people in Africa come to power. Why do you think they seek power? If for money, why do they continue to steal more and more without the nudging prickly conscience reminding them what is enough? Why don't they understand the positive role of governance? Why don't they think of developing Lubanda like the developed countries that their evil feet have graced abroad? What is the driving motivation of an African leader like Chimawanga?

"I know why I have decided to go into politics, not only for Able but to make a difference to the lives of the Lubandans, those whose lives are lived day in and day out scavenging for basic needs. No wonder we have not moved with the rest of the world, we have remained behind in more ways than one, slipping further back into the dark ages. Leadership, real leadership, is lacking. We need to change and the time to change is now. The generation for change is ours. I therefore put myself forward to champion the change. That, ladies and gentlemen, is my passionate mission and reason for being here, to tell you that I am going to stand for the presidency of Lubanda.

"I know the dangers," he continued. "Many have tried in the past thirty years and have either been killed in mysterious circumstances or banished to prison. As you will all remember only too well, one of the brightest sons of Lubanda was butchered by a heartless regime. I know. If need be, may my blood join that of the fallen as a libation for change for Lubanda and Lubandans." Poignant words delivered with passion, precision and reassuring calm and confidence.

There were some in the audience who were already struggling to hold back tears and others simply could not believe what they had just heard. Nobody has ever criticised Chimwanga and lived.

One man was heard muttering to himself: "This man is either very brave or a fool. If he is brave I shall support him, if he is a fool I shall mourn him; but at least he is man enough to raise his head where many of us duck ours."

"In three weeks from today, I shall hold a press conference to give you details about a new political party under which I shall fight the elections but for now, all those who would like to support the movement for change, please register your interest on www.dyingforwhatyoulove.na.afr or send emails to dyingforwhatyoulove@na.afr, thank you."

With this announcement, he sat down as the audience once again stood up to yet another burst of applause. Social media was running wild, wanting to know who this man committing suicide was. There were already predictions of how long he would live. His photos were popping out on watches, mobile gadgets and screens.

"Questions please, give us your name and the organisation you work for."

The first hand up belonged to the smiling woman.

"Yes, Madam?"

"I am... mmm... delighted to be here, Sir. Two questions. First, are you married?"

Laughter in the room.

"Sorry madam, what is your name?"

"I am sorry, I am Delilah Banda Mashidika from the *Citizen Chronicle*. This is gr..grea...great news for me indeed. How can... we... help the movement?"

Moses stood up. "Miss or Mrs Mashidika, Madam?"

"Miss Sir."

"Thank you Miss Mashidika. Firstly, ladies and gentlemen, give the lady a round of applause for leading us in the national anthem. I shall start with your last question. I am also delighted that you can so publicly come forward to join the movement for change. I think you are a great talent and I will be happy to work with you. Please leave your details at the end of the meeting."

Delighted, Delilah turned around, full of smiles as usual while paying attention to the next answer.

"The first question is easy to answer. Yes, I'm married to a beautiful woman like you with two little children. But Delilah, my family is much bigger; the children of Lubanda are my children, every Lubandan is part of my family. So Delilah, you too are my family – that is why I want to serve this great country."

"Next question please. Yes, Sir, the gentleman in a blue shirt," the chairman almost shouting across the room.

"I'm Thomas Kamushi from *The Times of Lubanda*. Sir, you have no party and followers, yet you believe you will win the elections in six months! How will you achieve that?"

"Mr. Kamushi, thank you for a very good question. You do not need to have a party to stand for an election. According to clause 132 section 4.1, you can stand for any office as a citizen. The party in itself is the machinery for organisation. Today I am launching the movement for change; in three weeks, I shall be launching our party and manifesto through which we shall fight the elections.

"Two more questions please."

Suddenly, there was a loud knock on the door and the Regional Police Commissioner rushed in sweating.

"You did not tell us the press conference was going to be streamed live on the internet. The meeting should therefore be brought to an end immediately. Everyone, please leave."

Moses calmly motioned to those who were standing ready to leave, to sit down. He stood up.

"Mr Commissioner, according to the constitution clause 7 section 2.1, you have trespassed my property, violated our freedom of speech and gathering. Your uniform suggests you are a servant of the people yet your actions show that you are a slave of the current regime. This is my house and these are my guests. We shall not be hurried to close this national event. We have the right to be in this country, to gather and discuss issues of importance for Lubanda; to enjoy all freedoms guaranteed in the original constitution of independence agreed by our founding fathers. If you want to arrest me I will come with you to the police station but not until my press conference is properly concluded. You are welcome to join us, Sir, have a cup of coffee and some cakes."

Moses was not a descendant of privilege and fortune but had a privileged upbringing. His mother grew up as a village girl, the daughter of a subsistence farmer in the central region of Lubanda. She went to the local village school and later earned her place at the District High School. Upon finishing high school, she went on to train as a nurse.

She knew Moses' father, Jonathan, from their days in the village. They both came from adjacent neighbouring villages. As children they played together, in fact, during *magogu*, the children's role play, Jonathan always picked her for a wife. Little did they know one day they would be married for real.

Jonathan grew up like most boys in his time, village boys with village aspirations. He finished his primary school but had no money to proceed to High School. He dropped out to do odd jobs for a living. He loved reading and school. After dropping out he decided to put aside any little extra money he had to spare to pay for evening classes. He did not earn much from doing chores for people but whatever he earned fed him, his disabled mother and younger sister. He was a young carer for himself, his sister and mother but he handled his responsibilities with complete loyalty and determination. He smiled more than he cried.

After five years, he got enough credits to be admitted to the local college where he studied public administration. Upon finishing his course, he got a job in a bank. He was known to be an organised, disciplined and hardworking man. He was the first to come to work and the last to leave. His hunger for knowledge did not end there. He knew the power of knowledge. Soon the company began promoting him through the ranks. One of his managers was quoted saying that "Through the conscientious effort of Jonathan, the company foiled a historical colossal fraud."

He went on to study law and rise until he became the company secretary. One day he had a conversation with an expatriate colleague who had come to train staff.

"Jonathan, why are some of the colleagues begging money from me? They work in the bank and are paid well."

"Because they have responsibilities."

"What do you mean? We all have responsibilities."

"No, you do not understand, they have bigger families than you. They have extended families to help. This makes us poor. I know, but to us relationships are more important than material things. My salary cheque feeds a village!"

"So you spend your money before you earn it and live on borrowing?"

"Do not patronise me please, I have never asked for money from you."

"I am sorry, I didn't mean to offend you. I just want to understand the culture here. The other day a bank manager asked me for money yet he is paid a lot of money."

"You white people are rich, you have a lot of money you spend on luxurious lifestyles, but we don't have extra money to enjoy like you. We enjoy the company and love of our relatives."

"Can I ask you one question, Jonathan – do you people budget your money?"

"That is patronising! What do you mean by 'you people'? Do you mean me, or Lubadans?"

"You!"

"To be honest, not quite. I know how I spend my money."

"Do you think the extended family can be abused and also develop a culture of dependence?"

"I think yes, to some extent, but it is part of our culture."

"Even when it holds you and countries back?"

"Even when it holds us back. Please do not insult my culture."

"No, of course not. I am just curious."

"There is nothing wrong with the extended family but you should make each member of the family understand their responsibilities."

"What exactly are you saying?"

"That is why you should have a budget and a plan for your finances. I have money not because there is a mine where every white person goes to fill their pockets but because I have a plan for my financial wellbeing and I budget. I know how to manage my finances. It is not how much money one earns or makes but how much he keeps."

"Good for you, but it does not work like that here, I am afraid."

"It is not easy to budget because there are needs in the family daily."

"Well Jonathan, one day before I go back, ask me how to keep money and let money work for you. Maybe that is what's lacking; financial literacy is discipline, not money. You are a good young man, I like you. Good night."

"I will think about it, but please no colonial lessons! What are you doing this weekend?"

"Reading newspapers and talking to family, nothing special."

"Do you play golf?"

"A little."

I am thinking of playing golf but I have no idea what it is because there is no golf course in my village! Can you teach me please?"

"Only if you stop accusing me of making colonial references!"

"It comes as a natural guard to us! No, I think you are a decent man."

"I shall come with a taxi to pick you up from the hotel at 10.00 am."

"See you tomorrow Jonathan."

On the way home and throughout the night Jonathan was thinking about the conversation. "I detest the arrogance of these chaps but it is true I do not budget. Lately my finances have been stressed. Does he have a point? It is funny, I work in the bank yet I do not budget! Is this the reason most of us live a life of hand to mouth?" He thought of bank workers in financial distress, corruption, the country's bankruptcy. "Could this be a result of poor personal and financial management?" He was fast going down that poor road too. He hardly had money left for the last week to his next payment. He did not understand where his money went. It was impossible to prosper under the current situation – but he loved his family and he was expected to help. After all, abroad, old people and the unemployed were looked after by the state, but not in developing countries like Lubanda. So he has become a source for social welfare. Surely, the financial pressure with greed lurking in the corners was one of the causes of poor governance, corruption and perhaps premature deaths. "Oh, well, I should stop worrying because I cannot change the world. But can I change *my* world?" he asked himself as he drifted into sleep.

The golf lesson was the most valuable life lesson Jonathan had ever received. He learnt the rules of two games. His new friend told him how it was important to have a financial plan. The key was to budget. He explained that although he did not have the weight of extended family responsibilities, he had financial commitments.

After the golf lesson, Jonathan wrote down his financial plan and drew up his budget. In it he put 5% for his children although he was not married. 10% went to his wedding plan, 15% to helping family, 10% for a car, 30% savings and 30% for monthly upkeep.

As a much disciplined man, Jonathan followed this plan religiously. He saw the wisdom of the plan as his investments grew. He diversified into property. He had a lavish wedding to his long-time neighbour girlfriend. When Moses was born, three years after their marriage, the children's trust fund had enough money to send him to a very good private school.

Moses therefore grew up in a life different to his father. He went to private schools and excelled. He was more focused and intelligent than many of his peers. It was no accident that when he went to the university, he stood out and attracted both admirers and adversaries. It was events at the university that shaped his life and carved his destiny.

Chapter Three

REACTIONS TO MOSES' ANNOUNCEMENT were mixed. The general public did not seem to have an opinion and of course they dared not express their opinions publicly as doing so was tantamount to an application for sudden death or a beating from the cadres that were paid meagre periodic allowances to intimidate, maim and kill dissenting voices at whatever level of society. However, the middle classes appeared to have noted the event and hushed conversations could be heard in corridors and corners. Much of the reaction was in the private and foreign media. They splashed the handsome image of Moses accompanied by his verbatim speech. Some praised him for his courage for rising against a tyrannical regime whose mercilessness chilled every spine in the land. In contrast, they compared him to the incumbent whose virtues were all but in spilt blood.

The following morning Moses sat down to read the newspapers. The headlines that enthused him the most were outrageously wild with a tone of national rebellion, calling him "The Messiah," "The True Leader" and "The Best of Lubanda."

The government-controlled media either hardly mentioned the press conference or belittled the candidate. One paper called him a little baby that was crying for attention.

The telephone rang. "Hullo mum, how are you?"

"Have you seen what is in the papers?"

"What do you think, mum?"

"I am worried, Son, he will unleash his forces of evil on you and us. Are you sure you want to do this? They are calling you a saviour! This is dangerous."

"Yes, mum, that is the reason I want to stand so you will not be living in fear. I am aware it is a dangerous undertaking but God will be on the side of good. Do not worry too much. It is not a gamble but I know it is a risk. I am sure God will not allow me to die twice."

After a deep sigh at the other end, in a shaky voice, "Son, we shall fight with you but from now on, remember you are the enemy of the state."

"Thanks mum, but not enemy of the state, enemy of the corrupt regime, enemy of Chimwanga and his henchmen. In their hearts, the majority of the people are on our side."

"Bye Son, I love you, please take care."

"Bye mum," as he slowly put his phone down.

Rachel who had sneaked into the room drew close to him, kissed him and embraced him like a child who will not let go.

"Who rang?"

"Mum."

"How is she?"

"Worried, uneasy, fearful, scared, concerned, anxious, apprehensive…"

"That is how we are all feeling, Moses; your parents, sister, and friends and…"

"And who?"

"Me. In spite of the many hours of discussions we have had about this move, I am worried and fearful."

Moses walked to the window, looked at his beautiful garden, and picked up the papers strewn everywhere around the breakfast table before putting them away in a pile. He turned round, held Rachel's hand and went into the garden without uttering a word. He grabbed a fruit, took a bite and offered it to Rachel who also took a bite and handed it back to him.

"Rachel, the beginning is hard and will be hard. First we have to win the people over and persuade them to fight with us. We shall do this not by giving money or goods, but by sharing our dream and offering them partnership in the dream for this country. The power of our ideas and the power of our convictions will win hearts and minds. Our opponent has built a machinery of intimidation and oppression; nobody likes the acts and behaviour of a tyranny. The people submit because they think they are not strong enough to fight back. The ordinary person does not realise the power he or she has to fight oppression. My task is to convince them that they are powerful, harness that power and together we can win. We *shall* win. But you need to sow the seed, tender the plant and harvest the fruit of peace, dignity and prosperity for this nation."

He gripped the remaining fruit and munched it ferociously, turned round and held Rachel by the shoulders and looked straight into her eyes: "Are you ready for this fight?"

"Yes. But that does not mean I am not fearful darling," she said as tears ran down her cheeks.

"My father often quoted a verse from the Bible: 'God has not given us the spirit of fear, but of power and love, and a sound mind' – with these words we shall overcome."

"Come on, let us go, we have a long and busy day ahead."

While Moses was dealing with these emotional battles, there was a battle taking place in the Cabinet office. Either by coincidence or design, there was a rare cabinet meeting called the morning following Moses' announcement. All cabinet ministers were in attendance.

As usual, these events were rare because the president opted to do whatever he wanted without consulting the cabinet. When a cabinet meeting was held, it was an excuse for pomp and ceremony. First, there was a knock on the door and everybody in the room stood up to attention. Two policemen walked in, to stand at the back of the room. Two bodyguards follow the advance group.

Then praise singer entered showering the President with undeserved acclaim. The President entered slowly, like a bride.

"Here comes the President, here comes the King, here comes the lion, do you all hear me?"

"Yes, we do!" the ministers responded with false smiles.

"The lion that devours its enemies, the lion that breaks bones, the lion the king of the jungle. Who can stand in his way, who can challenge him, who is above our leader?"

"No one," the audience responded.

"Here comes our leader, the only leader, the true leader, His Excellency President Chimwanga!"

Finally, two more policemen come in and stood in front followed by two more bodyguards behind the procession. Two of the policemen, in a rehearsed movement, draw the big chair and the President sat down. All policemen except the senior bodyguard who stood directly behind the president left the room.

The only difference this time was that the President was wearing a broad smile as he entered the room. When this happened, it was a sign of good things to come.

"Good morning ladies and gentlemen, there is only one agenda today. Professor Chilomba, our new Minister of finance, successfully negotiated with the donors and secured one hundred million dollars for projects. Congratulations, Mr Professor. I was right to bring you on board. Although you have not been a minister for a long time, you know the tricks. Professor, the tricks of the lecture room are different from those of the Cabinet Office and politics. You have to learn and you will do so quickly. Well done."

"Sir," interjected one of the inner circle ministers, "Did you hear the press conference?"

"Hon Chimovu, please be serious, we are here to talk about serious matters, not boys playing imitation football in the streets. Please do not talk to me about this nonsense again; you know what we do with our opponents so do not waste my time. I am here until death do me part."

He turned to face those assembled before him. "Ladies and gentlemen, I have decided to award each of you, the ministers, the chief police officers and the chiefs of defence, a hundred percent salary increase from today. The loan secured last week by our professor will pay for this."

"Yeeeeesssss, hear hear! Thank you Mr President. I need another farm."

"Excuse me Mr President, I'm sorry, Sir, the loan was not for salaries," protested the Minister of Finance.

"Professor, Professor Chilomba, please calm down. This is the way it works. When the money comes to my government, I am in charge and I can do whatever I want to do with it. So I have decided to give you a share for your hard work."

"I am sorry Sir, I cannot be part of this."

"Professor, are you challenging the President?" shouted Mr. Chimovu.

"No. I am sorry Sir, I am not challenging but I have a different point of view to yours."

"Come on Professor, do not spoil the day, take the money and give it to your grandmother if you do not need it!" screamed the man who was grinning since the president entered the room.

"Listen gentlemen, this is not a challenge, I gave my word in the negotiations that every dollar shall be spent on the projects and I stick to it. I negotiated funding for projects, not salaries. The projects are all ready to start and some have started already. These projects are essential for all our people. I have my own principles. Mr President, I am sorry but I have to resign my post. Thank you for appointing me, Sir. It is just that we have different points of view on life and on this matter."

With that, Professor Chilomba stood up and walked out of the room. Silence descended upon the assembly. It had never happened in the decades since Chimwanga came to power and all knew a red line had been crossed. "It is treason," someone whispered. They all looked down as if in shame, or was it in awe of the lion?

"Mr President, please do not bring in another professor, they spoil things. You have to fire him."

"Shut up; I will fire you too, don't tell me what to do! Do you understand Honourable Chimovu?"

"Yes, Sir, I am sorry. I am very sorry. I am very, very sorry, Sir."

At midnight on the second night after Moses' press conference, Moses was awakened by wild banging on the main front gate of his property. As if he knew who was coming, he dressed in his suit, told Rachel it was not a friendly caller and that he was prepared for any eventuality; he told her to be strong, kissed the children and walked to the gate with two of his guards. Rachel forced her way behind the guards. Moses told her to go back into the house because he would not like the children to lose two parents in a night. "I want to see them kill you," she protested. He then told the guards not to fight but take in as much detail as possible about the people at the gate. At the gate the two guards on duty were in a pool of blood. Moses stood still, looked at the policemen who had come to arrest him from their toes to their eyes in subdued anger, and walked to the injured men. He called the other guards to attend to the injured guards.

"Why did you have to do this? What did they do to deserve this? They were just doing their work to earn a living for their children like you do. If people attacked you like you have done for simply working, how would you feel? One day in Lubanda or in hell you shall not only answer but pay for this."

Moses was not to be seen for a while. Word had gone round that he had been arrested and locked up in prison. The public were expecting this to happen but what they were not expecting was what was to follow.

The Citizen Chronicle published a report about the arrest, with detailed and graphic pictures of the guards. The article called upon Lubandans to stand up for Moses as the last hope for the country. Rachel was pleased with this article. The following day she visited all the foreign embassies in the capital to ask for help to protect her husband. Many Lubandans came forward to offer support and even volunteer to fight for him. The seed had started germinating and the movement was born.

On the third day, Rachel was allowed to visit him in prison. Surprisingly, he looked clean shaven, wearing a dirty suit but cheerful. Rachel who was visibly pleased wondered how he could be so strong. As they sat together for a short private conversation, he told her to continue preparations for the launch. "They will break my body, not my spirit," he said. "I am innocent but innocence in Lubanda does not give you freedom." The fifteen-minute visit turned into an hour as the prison wards did not seem to bother about the time. When they finally came to tell her to go she carried papers and recordings of things to be done.

Before she left the prison, the commander beckoned her to his office. "Mum, do not worry, we shall look after him and do the best. He is a good man. He is our leader. I had a meeting with him, he is powerful. He told me that he does not need to fight for the freedom of Lubanda because he has all that he needs, but he is obliged to do it because he loves this country. He told me that my children and grandchildren will continue to suffer if nothing is done. I believe him and we shall do all we can to look after him. We give him good food and more blankets. Be careful yourself. We are behind you. Please mum, visit him daily, if you want; bring the children to see him but do not talk about the visits publicly."

Rachel remembered the conversation they had; it was not their battle alone and winning hearts and minds would be the key. She resolved to do something every day that would bring her into contact with people. Her first visit was to the children's ward at the main hospital where she donated food and toys. She spoke to the mothers and the staff. Through the discussions, she told the mothers how life for their children would change when Moses became president. Her next assignment was to visit the district shops they owned. She had never visited the shops alone but this time she did it in order to gauge the mood of the country. Well-wishers gathered each time she turned up and they offered support. She appealed to the people to be strong and support Moses. During her daily visits to prison, she briefed him and they planned what to do next. There was enough evidence that the movement for change was gaining ground. Hundreds of thousands had expressed interest by registering on the website.

Moses told Rachel to give an interview to the foreign press to call for his release. These interviews proved invaluable because she would call for his release and remind people about his circumstances. She seemed to be outsmarting the government in this fight. The latter did not regard her as a threat but as a desperate wife. In three weeks many volunteers were actively involved in secret recruitment and new leaders had emerged.

Moses kept contact with his followers through his wife. He used the time he had reading books and newspapers and writing. He worked on his plans, and these were given to Rachel to take home. He regarded the imprisonment as a retreat.

Other inmates respected him and they too protected him. They knew he was in prison because he wanted to help the nation. On few occasions they would ask him about his time at university. Most of the prisoners had never gone beyond primary-school level. When they learnt he spent time abroad, they became more interested in his time in America.

After three weeks, the date for his treason trial arrived. By coincidence, the judge called upon him at 1.30 pm to speak. The court was full and there was a sizable curious crowd outside.

"Your honour and Countrymen, I stand in this court on this day, so many years after independence as a captive of freedom. My crime is being a citizen, a citizen with opinion and ideas, a citizen with an alternative vision and mission to take our country away from chaos onto a road of prosperity."

"Objection," screamed the prosecutor, "this is a court case, not a political rally!"

"The defendant has the right to state his case. You may continue, Sir."

"Thank you, your honour. I am here in this court because I said to the people of Lubanda that we can do better and I appealed to them to join me in the pursuit of happiness for all Lubandans. According to article 149 of the independence constitution which should be guiding this nation but has since been ripped apart at will by President Chimwanga, I am as entitled as Chimwanga is to stand for the presidency of this nation. According to Chimwanga's handbook of chaos being used by this government, I have been accused of treason. Those who hold power and do not adhere to the law are accusing me of treason, using the law they don't respect. Shouldn't they themselves be charged with treason?

"Your honour, I have now been in prison for three weeks, not to mention the inhumane conditions of our prisons. Who is violating the law, and peace? Inciting hatred? Me or President Chimwanga?

"Look at my chains, the symbol of hatred, misrule and failed state. They can't even unlock them. This is how the people of Lubanda have been chained for the thirty years of Chimwanga's rule. They want a country without opposition so they can continue rolling in mud and dining on gold platters without question.

"Your honour, I don't know how free your judgement is going to be: between your conscience, God and the law, with the pressures brought to bear on you, for once Judge, in light of justice and in the interest of your country. I am moved to believe that you will make the right judgement."

The judge who had been listening attentively and followed every word and gesture, dismissed the case with costs and ordered his release. He did not see the need to proceed with the case beyond the first hearing. While commotion rose in court, Moses slipped out and went home. Three hours later there was an announcement in the news that the judge had been dismissed and placed under house arrest.

Later in the evening, Moses was in his pyjamas talking to the children when the police rushed in to re-arrest him. He was not even allowed to change into his suit this time. He was charged with insulting the President in court. Rachel had the presence of mind to take a picture and put it online and within a short time, he had become the topic of discussions and muted protests. The foreign embassies could not accept the pyjama pictures with equanimity; they issued timid threats and protestations.

Word had gone round that in three days he would be taken to court in the morning and locked up for a long time. The public started organising themselves. Social media ran crazy with secret followers daring each other to appear at court in the morning, ready to die. The Internet streamed videos of Moses in handcuffs in his pyjamas, being dragged into a police van – videos that became a magnet for recruitment of followers. On the day of his next appearance, the streets filled with people. Traffic was at a standstill and thousands of people were on the march to court.

"This is worse than what the colonialists had done. We are fighting an independence struggle. Lubanda, freedom will prevail. Do you hear me?" he shouted as the policemen dragged him into court. As though the whole nation was listening, there was a roar, seven times: "Yes, we hear you, be strong! We are behind you!"

The sea of people had never been seen before around the court. The judge ordered that Moses be loosened from the chains immediately and told them Moses was not a dog but a political prisoner who deserved to die with dignity. He refused to preside over the case. He was heard telling the prosecutor to go and tell Chimwanga to hear the case himself.

Just as violence was about to erupt between the policemen and the supporters, Moses stepped out of court to much cheering. He told them not to beat the policemen. "Thank you countrymen, I owe my temporary freedom to you all. I ask you not to manhandle the policemen because they simply act on orders. They too are prisoners of Chimwanga. They need to be freed and we shall free them and give them dignity. I don't know what is happening but I have been released. In my humiliation I have found strength in you. They undressed me but you have dressed me with new clothes of confidence. I am going home for at least a shower and a cup of tea before they come again. Please go home peacefully."

By the time Moses finished his brief speech, the policemen had fled and locked themselves up in the courtroom. The people commandeered a car that was stuck in traffic, put Moses in and escorted it to his residence five miles away singing and shouting "Down with Chimwanga!" As he was partly pushed and partly driven to his house Moses waved and kept whispering, "It is the beginning of a people's revolution."

The midday news reported that the President had dismissed all the policemen that were at the court for incompetence. In spite of his action, the crowds seem to have sent a shiver down Chimwanga's spine. His advisers urged him not to give any more orders to arrest Moses. They acknowledged that if he had not spoken to his supporters so calmly, something bad would have happened in the country. Chimwanga himself had received a distressing telephone call early in the morning. The last remaining donors that kept his corrupt regime running had telephoned him and warned him against further imprisonment or harming of Moses. They announced delays in payment of the next instalments of the money they were giving him. The people's reaction and the reaction of the international community, particularly the few supporters, took the government by surprise. They were perplexed about what to do next.

Chapter Four

THE EVENTS of the past month were unprecedented in the thirty years President Chimwanga had been in the office; he had never been so directly challenged before a full cabinet. This was a humiliation but he was more stunned than angry. Until recently, all foreign media was banned and any dissent was crushed. Things had been changing and his power structures, once solid, had shown signs of weakening with infighting and cliques.

Chimwanga was of average height. The protruding scarred cheeks and the pot belly made him ugly and clumsy. His opponents at their worst called him a hippopotamus. I am sure tailors had a problem in designing suits that sat on him well. Women who fancied him of course dared not look at his face but his pocket.

However, the worst of him was what could not be seen with the naked eye – his 'heart'. He was a very cruel man who exterminated his opponents at leisure. By conventional leadership qualities he was doubly incompetent. His administration was in shambles. He had caused innumerable political tensions in the country, dividing what was previously a united nation, plundered the treasury into bankruptcy and exasperated the citizens. The evangelical Christians 'complimented' him as being possessed with evil spirits with a soul far beyond redemption.

But how did such a man become a president in the first place? One respected journalist summed it up well: "Through masterful lies, corruption, theft, callousness, with a cherry of cruelty and brutality on top of a conspiracy of misfortunes."

At public rallies he sounded populist bells by giving false hopes to the poor who, although they did not understand the political gibberish, responded to an effervescence of emotions that his talk provoked into voting for him. He threatened violence in the event of loss and behind the doors he made alliances with the opportunist media, businessmen and government officials. Fortunately for him, at the time there was clearly a lack of inspirational and creative leadership.

He had since acquired a series of names from friends and foes. In one of the languages in the country his name Chimwanga meant someone who spills, destroys, scatters, and divides. There would be no better irony than this. Such is the reputation of this leader.

When he assumed power he was in complete control. He was brutal, merciless and arrogant. Soon the country was in shambles, a failed state; all state functions and systems were not working as they were meant to. He controlled the judiciary and the police. There was no professional integrity in these institutions. He was presiding over a complete parliamentary mockery. Everyone knew the country was ruled like a personal farm. He and his avaricious supporters were the only human beings and the rest were animals to be driven in any direction, with whips and dogs. The armed forces were placed under incompetent leaders paid to keep them happy and out of mischief, in case they had any competence to think rationally. He changed them regularly to assert his authority. Few people in Lubanda were happy; money was spent on the ruling elite's personal pleasure.

Under Chimwanga, government and parastatal organisation posts were filled by his uneducated children, relatives or friends. Thirty years on, the hospitals were partially open, no medicine or doctors. The few doctors employed were busy making ends meet in various non-professional activities. The country was in great fear because the many unemployed unruly youths indoctrinated into party cadres would do anything for Chimwanga for a few coins. They killed for him, they destroyed property for him, attacked political leaders for him and they terrorised the communities in his name. The thirty years of his leadership had been a catastrophe to say the least. There had been no development, all government institutions were corrupt and inefficient, once tarred roads were reduced to narrow strips in the centre causing regular road accidents. Schools under Chimwanga had no sensible curriculum. He issued meaningless instructions to what schools should teach. Truancy and indiscipline by teachers and pupils alike made any teaching and learning impossible.

His administration was widely believed to be the worst not only in the history of Lubanda but the world. It had no control, no purpose, was devoid of virtues but had a multiplicity of vices. Ministers and senior servants behaved like proxy presidents, making decisions that hurt the people and the economy. The leader himself had a reputation for making decisions on the hoof and lacked understanding of policy or governance. Some people saw him as a sleeping president who only awoke to order murder and indulge himself.

People felt trapped and hopeless. Everyone knew they wanted change and prayed for change but nobody had the courage to challenge him. All who tried to stand against him were dealt with ruthlessly or simply disappeared only to remain as statistical memories. Meanwhile, Chimwanga, and those around him were enjoying lavish living; oblivious of the pain, hatred, carnage and dissent around him.

The past ten years had been the most chaotic. Everything was at the extreme end of wickedness and depravity. Corruption had become an accepted norm and had reached unbelievable proportions.

Two years ago, Chimwanga carried out a massive internal purge of his party. The succession feud that had been building for years exploded at a family party. Chimwanga was too drunk to control the situation and the brawl that ensued could still be seen in the scars of scores of the Chimwanga clan. His nephew Absalom took over control as he had done with most functional powers of his uncle. He managed to stop the fight and he was rumoured to have carried out the purge with the blessings of his uncle.

More disturbing was that the purge, reminiscent of Stalin, started with Absalom personally shooting his older brother in his bed. It was believed that his brother was the favourite of half of the family. He was measured, intelligent and much wiser than Absalom. Absalom was more physical, short tempered and intellectually weak. Much like his uncle, he was ruthless and brutal. Close members of the family often whispered that even the President feared this monster.

The family brawl was a clash between Absalom, his brother and their supporters. Although Absalom's brother managed to sneak away, Absalom followed him to his house at 4.00 a.m. He found him sleeping and shot him in bed. Since then, he was the most feared and hated person in the country and government but he remained as the Secretary to the Cabinet, intimidating ministers and functioning as a de facto first vice president.

He often glamorised the atrocities his uncle had carried out and had been understudying him with a view to succeeding him. He was often heard boasting:

"If the love of my brother could not stop me, no one will stop me from becoming a president. I am just waiting for the right moment."

However, the family feud, chaos in the government, broken down economy and empty treasury forced Chimwanga into relenting and making small compromises like press freedom to please the international community. The result, voices of dissent become louder.

It is in this chaos and shambles that Moses entered the political scene. The events of the past month had already made him look like the star of David shining in the distance, full of hope, yet still not well known.

The days following Moses' announcement were full of confusion with so many stories and articles written about Moses. The arrests did not help the situation either although it had helped him more than it helped the government. The government media led on a personal malicious attack on Moses. Some reports in the private media were inaccurate and could not capture the true understanding of Moses. One paper, *The Citizen Chronicle,* took the centre stage and changed all this.

There was a national dialogue about Moses since his release. People were talking more openly. Momentum was certainly building since his first press conference. However, to make him a household name, the public needed to know the candidate's story. To his advantage though not linked, his cause also benefited from the confusion arising from the resignation of the Minister of Finance, Professor Chilomba.

Many people took the resignation as a direct outcome of Moses' bravery to stand up to a dictator. The shambolic way the government handled the issue, the conflicting announcements, the following spat with the donors and the revelations by the now self-exiled Professor Chilomba, added credibility to this narrative. Two newspapers had the following headlines: "Moses Shakes up the Government" and "The Next President of Lubanda." Absalom was incensed with these headlines.

However, the great breakthrough came through the articles of *The Citizen Chronicle.*

Soon after the press conference, Delilah had handed in her business card and they promised to get back to her. The following day Delilah published the most interesting article about Moses' announcement. This article caught Moses' attention. It was warm and, in particular, one paragraph was interesting:

"This handsome, rich and intelligent young man is the one the country has been waiting for. He is warm and graceful yet tougher than a lion, wiser than most men of his age. A man with a clear vision for this country and committed to bringing change for the better, to all Lubandans. Ladies, be careful, he is married to a beautiful wife. But this is the man you can entrust with the future of your children. If you are unemployed, this is the man who has a clear plan and understanding of the economy and how to create jobs. If you are a professional, he appreciates your value to the nation. If you are a businessman, you will not have a better ally than a successful self-made businessman. If you are an ordinary Lubandan, he says you are part of his family. He has a message of genuine unity and he is a true patriot. We at *The Citizen Chronicle* shall do whatever it takes to support him all the way to inauguration day. Will You?"

This was a very brave article in a totalitarian state. Delilah had so much hatred for the present government that she was prepared to risk her life even though her uncle was one of the ministers. Perhaps this is one of the reasons she was so bold because she had someone in the government.

This article certainly won her friends in Moses' camp but never endeared her with the government of Chimwanga, especially Absalom. Within hours of the article's publication, Delilah received an invitation to attend a meeting with Mr Kamawu at his farm. Unfortunately, she had to wait for a month because Moses was arrested before they could meet but when they eventually met, it marked the beginning of a special relationship.

She was met at the office by a smartly dressed aide who was very polite. He escorted her to an annex of the house. After the protocols and security checks, she was ushered into what looked like a board room. She sat down and waited. The room was beautifully designed with gorgeous flowers in a glass vase in the middle of the table. There were pictures of famous people on the wall, Nelson Mandela, Winston Churchill, Abraham Lincoln, to name but a few. The solid mahogany table and the twelve blending chairs around the table constituted a unique collection. In fact, she did not remember seeing them in any of the local furniture shops. She wondered what the man was worth.

A worker came in to offer her a drink while she waited. The longer she waited the more impatient and anxious she became but she urged herself to be calm and patient. A door she had not noticed before swung open and Moses stepped in.

"I am sorry to keep you waiting Miss Mashidika. Someone rang just as you were coming in."

"Good afternoon!" she said as she stretched out her hand. The firm but gentle handshake with searching eyes paralysed her briefly.

"Welcome to my office, and please take a seat. "

He offered her a cup of tea. Although she had just finished one, she could not refuse the pleasure of being served by this interesting man.

"Miss Delilah, tell me about yourself."

"I am a journalist, Sir. I am the co-founder of *The Citizen Chronicle*."

He did not seem to be impressed with this brief résumé. Delilah was clearly nervous. He went on to ask her about her training, education and future plans. He was very formal throughout the discussion. She was more nervous that he may ask her about her uncle, a prospect that would end the interview abruptly. Delilah used a different family surname to her uncle's. The questioning was more of a job interview. He was calm, reflective but engaging and his eyes had an intimidating edge

"Miss Delilah, from the way you sang the national anthem, you are a patriotic Lubandan. What do you think of the state of our nation?"

"Sir, it is terrible. The youth are told the country was better under the colonial settlers but who would like to be colonised again?"

"But we have been colonised by Chimwanga, Miss Delilah," he interjected.

"Sir, the reason I want to be involved with the movement for change is because I believe this country has a chance to change."

"Are you sure you do not want to sell more newspapers?"

"No, Sir," she quickly chipped in with a frown on her face and bit her lip.

"The country needs new leadership that will look at things differently and have no cause to fear reprisals. People of Lubanda are good and hardworking, they have ambitions but they are imprisoned."

He kept listening attentively to her rant about all the ills the country was facing and how she thought the country could change course and develop. Then she said, "I believe there is promise in you and I believe you." At which point he smiled for the first time, moved his chair closer and said,

"Delilah, you come across as an intelligent woman. You are articulate and wise. Why would you trust a new person you hardly know well, who may not succeed as some people are saying? Who may be killed before he starts campaigning? Why will you be taking a risk to support me?"

"Conviction, Sir. Conviction and love of the country. Yes, conviction. I saw something in you that I have never seen before. You said you are prepared to die for your convictions and ideals. I am convinced I share your convictions and I have hope in your dream. That alone, Sir, is worth dying for."

He gave Delilah a short trip into his vision. Delilah sat in admiration as Moses sprang into life, explaining the state of the nation as never heard before. The picture of the country he wanted to create was as vivid as a trip to a new heaven. In the fifteen minutes he spoke, she was stirred even more. When he finished she remained speechless. They seemed to have been connected by a deep understanding. She decided there and then that she would support this man beyond the call of journalistic duty; she indeed would support him with her soul.

"Delilah, I do not know you. You will either support me wholeheartedly or betray me wholeheartedly. I have decided to work with you. If what I have seen in you is not Hollywood then you will be a strong ally in the movement. What do you want to help me with?"

"To help you connect with the people. I suggest we run a series of articles to inform the nation who you are and your vision. You may need to give me a couple of interviews, Sir. I will also be covering your party and campaigns. But I have one request."

"What is it?"

"I want to have exclusive rights to the official story."

"Locally, yes. And on condition that you show me all articles about me and my party before you publish them. I also reserve the right to cancel this agreement if you misrepresent me. Finally, the agreement is for the initial three months only."

"It's a deal, Sir."

"Let me see what you come up with in your next issue."

"I need to interview you, Sir."

"Come tomorrow in the afternoon."

He called one of the workers to take her round the orchard to harvest fresh fruits for herself, a Lumbadan tradition now forgotten. When she came back he had drawn up a contract of the agreement. Although she was surprised by how formal he was behaving, she signed it and told him that this should not be in the public domain. This decision alone would change their lives for ever.

The agreement was not without its critics. Some people around Moses did not like her flirtations at the press conference and Rachel thought he had acted a bit too hastily. Most of the inner circle was pleased with her forthright support. One person who was very upset was Moses' uncle.

"Moses, did you know that Delilah is the niece of a minister?"

"No, I did not."

"I suggest you do not open up to her because she will be your weakest defence against the regime. They are planting her into the movement. How closer can you be than she is now to you? Cancel the agreement."

"No, uncle, I have given her my word and it will stay. I made a decision not out of desperation for media support but I saw in her heart that she is genuine. If I have made a wrong judgement, I will have to live with the consequences."

"Moses, I think sometimes you are too stubborn, you should be listening to other people," his uncle said almost shouting.

Moses smiled. "A leader sometimes makes judgements and decisions based on intuitions," he said. "It's healthy to get advice but not to surrender leadership; you have to make the decision. I appreciate what you have said, invaluable observations that will inform this relationship until we are completely confident she is not a mole in our midst."

Meanwhile, Delilah went home thrilled. The meeting with Moses had gone rather well and to secure almost exclusive rights to the story of the year was not bad business. She always proudly recalled this meeting as the defining achievement of her career as a journalist. She worked throughout the night drawing up an elaborate plan of her articles and how she would serialise his biographical articles. She knew that supporting Moses was going to put her and her family in harm's way but she was completely committed to it. Her next article was even more interesting.

Mr Moses Kabwibu Kamawu's upbringing was intriguing. From the age of five he was talkative and very inquisitive like all other children. He would not only trick others but make them cry with words. What was unique about him was the cleverness of his questions and the depth of his thoughts. He was always curious and asked tough questions. Once at the age of six he sat with his grandmother listening to the story of Jesus, the little boy born in Bethlehem. He had turned to her and said,

"*Nkaka* (grandma), did you see Jesus?"

"No."

"Did you see his mother?"

"No."

"What colour was his hair?"

"I don't know."

"How about his father, what is God like? An old man, young man, tall, fat?"

"I don't know!"

"Did God stop growing to remain the same age?"

"I do not know."

"*Nkaka*, you have talked about God having a son, how many daughters does God have?"

"None. Moses, I do not know. Stop asking me those questions, just listen. We may not understand everything about God. If we did he would not be God. He loves you, you know."

He smiled and looked at her. "Don't be angry, *nkaka*; I know you are making up the story. I do not believe there was ever a Jesus. God lives too far to come down here."

"No, Thomas! It is true. God is spirit, we cannot see him."

"I'm not Thomas, I am Moses," he protested

"You're now the doubting Thomas!"

He had just earned himself his first nickname of *Thomas* after the doubting disciple of Jesus.

The following day Delilah arrived promptly. She went through the security checks and was shown the same room and the same chair. As she waited she wondered what was in the actual office. Who worked there, why was there no noise?

"Good afternoon Miss Delilah." She soon realised that was his way of being semi-formal.

Moses always had ambitions of becoming a politician, ever since he won every school debate he entered at school. As he grew up he liked discussing politics and reading about politics. He grew up an intelligent masterful communicator. Others thought he was shrewd and tactful. He also won many prizes at school for attainment and extra curricula activities. It was no wonder he cherished the debating prizes the most.

The story he first told Delilah was sad. As she listened, she realised this story was the spirit behind the man's ambitions. He narrated it with a mixture of anger, pride and much reflection. It started when he was in his last year at university. After completing secondary school he applied to study law at the national university even though he had qualified to study medicine or engineering which his parents would have preferred.

His political ambitions appeared to have been shattered in the last three months of his university studies. He was the Chairman of a student *Think Tank* that met once a week to discuss various pertinent issues that they identified with. Moses enjoyed this role more than topics such as contract and criminal law. He kept a record of all topics, minutes and issues they discussed. He seemed to remember much of what they discussed and became animated when recalling these discussions.

"We discussed every topic we considered relevant: democracy, traditional values, governance, weddings, history and many more." He leaned forward as he explained. "We talked about democracy. What is democracy? Is there a thing called African democracy? Why was African democracy failing? Listen, Miss Delilah, democracy is not simply casting your vote – that is only the first step of a democratic society. In fact a true democratic vote is one that is cast freely with all parties treated fairly. The concept of democracy has not been well understood by most Africans and sadly, African democracy seems to start and end with the casting of votes. The vote becomes powerful if accompanied by the rule of law and powerful democratic institutions and systems that regulate the exercise of power. African democracy should be spiced, enriched and influenced by the traditional African values of respect, communalism, honesty and brotherhood. Unfortunately, political leaders behave like supreme paramount chiefs who exercise autocratic feudal powers. Until the systems are well constituted, clearly understood and the rule of law embraced by all citizens, poor governance and failed experiments of democracy will continue to litter the continent with devastating human tragedies."

As he mentioned the last point, he took in a deep breath, sipped some water and paused as though lost in his own mind, continuing the conversation in the inner heart.

"During my term in office, every school, college and university shall have a state-sponsored think tank." His eyes lightened up and he smiled.

"In my fourth year, three months from graduation, the think tank organised a symposium and invited Professor Elijah Kamona, our patron, to give the keynote speech. He walked in, stone faced, visibly troubled. I introduced him to the audience. What stunned the audience was not the flouted protocols; they would gladly forgive him for such etiquette failures as professors are often half way to a mental asylum. The bombshell that took the audience by surprise was what he said and how he said it:

" 'Shame upon you ladies and gentlemen and your leaders; there is a high probability or I dare even say a possibility that your children or great grandchildren will be sold as slaves to Europe and the far East again; only this time, it will be a circular slave trade!'

" 'Never!' the audience, coming to their feet, shouted at the top of their voices in unison.

" 'Professor, that is an outrageous exaggeration, we are free people and we shall never be slaves again,' I screamed in my chairman's big chair.

"He paused, looked at me sternly and in a slow tone he said, 'What freedom do you have? You have no economic power, you have no military power and you have no technological power. You are wrong, you have no freedom. Who listens to you in the world, what dignity do you have? No, Moses, you have no freedom.' And like thunder he broke into what appeared to be a soliloquy. 'It is all in the air, you are all imbeciles – that is why you cannot see, hear or feel it. Your leaders are morons with the brains of a fly. It is in the air; look at how blacks are being treated in this country, in their own country, in Europe and in the media. Black children are paraded in western media as objects of pity by charity appeals. What is disheartening is that they are presented in the same way that appeals for donations for preserving animals are made. Though not intended, this practice dehumanises and steals the dignity of the black child. Dignity stolen by slavery, colonisation and continues to be undermined. This is part of the lynching of the black race that has been going on for years. That is why black life is not treated as human and black people and governments are patronised and treated in a condescending manner. Your potbellied politicians go with open palms to beg for the Euro, Yuan and dollar. In Africa, the so-called leaders are selling the land to fulfil their insatiable appetites. Black people: the unwanted race, unwanted communities, unwanted children. Unwanted in the neighbourhood, unwanted in schools, unwanted travellers… Look, the foundations of slavery are in the air. Why and how did slavery start, you may ask? What were the conditions? Today black people everywhere are economically weak, politically weak, militarily weak and technologically weak. The weaker you are the less likely you will be to defend yourself and in the grand scheme of racial supremacy, the more likely you or your descendants will be likely to be enslaved. Even as I speak, the drums of slavery are beating. It is in the air. Foundations are being laid. Look at the rise in racism and fascism all around the world! Look at the plunder of African resources.'

"The tone of his voice, the certainty of delivery and the passion and anger with which every word was said plunged the large theatre into complete silence. He spoke for fifteen more minutes uninterrupted. As he concluded his remarkable speech he challenged the audience:

" 'Ladies and gentlemen, how can we stop this? What will stop the inevitable lynching of your children which the satanic racists are itching to do? What will stop black people becoming a product once more? It is leadership. Leadership that understands the forces of history and helps to predict the future; leadership that sees beyond the horizons of today; leadership that has a vision not only of their countries but the black community; leadership that understands their responsibilities to their nations and future generations, leadership that is wise enough to harness the forces and resources available to build strong nations, respected and revered by others; leadership that desires to lift people out of poverty and misery; leadership that has a long perspective on life; leadership endowed with intelligence and wisdom. What you have are *magogu*, like children playing leadership. That is your current leaders. Devoid of true qualities of leadership. They cannot hear what others are saying, incapable of seeing what others are doing. This is the tragedy of the black people. What are you people going to do? Will you perpetuate the collusion to black people's indignity and suffering? Or will you stand up for your children, grandchildren and great grandchildren and the black race?'

"Finally, he declared that he was not drunk because he did not drink but he was the voice of the voiceless, the voice of the helpless, of unborn children who would have the misfortune of turning up in this world black or in an African country. He was fearful of the future of the black people .He could hear the cries of children, men and women as they would be chained into servitude. At this point he stormed out, throwing his speech at the Chairman as he went past him."

Delilah who had been listening to this was visibly shaken with tears streaming uncontrollable down her face. She had heard about this lecture but it was through one of the banned canons under Chimwanga. After gaining her composure she asked what happened next.

Moses stood up and poured some coffee for himself and Delilah.

"The following day the speech was reported in the papers and Professor Elijah as we called him was arrested for insulting the president and falsely alarming the nation. I was livid and took his arrest personally. I mobilised students to march to the presidential mansion. Before we could reach the presidential mansion, for some reason which I have never found out, President Chimwanga released the Professor. This took place fifteen years ago. Some of your readers will remember the event although the media was barred from reporting it.

In the evening following his release, I was called to the Vice Chancellor's office at midnight and given an expulsion letter. Policemen escorted me off the university compass. The following day it was Professor Elijah's turn to organise all the lecturers to strike over my expulsion. The expulsion was rescinded and a compromise was reached. I was told to leave the university accommodation but allowed to write my final examinations and told not to attend the graduation ceremony. What happened after this event was diabolical, abhorrent and inhumane." He kept quiet for several minutes.

"By the way, I was known by the name Thomas. When I returned from my exile, I insisted on using my real names to avoid any special attention and somehow, the open disguise hid me from public focus."

Chapter Five

"**GOOD AFTERNOON**, Sir?" "Good afternoon Miss Delilah, thank you for coming. Thank you too for the brilliant articles. They appear to have been received well by the public."

"Yes, Sir. We have been getting many telephone calls in the office. We have already registered hundreds of thousands of members and I am hopeful this number will grow."

"Please sit down, Miss Delilah."

Today he was the first in the room, seated with a small bundle of papers tied together with a thin string wrapped round and neatly placed on the table.

His gamble had paid off and he had made a good judgement with this young lady. Delilah was now accepted as part of the movement for change. She was given access to people and sensitive personal information – though under the watchful eye of Rachel.

When the two women first met, there was respectful affection. Rachel liked Delilah not because her husband had so warmly talked about her but the exuberance of her personality was efficacious. Always with a smile that made her more attractive. In spite of the five-year difference in age, Rachel was equally stunning. On this first occasion, she made sure she established the boundaries and with stern looks and instructive commands, everyone knew who the lady of the house was.

The clever Delilah understood the feminine rivalry and decided she would have to conduct herself formally. She also knew the power of her personality that often left men on the trail and often swayed arguments in her favour. Nobody understood why she was still a spinster with such a flock of suitors: rich, educated professionals and a few sugar daddies to boot.

Since then, Rachel and Delilah were allies, not agreeing on all things but broadly united behind their man. On this occasion Delilah quickly settled down to business.

"Sir, I cannot wait to hear the stories of your exile."

Delilah did not mind that Moses was a very calculative and cautious man. He was controlling the publication of his story and yet growing in his trust in Delilah.

"Would you like a drink Miss Delilah?"

Rachel entered the office, perhaps to check lines were not being crossed. With dominant defiance, she walked over to Moses and kissed him with a slight jealous look of insecurity. The message was clear: this is my man, hands off, Delilah. The latter smiled and complemented her on her beautiful dress.

With peace temporarily restored, Moses who appeared to be far removed from the rivalry was lost in thought. He had anticipated this rivalry because the two women were both beautiful and had strong personalities. His job was to maintain peace and maximise their unique talents. He knew he was the unquestionable adjudicator. Rachel would be the strategist and the Secretary General. Delilah would be the head of communication and personal adviser. Although the roles were explained clearly, the grey areas of unique charm were not easy to navigate.

"Let me leave you two to work, please let me know if you need anything. Delilah, I loved those articles, thank you. You are an asset to the movement," Rachel said as she swept past her.

"Thank you, Mrs Kamawu, it is our mission."

With the peace treaty for the day declared, Moses stood up and went to join Delilah on the big elegant conference table.

"What is your plan today?"

"I suggest we write a few articles about your time in exile. My readers are following your story so we give it to them strategically, sustain interest and reveal your character to help them make up their own judgements. This part will then link in with the rallies when they will start listening to you directly."

"Very good, I am for it. What do you want to know?"

"Everything. How you ended up abroad, your studies, what happened after the graduation and what you were doing whilst you were abroad?"

"I will tell you the story but do not write everything. As I told you last time, I was asked to leave the campus and only go there to write examinations. If I passed, my certificate would be posted or collected by my relatives. I could not attend the graduation ceremony to keep me away from the President's *holy hands*." The sarcasm could be heard in each syllable.

"Two days after being sent away from the university campus, my father lost his job."

"Why?" Delilah asked, surprised. "Was he working for the government?"

"No. He was the Company Secretary of a bank, a private company. He was a very hard working man, the first to arrive and last to leave the office. On this day, he found the Chief executive already at the office. As he walked past the Chief executive's office, the latter called him in. He said, 'I am sorry Mr Kamawu, your employment has been terminated with immediate effect. It was not my decision. I was called to the President's residence at 1.00am this morning. I tried to argue but I was told I had to choose between you and the company. What can I do for you?'

"My father was shocked but he had the presence of mind to request that as part of his severance pay, they should sponsor me abroad for studies and any extra money be transferred into an account abroad. He told his boss that they should act quickly because he suspected more bad things were on the way. His wishes were granted. He was given a handsome pay packet which was transferred into a foreign account the same day.

"Dad called the family together and told us what had happened. He said he believed it was related to the protest. We all knew it had to do with the university demonstration. I apologised to the family that it was my fault. He was not having that and chided me for apologising. He said I was a victim so I should not feel guilty. He advised us to be careful and I was asked to apply to a university of my choice abroad for a master's degree and a Ph.D.

"I did not have much time to research. I decided to apply to a few universities in America and the U.K. For some unknown reason, I applied to the universities on the basis of how many presidents and prime ministers had studied at that university. I was happy to be offered a place at Harvard. Tickets were bought secretly and I was scheduled to leave in three months after my final examinations as most universities were in recess.

"On the last day of my examinations, I finished the examination at 3.00pm and decided to go home while everybody was trooping into town to celebrate. I was feeling very low although I knew I had done well in the examinations. As I approached home, I saw people gathered around our house. I knew something had gone terribly wrong. I ran. As I approached the house, there were uncontrollable wailings. This only happened if a relative or beloved one had passed away. I was confused. Who had died? My father? My Uncle? A distant relative? Why did they die? Am I responsible? Is everyone fine? I ran straight in and found my mother and sister crying and all the women started crying when they saw me. There was no need for a narrative. My young brother was lying in a pool of blood."

Moses stopped talking. He was gazing at the ceiling. He stood up and walked to the window looking into the distance like a father waiting for a lost son. He slowly walked to his chair and resumed the story.

"I dived across the room, lifted him up. He was dead. I remember carrying him in my arms and walking around the room, asking mum and whoever cared to reply what happened. Where Dad was and who did it? No one answered. I remember that I stood by the window, got choked up, tears flowing down my cheek. I must have been standing by the window for quite a while looking at the garden in silence, flooding myself with memories of Abel and with all the activities we did together. Gone. My little brother that I loved so much was gone. I remember feeling then as I feel now, something had been ripped within me, there was a vacuum I could not fill and I have never filled it. There was no purpose for living. My father who apparently was out at the time of the attack walked in with men carrying a coffin but had been standing behind me for some time and had decided not to disturb my moments of loss. He walked over to me, took the body of my ten-year-old brother and placed it gently in the coffin on the dining table. We both stood over the coffin for a while and he walked over to me and embraced me."

"He is dead," I said after a long pause, the only words I could manage to say.

My father looked at me straight in the eye and said, "Yes, he is dead. He is a martyr for Lubanda. Do not blame yourself because that is what they want you to do. To break your will and your soul. I do not want you to blame yourself for what happened to me or for the cold blooded slaughter of your brother. President Chimwanga is wholly responsible and one day he shall pay for Abel and for all Lubandans he has killed. But be strong, one day you shall revenge and avenge. They think they can get away with it because they have the power of the government but one day, you or your children or even grandchildren shall avenge your brother. Perhaps, you shall be the real president this country so badly needs."

"What happened next?" Delilah asked through her tears after a very long pause.

In exactly the same way, he gazed at the ceiling, walked over to the window and stood there in silence for several minutes.

"Miss Delilah, this is one of my reasons for going into politics – because my brother died for me. I feel as though all the Lubandans who have been killed died for me. The other reason I have chosen to be in politics is to bring dignity, hope and development to the Lubandans." He walked back to his chair and sat down. "I have never discussed this with anybody other than family. Please respect this. It is not for a newspaper article. I shall fight Chimwanga day and night trusting God is on my side."

There was defiance in his voice and the determination was unmistakable.

"Masked men had come to the house, found my mother and her two children; they asked for me. My brother challenged them as they threw my protesting mum on the floor and tried to hit her. The little man put up a fight – he is my hero because he died fighting. One of the gunmen shot him in the head. They went into my room looking for me. They trashed my room; everything was broken before they fled. Our maid saw the getaway car and I have the number plate written on this piece of paper." He took out an old piece of paper and waved it. "But I will not give it to you, at least not just yet. I wanted to fight back but my father insisted he would not lose two sons. He said my revenge will come. I hope he was right.

"Nothing was reported in the media about this attack. We buried my brother the following day and my father who escaped the attack because he had gone out to visit a friend told me to get whatever was left of my belongings and we left for the airport that evening. He pleaded with the airline to take me aboard. He put one hundred dollars in my hand, gave me the longest hug I have ever got from him and after our hearts had communicated, he let go and told me to book into a hotel and wait for further instructions.

"Life in America was not easy. I had money to live on but the bloody memories of my brother, my haggard mother lying helpless and my traumatised little sister trembling under the table were too strong to forget. I have spent long hours thinking of him since and I know his spirit walks with me. The thought of my father, blacklisted with hardly a source of income, was depressing. I feared for them daily. But it was also the major driving force in my studies. It was not until my son Abel, named after my brother, was born that I have some consolation in my heart. Look at the papers in the folder for the rest of the story."

He gently pushed the little bundle of papers towards Delilah and instructed her not to take them out of the room, to make copies or copy the content by way of a few notes.

The papers provided fascinating glimpses into Moses' time abroad. He studied politics, philosophy and economics (PPE). He had graduated with a first class. In addition to the prescribed courses, he enrolled for courses of interest such as banking, international law and finance and investment. He attended several economics lectures from leading scholars.

At the end of the first year, he performed so well that he was given a full scholarship. He had made a note to the effect that he probably won it with his essay entitled *The Weakness of the Strong.* In this essay he analysed the weaknesses of five of America's most famous former presidents.

Now that he had a scholarship, he used the money saved for his tuition fees to buy a two-bedroom flat. He let out the second bedroom to other international students, which gave him enough money to pay for the mortgage and a little to invest in shares.

Moses kept two diaries: one was a factual diary which provided excerpts that were in the pile. The other was a reflective diary in which he wrote his reflections on events. In the pile there were only two pages from the reflective diary. One was about his reaction when he was offered the scholarship. He was very happy and rang his father. He was jumping up and down like a small boy who had just got his first toy.

The second page was about the death of his friend, his first love. He had met Mary in his philosophy class. They had argued about the achievements of black people over the past five centuries. Mary was convinced the Civil Rights Movement died with Martin Luther King. Moses on the other hand believed the movement existed before Martin Luther and still exists. What was lacking was leadership. Martin Luther King Jr provided leadership in his time, as did Nelson Mandela. He believed the movement was in the hearts of all black people but most black people lacked the determination and will to strive for leadership.

After this exchange, they became close friends, argued many times and shared many experiences. Unfortunately, she died prematurely of cancer. He wrote a tribute to her which must be somewhere because it was published, according to the factual diary. He described the time she died:

"Mary was striking. As she lay on her death bed, she was like an angel to me. In pain yet with a smile on her face, she looked right at her parents who were holding her right hand together. She turned left, in a goodbye sweetheart final look to the left where I was holding her left hand. She smiled, closed her eyes, and opened them again. Turned right to her parents and smiled. Was she saying mum and dad here is your son Moses or Moses, look after my parents? She looked up, closed her eyes. Instinctively, the three of us kissed her simultaneously. Goodbye sweetheart, I whispered. She opened her eyes for the last time. The last breathe, the warmth in her hands and the smile on her face remain memories of love unfinished, of joy exported to the heavens and memories of a short life lived well."

Delilah asked whether he was going to marry her. Moses said, "You will read that in my autobiography but you will soon meet her parents if I win the elections. They are my adopted parents. To lose an only child is to lose half your life. One thing you should know is that she saved my life but she could not save hers. She loved me. I loved her. I hope she is looking after Abel for me."

One other interesting observation in the notes was an extract from his factual diary. Three entries recorded the places he visited. One was a beautiful building. He recorded what it was, the companies that built it, how much was spent on it, who funded the project, how it was maintained and the financial benefit. There were even comments from tourists, what they said of it. Delilah was surprised at the level of detail and wondered whether there was a code or whether it was all simply a result of his fascination of the building.

His return five years ago was not planned. His father had been taken ill so he came back to see him against protestations from his father about coming back to an enemy still in power.

"I need you alive, Moses. A living Moses is a gift to me and the country."

But Moses felt it was time to come back. He would come back quietly and run businesses for five years before thinking of joining politics. When he went back to America, he sold one of the houses he bought and used the money to invest in businesses. He kept to his promise and upon his arrival, he established a chain of supermarkets in every district in the country. The supermarkets were dedicated to selling local produce. He said it was not a silent period but a learning and planning period. It helped him analyse the issues the country was facing and through the businesses, he interacted with both rural and urban populations and learnt five of the six major languages. He knew the country more than some of his opponents. His supermarkets were designed to provide markets to the local farmers and they had made a difference to the local economy and boosted food production in the country.

When Delilah came to the last page in the bundle, she realised there were more fascinating stories. He had only been given a bird's eye view. It was obvious that Moses had a sophisticated plan for his political career. It was not an impromptu decision as some commentators had speculated. The decision to stand had been long in the making. She was now more enthralled with both the man and his story. It would not be easy to just ask him for the blueprint; she was more determined than ever to understand this intriguing candidate. She would be completing the puzzle as the story unfolded.

The Citizen Chronicle was now the political focus for both the friends and foes of Moses. They were making reprints regularly. Delilah thought she had enough content to run a daily paper. It became the largest circulation paper. Delilah was becoming as famous as Moses. Many people were registering to join the movement and Moses was fast becoming a household name.

In less than three weeks, *The Chronicle* had become the fastest and biggest selling paper in the country, much to the envy of the other newspaper publishers. Royalties and commissions rolled in from associated internet articles. Delilah sponsored the upcoming launch event as part of the support for the movement and also hopefully, to renew the exclusive agreement when the time came.

It was obvious that they would not have a placid sea to sail. Their rivals, both media and politicians had finally realised that the Moses phenomena was not a fluke event. The first attack came from the government associated newspapers. They accused Moses of being in a sexual relationship with Delilah. They reported that Moses was about to divorce his wife in order to marry Delilah.

One strategy Moses employed was to be ahead of the enemy. Two days before the publications, he called his inner circle excluding Delilah. He told them that he had called them to discuss possible lines of attack from the government. He presented a paper which was discussed at length. What they did not know was that he had been collecting evidence for a long time about his opponents. When the accusations broke out, Delilah rang Rachel to tell her. She was distraught.

"Have you seen today's papers?" she asked Rachel anxiously.

"Yes, we have. Do not worry about it. It is part of their tactics and Mr Kamawu will respond."

"Would you mind coming to dinner tonight?"

"I shall be delighted, thank you. What time, mum?"

"Seven would do."

"Thank you, see you then."

Delilah was surprised how calm Rachel was. She had been agonizing about it since she saw the newspapers, wondering how Rachel would respond to the articles. She had discussed the potential loss of business with her business partner and staff as a result of the malicious articles.

There was a knock on the door. Moses' driver came in with an envelope. In it was an article and photos about relationships. The note read: "Please publish in response." The photos were evidence of promiscuous activities of the editors who published the false information. After a quick liaison with the lawyers and her partner, the article was sent for publication.

During the day, Moses decided to visit a relative at the central hospital in the company of his wife. Well-wishers came over and asked him questions.

"Do we look like we are about to divorce? This was malicious propaganda which they will pay for." Pictures of him talking to the people and hand-in-hand with the wife began circulating on social media. By the end of the day, most people had dismissed the articles.

The following day, it was their turn to laugh out loudly as *The Citizen Chronicle* splashed government owned newspaper editors on the front pages. This caught people by surprise. Wives were irate and concubines came forward for interviews. Hidden children surfaced.

President Chimwanga called for a Cabinet meeting in the evening. Everybody was ordered to attend. Mr Katooka, Delilah's uncle, was late because of a prior engagement with foreign dignitaries. As he entered the room, there was no seat for him. This had never happened before. The President started shouting:

"You are all useless and idiots, how could you not stop this boy and his girlfriend!. Stop him. He has gone too far. Stop them at any cost. Do you hear me?" as he banged on the table and stood up.

"Honourable Katooka, will you please see me in my office in fifteen minutes?"

Mr Katooka knew there was a problem. His colleagues each filed past him, looked at him, shook their heads and without a word, left pensively. He knew there was trouble. In what appeared to be a rehearsed plan, he went to his office for a little while before the meeting with the President.

"Sit down Mr Katooka!" the President said, almost shouting. Only a few people and the walls would testify to the shouting matches that took place in this office. The shouting was often followed by bad news thereafter.

"Will you please ask Absalom to leave us alone," Mr Katooka said.

Absalom angrily left the office protesting loudly.

"Hon. Katooka, what has happened to you? You have been my supporter for many years. I trusted you to control your niece. See now what she has done. Why couldn't you stop her?"

"Mr President, my relatives are free to choose to do what they want. If you are asking me whether I have joined the movement, the answer is no. Is that the reason there was no chair for me in the meeting?"

"Hon Katooka, I want you to go and stop your niece tonight. If you do not, I shall deal with her myself. Do you understand me?"

"Are you threatening me?"

"Hon. Katooka, you are a senior minister in my government, I expect complete loyalty even in tough situations. As a friend, I am advising you to stop your niece. In fact, ask her to work for me. I shall give her a lot of money."

Hon. Katooka stood up. "Mr. President, thank you for letting me serve in your government, but I am sorry I have to resign."

He took a letter from his jacket and placed it on the table in front of the stunned Chimwanga. The President tried to talk him out of it but it was too late, all doors for negotiation were closed.

"Chimwanga, deal with *me*. If you ever touch my family you shall regret it for the rest of your life. Remember we have been together for a long time. I know you too well, perhaps more than you know yourself. Even if you kill me, you shall still regret your actions. Good luck Mr President Chimwanga."

Hon .Katooka quickly left the office, looked searchingly at Absalom who seemed to have been eavesdropping in the doorway, and said, "You too will regret."

That evening, Mr Katooka made a few phone calls. The last one to call was Delilah. They met and discussed what had happened and he told her he was leaving the country to protect them. If he remained, he would be killed and he did not want to give Chimwanga an opportunity. He told Delilah that he was anticipating events would turn nasty and he expected this since her first article about Moses. He had been thinking about it and had a plan. He sensed his time had come because of the reaction he was given when he went into the cabinet office. He told her she was in serious danger but she should continue what she was doing because it was good for the country.

"As long as I am alive, I shall support you. I do not think the President has asked people to get you and Moses. Be strong. I will go to one of the embassies and a friend will drive me to the airport. I know how he thinks and acts. He has not yet taken my diplomatic passport and there is a plane at 9.00pm tonight. I shall use what I know to fight back from abroad."

He told Delilah what to do if they came to the house, where to go and hide and who to call for help, '*his boys.*' He went into the bedroom and came out dressed in his wife's dress with her veil on his head. He carried one medium size suitcase. "Delilah, take care. I can't give Chimwanga time to think otherwise I will be dead tomorrow," he whispered as he rushed out of the house. A vehicle drew by at what appeared an exact arranged time, picked him up and left. This appeared to be another rehearsed plan. Delilah was worried they might catch up with him before he left.

Next up in the President's Office were the defence and secret service commanders.

"Gentlemen, I have called you because we have a big national threat. This boy who wants to be a president is causing much trouble. We need to stop him and his girlfriend. I do not care what you do but use whatever powers you have to stop them. If you have to use live ammunitions, please go ahead."

"No, Mr President, I will not order my men to shoot civilians," said the army general. "My forces are to protect the country against external enemies, not against Lubandans."

"Yes, you will," snapped Absalom with a pistol in his hand.

"No I won't," said General Aaron Makwayanga. "You can shoot me if you like, I will not."

"Put the gun away!" shouted President Chimwanga who appeared bewildered.

As Absalom slowly put his gun in his jacket, General Makwayanga stood up and took two slow steps to within half a metre of Absalom and said:

"Never, ever, ever draw your gun at a general again. Never. I can shoot you and your uncle here now, no one will stop me. But thank God we are not all as insane as you."

Later, President Chimwanga lay in bed, troubled. He kept turning from side to side and standing up. At some point he walked to the lounge and watched the television for an hour, something he only did if he was troubled. He had never had any such problems before. In less than eight weeks he had lost two ministers and he had a potentially mutinous general. Why were people deserting him? Was his government crumbling? He was worried too about Absalom. What kind of a president will he be?

Most troubling was the Minister of Foreign affairs, Hon. Katooka. What should he do with him? He knew too much about Chimwanga – he was the one who opened foreign accounts for him. He was the one who controlled secret businesses and had made several investments for him in his name. "This was my most trusted minister. What has happened to him to change so quickly?" If he killed him, he would never recover the money and if he escaped, he would vengefully wash all the dirty linen in public. After the troubles from the Minister of Finance, what was in store for him from Hon. Katooka?

He was drifting to sleep when the telephone rang. "Mr President, Sir, your nephew Absalom has attacked the Editor of *The Citizen Chronicle.* She was not in her house and she is not hurt. There is a video of the attack on the internet. We understand he also broke into Hon. Katooka's home but he was not in his house. He must have gone into hiding. Absalom is reported to have been shouting that he will kill him as soon as he finds him."

Chimwanga thought that the only way to stop Moses was to hit him financially. Lack of finances would disrupt his campaign. A team of loyal intelligence officers were assembled to investigate Moses' bank accounts. There were two reasons for this strategy. Frist, they were looking for evidence of wrongdoing in order to arrest him. Secondly, to assess how much he was worth and freeze his accounts to disrupt his campaign. They discovered that Lubanda Standard Chartered Bank was his main bank holding millions in his personal accounts.

The managing director of Lubanda Standard Bank was having a late dinner with his family when his telephone rang.

"Hullo!"

This is President Chimwanga. How much does this thing have in your bank?"

"Good evening, Sir, which thing?"

"Don't mess around with me, you know this shit of yours wishing to be president."

"Sir, I can't discuss client details with a third party. The law and bank ethics do not allow it."

"Stupid man, don't you know that I *am* the law and the ethics. You are so foolish – do you not understand this? How long have you lived in Lubanda?"

"Your Excellency, Sir, with all due respect, I can't discuss this with you."

"Listen you bastard, I have not telephoned you to discuss your ethics; I called to give you a presidential order to close all his account holdings in your bank immediately. Do it now!"

"Sir, what is the reason for closing the accounts so that I can tell the Board. He is our largest customer. He also deserves an explanation."

"He deserves nothing! A dog does not deserve more than his master. I am the most important board, close the account or I close you," shouted Chimwanga as he hung up.

Minutes later there was a loud knock on the managing director's front door. Two men entered pushing him aside as they walked past him.

"Can I help you gentlemen?

"You don't say no to the President of Lubanda, Mr Director," rudely answered the first man to enter. "Look, you have so many nice things: the house, the furniture and your family. Do you want to lose all these?" the man continued. "You must be out of your mind Mr Managing Director."

"Why should I lose them? What have I done? Please don't harm my family. Take anything that you want but please don't touch my family."

A family cat that was coiled up sleeping in the corner stood up, stretched, mewed and leapt onto the coffee table in the middle of the room gazing at the intruders. One of the men drew a pistol and shot it in the head. He turned, looked at the terrified family and pointed his gun at the Managing Director.

"When President Chimwanga tells you to do something, you do it or die."

The telephone conversation with the Police Chief had gone very well. Moses had got the assurance he wanted to make sure there was no loss of life or violence at the launch of his party.

"It is logical to see how the police and the army and other defence institutions find it hard to say 'No, Sir' to the president," Moses whispered to himself.

"Yes, Sir," agreed Kashimbi, the trusted P.A.

Kashimbi had been working for Moses for the past five years. She had collated a lot of information, for much of it; she did not know why she was keeping such data bases until the day Moses made the announcement to become president. She had been listening into the conversation with the Police Chief with great amusement. Moses had a file on every senior police officer and kept a log of crucial decisions and actions. He also kept personal information on them. He knew the villages they came from and their parents.

"Chief, tomorrow is the launch of the party and I would like to get assurances from you. I have been told you have received orders to shoot to kill. I do not want anybody killed tomorrow, neither do I want people to come and stop my meeting," said Moses in a reassuring and polite tone.

"Sir, we work by orders," said the Police Chief.

"If I asked you to kill your son, would you do it?" Moses replied.

"No, Sir, I will not."

"The people you have been ordered to kill are other people's children. They will feel the pain you would feel," Moses said in a firm and assertive voice. "Please, find an excuse not to kill. When I take office, I shall account for every political soul you people have killed."

"You are asking me to disobey, Sir, should I disobey you when you become president?"

"No, Chief, I do not expect you to disobey any order. I am asking you to disobey unconstitutional and personal orders that kill people you are meant to protect. You are employed to keep order for the citizens on behalf of the citizens. Many countries in the world hold large demonstrations and rarely do people die, so why are you so predisposed to killing? I shall tell my people that the police are not their enemy and therefore, they should not fight with you. What will you tell your officers?"

"Sir, you know General Aaron Makwayanga is under house arrest for saying, No."

"Chief, what will you tell your policemen and women? General Aaron Makwayanga is a very brave soldier. I have never met him but I respect him, he is a hero and one day he shall be honoured. What will you do?"

"Sir, if they do not attack us, we shall keep a distance."

"You will come to protect, not to kill, will you?"

"Correct, Sir."

"Chief, if you are fired for not killing my people, I shall remember your sacrifice, thank you and goodbye."

"Goodbye."

Kashimbi had listened to thousands of these tough conversations. What was remarkable is that he always got what he wanted. She was sure that if he negotiated with President Chimwanga, he would get the presidency from him without casting a single vote. She indexed the conversation and filed it in time to answer the buzzing telephone.

This particular Tuesday morning was the busiest she had ever been. People were calling to ask for tickets to attend the launch. Others were complaining they had not received their tickets. Moses and Rachel had drafted themselves in to answer difficult telephone calls.

Soon after they left to go and see what Delilah and her team had done at the lecture theatre, the venue for the launch, there was an angry worrying call from someone in the government.

"Where is Moses?"

"He has gone out, Sir; may I know who is calling?"

"Tell him to write his will today because tomorrow he will be dead. Do you hear that? He will join his brother Abel. If he does not want to die, he should renounce his candidature! Tell him, tell him, tell this bastard!"

Kashimbi stood sweating and shivering. She went into the secret room and told the two security men on duty. They quickly traced the call to Absalom, the Secretary to the Cabinet and notorious nephew of the President. They then rang Moses to advise him of the threat.

He sounded very calm, thanked them for their quick action and told them he had expected such calls from him. He ordered extra security round the house. An hour later, an audio clip of Absalom's threat was available on the internet, with his picture displayed.

When Moses came back from the venue, he was smiling calmly, relaxed as ever. Kashimbi who ran to meet him to inquire whether he was alright could not understand why this man was so calm under a death threat.

"Thank you, Kashimbi, for your vigilance. The hunter is said to have gone into hiding because people have been ringing him and threatening him. His personal details have been disclosed on the internet including an affair he had with his secretary, the wife of the Air Force commander," said Moses as he sipped his coffee.

"Sir, how did you do it?" inquired the puzzled but relieved Kashimbi.

"You have to be ahead of your enemy. I don't fight with guns but with my brain. We made the threat public because it is my first line of defence. Bad people love darkness and secret places. If you shine a light into these places, they flee the camp. At least I shall live to die another day. By the way, the hall looks excellent and everything is in place for tomorrow." He laughed and walked away to play with his children.

The theatre was full of people, far outnumbering the media who attended his first press conference. People had been filing past the security since daybreak. A big screen had been placed outside in the ground for those who did not have tickets and there were tens of thousands. They all said they had come to support him and will be looking forward to meeting him at the rallies. Asked whether they were scared the police would attack them, they said the policemen and women they saw were friendly and smiling. If they attacked them they were ready to die for Moses. The people had lost all the fear they had for many, many years; as one said:

"Whatever happens after the election, Moses has already won the battle for us because we are FREE to think and act."

Of course, not quite yet. Some people were still scared of the brutality they had experienced over the years. They thought it would be a question of time before Chimwanga struck back. And struck back hard.

The room erupted into cheers and ululations as Moses entered dressed in his trademark navy blue suit, white shirt and a red and green tie. His team were all adorned in party colours; a mixture of blue, red and green. He waved and smiled. They did not care he was thirty minutes late because he spent the time greeting the supporters gathered outside.

"Shall we please sing the national anthem?" Who but Delilah would burst into her lovely voice to lead the audience! The energy and enthusiasm in the room was beyond what they expected. Delilah was beaming with satisfaction at the work her team had done and for being part of this historical movement. Whatever danger was to come, her loyalties were unquestionably declared fully to Moses.

After all the introductions, the master of ceremonies introduced the candidate: "Ladies and gentlemen... Mr Moses Kabwibu Kamawu!"

The noise was deafening. He stood up slowly and walked to the lectern in the middle of the platform.

"Thank you, ladies and gentlemen. Thank you for coming. Thank you too to the organising committee that has done such a fabulous job. Ladies and gentlemen, I would like to appeal to all the people that we must all behave sensibly, we should be peaceful, treat the policemen as being on our side because after all the police belong to the people of Lubanda.

"Today I am here to do a simple job, to launch the party under which we shall fight and win the elections. The party, ladies and gentlemen is: **The Democratic Progress Party of Lubanda (DPPL).**" This was followed by the usual fanfare of music, drums and clapping found at such occasions.

"Ladies and gentlemen, I should begin by reminding ourselves about the history behind why we are here and why we have chosen this name. Pre-colonial Africa was ruled by either warlords or traditional rulers, the chiefs. This rule was often autocratic and authoritarian. The people had little say although in the case of traditional rule, there were little elements of consensus especially when it came to bestowing power to the next hereditary descendant.

"Under the colonial rule, there were three types of ruling systems: the colonial government for the settlers, colonial systems for the blacks and limited powers for the traditional chiefs; to maximise divide and rule. There was therefore, no coherent central rule that affected everybody equally.

"The result of these systems was that at independence, the new rulers had neither a unified system of governance nor knowledge of governance. To unify the rules that applied to the whites only and those that applied to the blacks created a challenge because it meant dispensing with privilege. Divide and rule had evolved divisions usually along tribal lines. Traditional African society was a communal society with strong family and community links. Therefore, the lack of knowledge and governance skills, political ideology and prevailing African communal society made it difficult to evolve systems that would bring sustained development and compete with the developed countries of the West.

"What came out was confusion in policy and practice as the leaders of the newly independent countries tried to copy systems elsewhere or even to emulate the colonial system that had their roots in western culture, systems and institutions. The leaders that arose wanted in one respect, to behave like their colonial masters but in actual fact, they became the chief of all chiefs. The fluidity of past ruling systems did not help adherence to the constitution and rule of law. Pressures of the extended family and communal society were manipulated to foster corruption and nepotism. The ultimate result was failed governments, despotic leadership, lack of rule of law, unstable constitutions and governments. Policies based on fragmented ideologies not fully understood could not yield effective progressive outcomes. The public voted more on tribal affiliations rather than quality of leadership. This confusion continues to persist and weaken governance with no strong fabric to hold the whole society together.

"That is why our country is in such a terrible state: your children cannot get proper education, no medicines in hospitals, with a lack of commodities on shelves; there are no local industries, there are no jobs and opposition leaders are threatened and killed at the behest and pleasure of the serving president.

"The Democratic Progressive Party of Lubanda will change this situation. We shall constitute proper democracy founded on true universal franchise, backed by rule of law and strong institutions. The president is not an institution or a law, he is a person entrusted with finite state powers to exercise rule in the interest of all the Lubadans, a servant of the people."

There were standing ovations throughout the speech to this point. Heads were nodding vigorously and everyone including those outside listened attentively.

"We shall bring progress to every individual and corner of the country. The primary problem we have is not money, it is poor management and leadership in managing the resources we have to enable us to build on and expand our reserves. If my government shall not bring progress the country shall at least have the ability to kick us out of power and elect citizens who will have the capacity and ability to do better.

"Therefore ladies and gentlemen, our vision is to create a society where everyone is free, a society where there are opportunities for everyone, and a society where every child has a decent education and everyone has at least a decent sleeping place.

"We shall create this society with a strong constitution that will not be changed like underpants, rebuild institutions and systems that work for all and we shall replace the rule of the president with the rule of the law by providing authority for the rule of law.

"Some people seek power for the love of power. They enjoy power and all the trappings that come with power. They want to feel important and seeking power is the end in itself. Once in power, they enjoy it and make merry and a threat from anyone seeking power grants them an opportunity to exercise power in defence of the privileges they enjoy.

Others seek power because it gives them an opportunity to make money. The salary, allowances and influence bring them opportunities to increase wealth.

"I seek power for none of these reasons. I seek power not because I want to advance my fortunes; I do so out of a strong patriotic conviction that I can make a difference to the advancement of this country. I wish to make a difference not only to the living but to the dead and to those not yet born. To make a difference to the dead by honouring their dream of true freedom and the sacrifice they made for freedom. I want to make a difference to the living by restoring dignity, offering them the opportunity to make progress in life and to uplift society beyond the daily pursuit of basic needs. I want to make a difference to the unborn whose fate or blessing will be to be born in this land – they are the future of Lubanda.

"I therefore ask you to support us to make this dream a reality for all. Do not support me because I speak the same language with you, do not support me because we come from the same village or district; but support me because you believe I shall make a difference to this country, to your life and your children's lives. Five weeks ago I was asked how I could win an election without a party; well, here is one. It already has thousands of members. But I cannot win without you. The coming election is not mine but ours. I do not have a government machinery that my opponents have. I am only a leader of the movement. I will depend on you to protect me, to be my ears and eyes. Do not put yourselves in harm's way but pass on any vital information. This is as much my fight as it is yours and the victory shall be ours.

"Here is the interim committee: I am the president, these are the committee members drawn from every corner and tribe because we want a government for the whole nation. Everyone who registered online has already received the membership card. Recruit as many people as you can and register to vote. Next week, we expect twenty people coming from each district to our first ever conference at which we shall announce our policies and provide a complete list of our leadership. Thank you once again for your patience and interest in the Democratic Progressive Party of Lubanda."

Chapter Six

THE CAMPAIGN for the biggest and best job in the land had just started. Mr Kamawu was well known for his excellent organisational ability and meticulous planning. Whatever he had done so far had shown that he had put a lot of thinking into every action or word he had said.

His campaign plan looked like a Ph.D. thesis: it had three phases. The first phase would focus on universities, colleges and seats of higher education.

"Colleges and universities are nurturing grounds for ideas," he would explain to his team.

"Starting here will help us to clarify our thinking on the many ideas we have to offer our people. The students will ask searching questions and they will try to understand the vision by deconstructing it. Once they understand, they'll buy in and form a partnership with us. Another advantage is that young people are full of energy and action which we need in this campaign. This brings with it risks of explosions of emotions but that is where leadership comes in, leadership which we shall provide."

He had a list of all the colleges he would visit and the themes and sub-themes of the speeches to be delivered. He even had expected questions, opposition, and safety precautions for the students and his team. Rachel said that he had planned far even including the socks he would wear on the day.

The second phase of his campaign plan took the form of speeches and rallies in all towns and cities terminating in the capital which would host the last event. As a small country there were two cities and eight towns. There was a unique message specific for each city and town. The final rally would be held in the capital city three days before the election.

"In the cities and towns are the middle class who understand issues and systems. In them are also the poorest people in the land who live in poor housing or are semi-homeless. We should have a different way of talking to them, to give them hope and generate sustained support for the movement."

The third phase would be speeches and rallies in all rural areas and outposts. The encompassing theme of his campaign strategy was unity under the slogan "Lubanda for all." Moses had understood the psychology of the rural voters, conservative, pensive and reflective. The gift Lubanda had was that unlike the poor rural dwellers elsewhere, they had land. They grew their own crops and needed little money for their daily upkeep. However, they were also the areas of most need. Development trickled very slowly to villages if at all and often it did so because of poor infrastructure and communication. During the past five years, he had learnt to speak a language they understood. He will have to explain clearly what development meant to them and a vision different from the towns but compatible with unity among all.

One other fascinating point about the campaign strategy was the different methods of delivering his speeches. They all had a visual component to illustrate his ideas. When he was asked about this he said:

"Many of our folks have no idea of what is possible. Generations have by history and geography been prevented from participating in the world economy and positive outcomes of industrial revolutions. They grew up in the areas they were born under broken political and economic systems. These systems are all they know, the best of what can be and they suppose every country is run in the same way. We need to show them comparative reference points." He prepared film clips and photographs as visual prompts to go with his speeches. "The clips will help them to see what is possible and where we are going."

He had been gathering equipment for the campaign. He had ordered special adapted vehicles that carried screens and real time online broadcast equipment. He even had backups for each aspect of his programme in case he was sabotaged by Absalom and his uncle.

The last rally was planned for the capital city three days before the polls opened. He hoped this event would mark the climax of the campaign. He had no idea about the turnout but he had his estimates and a speech at the ready. There were only three people who were privy to the whole document – himself, his wife and his trusted secretary.

After launching the DPPL, the telephone was buzzing and everyone in the office was full of energy. People were calling to congratulate Moses on a wonderful speech and statesman behaviour. That morning alone, five million dollars had been pledged in support to help the party, much of it anonymously donated. Those who could not donate pledged to offer support in kind. Institutions and companies offered their support and good wishes. The movement for change was now in full swing.

Moses was most pleased that the event passed on smoothly and the message he received from the Police Chief was encouraging. He rang to thank him for managing the crowds peacefully and offered his support to work with him in future events. He was aware that the police force was in a difficult position so Moses had a plan to both manage their fears and exploit their concealed support for the movement for change. So far, it was reassuring.

Two telephone calls were memorable. The first was received by Kashimbi from an elderly sounding lady. She asked to speak to Moses personally. Kashimbi insisted in taking the message but the woman would have none of it.

"Can I talk to President Kamawu, madam?"

"Sorry mum. Can I have your name, mum?"

"Do you love Moses like I do? Do you want to save his life? Get me on to him, *now*, please!"

Moses who was walking in saw the expression on Kashimbi's face.

"Can I talk to the person?" He took the phone. "Hullo, mum, how are you? I'm Moses and thank you for calling. How can I help you?"

"Listen Son, I am a cleaner in a hotel and as you were delivering that wonderful speech, two men who were watching it from our hotel said things I must let you know."

"Thank you for your concern and care. I really appreciate it," said Moses who quickly walked back into his office.

"They were cursing you most of the time and said they will blow you up at the university. Son, if you are planning an event at any university, please be careful. Be very careful. They are evil," she stressed as she ended. "I secretly took a picture of these men on my phone – who should I send it to?"

Moses thanked the woman and told her that she had been brave and most likely, saved his life. He invited her to visit him when he had won the election. He asked her not to tell other people for her own security.

The second telephone came later in the evening when he was at the table with the family. He decided to answer the telephone himself.

"Good evening, Sir! I wonder whether you have a moment to talk."

"Good evening. Yes, I do. May I know who is speaking?" he asked curiously as he put down the food he was about to put in the mouth.

"My name is General Kalwiji Mufuka. I am calling to arrange a meeting on behalf of twenty other people."

"No problem General, but it might not be easy to meet with twenty people because I have to get permission for a meeting of more than five people."

"Five of us will attend the meeting. When do you want the meeting?"

"As soon as possible, Sir."

"Where do you want us to meet?"

"Your home may be ideal since you are under surveillance."

"Do you want to come now? Can you come by taxi?"

"Yes, Sir. We shall be there in an hour."

Rachel was not pleased and thought this was careless or too risky to arrange an impromptu meeting with strangers when he is wanted dead by the President. Moses alerted his security to find out about the incoming visitors. They found out that General Kalwiji had left the government ten years ago. He was a businessman and a decent citizen.

He decided to hold the meeting in the guest house panic room. Security was doubled and Rachel was told to look after the children much to her displeasure.

The men arrived by taxi which was immediately sent back as soon as they reached the gate. It was a company of five men. They were escorted to the empty guest house. Rachel insisted she should see the men and would leave them after introductions.

When the parties met, there was a friendly atmosphere. Rachel recognised one of the men, a husband to a distant relative who was fired from the army several years before for insubordination. He was a successful farmer in a town fifty miles away. She offered them coffee and cakes which were never in short supply. General Kalwiji insisted Rachel attend the meeting as well.

"Congratulations Sir, that speech has never been heard in our land and like many people, we loved it. We are convinced you have a real chance to change this country. However, we are concerned that you are up against a very dangerous enemy who has killed many people over the years. We have been picking up rumours that he wants to assassinate you during your campaign trips. We, five of us and fifteen others so far, have volunteered to support you by forming a special force. We understand security issues and we know the system well. We are all former soldiers. On our way here, we received a message that many former soldiers, intelligence officers and policemen would like to join. Your current security arrangements will not be affected. We want to offer another ring of security. If you are happy for us to go ahead, I, General Kalwiji will be the organiser and the five of us will form the command unit. We might need a bit of money for fuel and other logistical arrangements but we shall largely finance ourselves. As you may know, Sir, we have our boys too still serving and will have access to good intelligence."

Moses who was listening carefully and in his customary habit, studying their faces, smiled, stood up and hugged each of the men. Rachel was shocked to see this show of emotion from Moses. She did not recall seeing him so emotional before.

"Gentlemen, I have no words to thank you. When we began this journey, I never realized it would be a journey of so many people. I have no cause to distrust you except to admire your courage. This will be dangerous for you. I am happy for you to go ahead but please keep me informed of developments. Please be careful, too, that you are not infiltrated by President Chimwanga's men."

Business done, they talked about farms and business and how delighted they were to help. Moses provided two separate cars to take them home and arranged with General Kalwiji to come in the afternoon the following day for more discussions and to get money for fuel for the "special force."

Back in the house Rachel was convinced her husband was going to win the elections. The genuine outpouring of support was unprecedented.

"Honey, why did you hug those men, total strangers?"

"That is the point, Rachel – total strangers offering to die for you is overwhelming."

"What will you do for them when you become president?"

"Honour their sacrifice. You cannot pay for life but give honour. No sum of money is sufficient for a precious life."

Delilah drove to the farm very early in the morning. In her hands were photographs of the latest attack on her house. She had returned to her house a week before, reinforced security and had additional CCTV installed. Last night she went to her mum who insisted that after such positive publications of the launch, she would have provoked the President and his men.

The photographs showed what she had found when she had arrived. She had found the gate and the door wide open. In the dining room was a bottle filled with blood, suspended from the lampshade above the table. On the wall was written in blood:

"You, bitch, will be dead by six tomorrow. Say your goodbyes today. That is our kindness."

Moses stepped forward, embraced Delilah who was evidently shaken and escorted her to the sitting room. Rachel too was seriously concerned. The previous time they came to break the doors and windows but now they have directly threatened her life.

"Delilah, you will be fine. They do not want you to come to the conference tomorrow or to publish articles about the conference. It is a tactic," Moses said as calmly as ever. "Come, let us have breakfast – we shall fix him."

After breakfast Moses disappeared into his office and emerged thirty minutes later with a video of men attacking the house. These were the same men on the photograph supplied by the anonymous woman; the only person missing was Absalom. These were the men hired by Absalom to attack Moses and his supporters, especially Delilah.

The clip was placed on the internet and one of the international private television stations broadcast it on their news channel. By midday, police had picked up the men; Absalom was still in the wind, however.

Preparations for the conference were in full swing. Moses thanked the policemen for prompt action and reiterated his support. In a private conversation, Delilah told Moses that she was shaken but would not back out. She affirmed her support and accepted Rachel's invitation to relocate to their guest house for at least a week.

Late in the afternoon, one man decided to stage a protest at Delilah's house in support of her paper and the work she was doing. In less than three hours, ten thousand people had gathered. The policemen were scared there might be trouble. They called Moses who came and spoke to the people, praised them for their support and requested them to disperse assuring them that Delilah would be protected and that they should be vigilant. They chanted "Death to Absalom and away with Chimwanga!" as they dispersed. All the taboos were crumbling as fast as Chimwanga's regime.

Chapter Seven

PRESIDENT CHIMWANGA was an angry man and under siege. He was angry with his cabinet for not stopping Moses early. He was angry with General Aaron Makwayanga for refusing to obey orders and angry with Hon. Katooka for running away with his money and angry with himself for trusting him.

General Aaron Makwayanga was put on house arrest soon after refusing to kill civilians. The man he appointed as replacement apparently also refused as well to kill civilians. The agreement was that he was only acting for a short time. He demanded that the military guard General Aaron Makwayanga instead of the police. He posted a special unit to guard the General. This meant that the General would do whatever he wanted.

Hon. Katooka was at large, rumoured to be in either London or America. Efforts to track him were leading nowhere. He knew that if he saw the attack on his niece, he would not keep quiet. What was he going to do to stop him? What of Moses, how does he stop him? He had been gathering support and to be honest, he was more admirable than Absalom. But if he came to power, he might hang him or disgrace him even more. Old tactics should work.

He called for Absalom who was rarely seen in public and was jeered each time he showed up anywhere. Once he was seen with his children in the mall, without the quick action of the guards, he would have been lynched. Now he walked with a large group of armed men.

They met and hatched a plan. They should let Moses' conference pass but work to assassinate him afterwards. They knew what his engagements were and planned to attack him. Once he was dead, they would work on the other leaders.

Absalom and his uncle decided to form a hit squad since they did not trust the defence forces. They called a secret meeting of the soldiers from his village, promoted them and gave them large sums of money. They were asked to recruit at least thirty more men who would be taken to the President's village for special training. One man recruited was the cleaner's son and on the day of the secret midnight meeting with the men, she saw an army vehicle come for him. As a soldier he was regularly picked up but this time it had all the hallmarks of a clandestine activity.

When he came back two hours later, he said very little, hardly smiled and looked rather troubled. She tried to talk to him but he was not engaging well. He left the following evening after saying goodbye to his mother and said he was going on an operation for a week.

The conference was yet another resounding success; thanks to the threats issued to Chimwanga, there was no open attempt to disrupt the event. Credit too went to the Special Force who deployed security around the conference venue and organised air transport to pre-empt evil plans from the government. This reduced concerns of an ambush along the road. More importantly, they picked up information on the hit squad, traced the training camp in the President's village and found out how much money they had been paid. They decided not to release this information during the conference.

The two and half day long conference was extended to three. On the first day they started with a welcome speech by the interim president of the Party. He was clearly a delighted man. He spent breakfast meeting as many of the delegates as possible so when he stood up to welcome them, they all had a personal attachment to the man. The welcome speech was short:

"Fellow members, I warmly welcome each of you and all of you to this our first conference. It is a privilege to be found in this company. We are a party unlike other parties. We have a vision, we have a purpose, we have principles and values and we have a plan for change. Over the time we shall be together, we shall discuss and share the vision, principles and strategies. You are all history makers."

The rest of the morning was spent on team building activities and getting to know each other. Various activities encouraged people to mix and work together. He invited people from his companies and network to deliver some of the seminars. Moses himself spent the day meeting every single delegate and getting to know them. In the afternoon various members of the interim leadership delivered speeches and the day ended with entertainment. The special force sealed off the college.

The second day was spent on the party's vision, its values and accompanying manifesto. Moses strongly believed that a party must have these to govern. He took charge of the proceedings after an effective delivery by Rachel. Delegates started off with discussions in their district groups to draw up lists of the needs of the district and what could be done to bring development. They were asked to divide the list into three parts: short term, medium and long term. Two lists were further drawn: what needed money and what did not require much money. Then these were discussed as a region and developed into a regional plan. Finally, the various regional plans were collated and bound into a national aspiration plan.

Then Rachel delivered the draft manifesto developed in the office. The conference amended it with the national plan. By the end of day two, they all had what they named 'A people's manifesto.' On the morning of day three, there were elections for the district, regional and national executive committees.

In the afternoon Moses delivered a speech on strategies for winning the election. He finally gave a closing speech in the evening. The conference ended with a big party.

This was another milestone. Proceedings though were not smooth and straightforward. In the week leading up to the conference, Moses called Delilah into his office, the inner office, for the first time. It was a masterpiece. From the table and chairs to the books on the shelves, it was marvellous. The certificates on the walls and graduation pictures were impressive.

The reason for the meeting was to discuss the leadership of the party. Moses wanted Delilah to join the leadership team as secretary general because Rachel decided to focus on other responsibilities. However, he did not want her to leave the newspaper because the party was benefiting from the publications. They agreed that she would be Media and Communications Adviser until after the elections. Then after appointments to cabinet she would come in at the right opportunity. Delilah was happy with this plan. The post of Secretary General was openly contested at the conference and the two candidates who stood for it were very ambitious and forceful. They almost caused a division in the new party.

The second crack was between Moses and Yudas Yamba Mwale. When Moses decided to join politics, he thought of people who would help. He followed up on members of the *Think Tank.* Some had joined the government and were settled in their jobs. Three had joined international organisations. He followed these up. Most interesting was Yudas. Moses knew Yudas was a strong character and was concerned he might not work well with the rest of the team. In spite of this, he was such an intelligent man that he thought he would be the right person to head the ministry of finance or central bank.

Yudas was nominated for the post of Secretary General. Solomon Mayuka, a very intelligent and wise man who had held positions with the United Nations since completing university, was put forward as Vice President. Yudas was not happy with this snub. He decided to contest the post anyway but the delegates quickly saw his weaknesses and elected Solomon. Moses saved him from further embarrassment by pledging his support to have him elected as Secretary General. He probably was the only one who left the conference emotionally wounded. He blamed Moses for not nominating him as the Vice President.

Following the conference, the battle lines were drawn, Moses' movement had the momentum which he needed if he were to mount a serious challenge to Chimwanga. What he did not plan was the size and impact of the response from the public. Two questions occupied the people: How will Chimwanga respond and will the elections be free and fair?

Chapter Eight

THERE WAS DRAMA on the day for filing nomination papers for the election. The law required witnesses to accompany the candidate to the registration office. Chimwanga was told that Moses was going to register in the afternoon so he too decided to go in the afternoon in order to disrupt the process. Moses' Special Forces had learnt about this strategy and organised people to go in the morning instead. Standing a mile away and through social media and the internet, they marshalled their supporters to use different routes to the registration office. They were advised not to shout or make noise that may be used as an excuse to attack them. At ten hours, Moses arrived with thousands of supporters and registered his candidacy. He briefly addressed the crowd and they dispersed.

When President Chimwanga was told, he was so angry that he shot and badly wounded the head of the intelligence that went to inform him. When his turn to register came, there were no more than two hundred people, mainly passers-by who were rounded up by armed policemen to join the President. He was said to have abused the registering officer and threatened to fire him. Those who saw him thought the man was acting as though he was insane.

The shooting incident sent fear in the people but it also worked in his opponent's favour. The intelligence service got so upset that they began debriefing against him. Unfortunately for him, he did not seem to understand the mood in the country.

However, the biggest loser was going to be Absalom. He could not stand for the elections because his uncle was standing. If his uncle lost the elections and power, unthinkable as it was to him, his chances for ever becoming the next president were substantially diminished. He therefore took everything personally.

He visited the hit squad in the morning after the registration, addressed them with all the threats he could think of including burning their families and cutting their throats open. He called Moses names that cannot be repeated here. He ordered them to mercilessly slaughter him. His fit of rage and hatred had consumed him beyond any rational thinking.

"I will be president, no matter what happens. You all have to obey my orders or be slaughtered like I killed Abel, your stupid unionist and of course my brother. My own blood brother. You betray me and you are dead, you fail to kill Moses you are dead!" On this note he concluded his address to the petrified men. As if the threats were not enough, he gave them more money in what he called an advance payment.

The hit squad finished their training and was ready to be deployed. Kamonu, the cleaner, was very suspicious of her son's recent behaviour. He appeared to be restless and withdrawn but with a sudden fortune. He bought himself a new car and replaced the furniture in his house. She tried to talk to him about it but he refused to discuss anything. The day before Moses' first rally at the university, Kamonu went into her kitchen and, watching through the window, she could see the goings in and out of her son's house. Her son went out at the same time, picked up by the same car. She knew they would be coming for him but she wanted to see who was picking him up. When the car arrived, she recognised one face, Absalom. The car sped off in the darkness. She crept into her son's house and without causing suspicion, she searched the house and under the pillow found an envelope full of money with dates and locations for their plans in the upcoming weeks. It was a list of Moses' rallies and how they would cause enough confusion to mount an attack. "The first rally – university – plant a bomb; second rally – stadium-sniper, Rogers Chikomu", her son, and a list of others. She found some paper and copied whatever she could and sneaked out just in time before he returned. She was convinced her son was recruited to assassinate Moses. She had to stop the operations but what would happen to her or her son?

An hour before Moses started off for the university, Kamonu rang. Kashimbi recognised the voice of the woman and ran outside to call him to answer the telephone. Kamonu told Moses that she had more information about a threat to his life and urged him to be more careful. At the end of her telephone conversation she added:

"If I do not live to see the day you become president, my name is Kamonu Chikomu."

"Thanks Mum; I owe you so much. Listen to me, be careful and do not let anyone know about this. I hope we shall meet soon."

Students had gathered in the hall waiting for Moses, who ordered that the venue be evacuated and relocated to the open fields in the university grounds away from the hall. He told security to leave the secret cameras in the hall to continue filming but install feeds on the vehicles. It was all suspicion but he wanted any evidence he could use to hit back. It was like he had a plan B in place already. He jumped into the truck that was delivered the previous week, adapted with a stage and microphones.

The motorcade arrived but there was no Moses. The students were restlessly disappointed. Rachel and the Secretary General spoke to the people. They assured them that he was coming. After speaking to his security and the Police Chief, he arrived in the truck much to the astonishment of the excited crowd.

The truck was transformed with a stage and two large screens by the side. With formal procedures already announced, he went straight into addressing the people. He looked energetic with his characteristic calm and self-assured demeanour.

"Good morning everyone!" the loudspeakers rung out for miles around. "I am delighted to be here. Before I start to speak, ladies and gentlemen, I invite you to stand and observe a minute's silence for those who have been butchered and murdered by this government for their political opinions. Secondly, for my brother Abel, who was the first martyr to be slaughtered instead of me simply because he was my brother. His killer is still hunting me down this minute as though I were a rabid dog."

The silence was total, the faces tense.

"Thank you, please be seated. I am sorry for coming an hour late; I shall tell you the story next time. I am also sorry for changing the venue – both were for security reasons. For precautionary reasons, if there are any unusual noises please either remain where you are or in an orderly fashion, follow the instructions of the security personnel away from the noise and buildings.

"I am pleased to be here because this is where it all started for me. I learnt a lot of things when I was a student here and I was inspired within these buildings. I have not been in for a long time and sorry to see the state in which it has degenerated. When I become president, we shall transform this institution to its former glory and make it a world class institution competing with the best.

"First we have to kick out these murderers and bring them to justice. We are not sheep or cattle to be herded into a political kraal. Neither is the president of the time our God. I have offered myself for election because I want to make a lasting change. As I have told you, bombs have been planted to kill me. Hit squads have been trained to kill me. It's possible there are snipers in the trees or on buildings to shoot at me. I want you to know that I will not back away. I shall bring this fight to its bitter end. If that means shedding my blood, please step up and take on the fight until we bring change.

"Second, I want you to work harder. Do not only study to pass the examinations, study to increase your knowledge. I shall need educated men and women to turn round the economy and the country and to forge the path of development. I am not standing to make money – I am lucky to have enough to survive on; neither am I standing to enjoy power for its own sake. I am here to join you to rebuild this country – to put bread back onto the shelves in the shops, to bring dignity to Lubandans, to create jobs so all of you can fulfil your dreams and your children's dreams. I shall not be a president who is paid for spending time plotting to kill but to save lives. We shall revive education, healthy, democracy and revive your pride, not fear.

"Thirdly, I want you to be involved in this movement of change and hope. Do not put yourself in harm's way but be a foot soldier, recruiting and explaining to people what we intend to do. You all have been given a copy of our manifesto; explain to people who may be struggling to understand. Send us information of what may be troubling to the ear. I am here to speak to you because citizens have picked up information that has made a difference.

"Fourthly, I want you to..."

Boom! The ground shook and an electrified panic arose among the students. Moses was pushed into the bullet proof cabin as the security men and women darted here and there. He refused to leave the scene and told them he would be safe, much to the displeasure of all the security men and women.

He was briefed that a bomb had exploded in the hall, destroying the previously assembled stage. Had there been people the harm caused would have been tragic.

He emerged from the truck and shouted:

"Are you all okay?"

"Yes!" shouted the crowd in reassuring unison.

They flashed images of the hall on the screen.

"I would have been dead, my family would have been dead, all these noble men and women would have been dead. Some of you who would have been in front would have been dead.

"What kind of a person would do this?"

"A monster! Down, down, down with the monster!" they shouted.

"I don't want you to demonstrate because Chimwanga will unleash his anger of failing to kill me on you. Stay on the campus and continue your work," Moses exhorted the now angry and shouting crowd.

Back on the farm the Police Chief and security admonished Moses for not leaving the scene promptly. He had risked the lives of many people and he should never refuse security instructions again. He told them that it was hard for a general to run away from the battlefield. He wanted to send a message to Chimwanga he was not afraid to die.

Hon. Katooka popped up on some international television telling the world how dangerous Chimwanga and his nephew were. He gave graphic accounts of how other leaders had been assassinated in the past.

Foreign governments pledged their support to Moses and promised to do whatever they could to help him. All the institutions and governments that were lending money to Chimwanga's government suspended payments on Moses' request except money going directly to the people.

The assassination attempt occupied the media and people's conversations for the whole week. Delilah got more information from her uncle and printed more accounts of Chimwanga's dark regime. These helped Moses. His popularity had grown massively. In fact, the DPPL website crashed because of the sheer volume of traffic, people wanting to join. Various pieces of interesting and damaging information were published on the internet. It had now become a public fight. A list of the hit squad and how much they were paid was published and most of them were beaten up by the angry citizens. More of Absalom's promiscuous activities and abuse was in all the papers. Even the government controlled papers broke the taboo and began publishing damaging information. More information was released of how Absalom killed his brother in bed. By any measure, this was a revolution of the people.

Chimwanga had become a hostage. There was open rebellion and defiance to the President the likes of which he had never seen. But he wasn't down and out yet. In fact, he was now badly wounded and resolved to revenge.

Chapter Nine

PRESIDENT CHIMWANGA decided to replace all the heads of defence, demoted some ministers and filled the posts with people from his tribe. It was a wide ranging reshuffle intended to create a political fortress. Some soldiers were promoted from the rank of private to commander. This was an ill-advised and ill-thought out manoeuvre. There were ripples of resistance in the already disgruntled forces.

Moses called for calm and insisted the elections should go ahead and appealed to the armed forces to remain vigilant and assured them the situation would be resolved soon after the elections. He continued with his campaign.

After the setback of the first rally, the rest of the rallies at the colleges, universities, cities and towns went very well. He decided no rally would take place indoors to minimise the risks. They moved with their own platforms and the trucks became key features.

The message to the young people was to sell them the vision. He showed them how the subjects they were studying would impact on development. He showed them how they had a future in spite of the record unemployment. At every rally, he asked for a dream from the students and he took them through the stages of fulfilling that dream. The core message was that there was still hope and a change of leadership would deliver opportunities for them. He explained to them the role he wanted them to play in the election. At the end of the first phase, there were armies of followers volunteering to campaign for him.

The second phase of Moses' campaign passed off peacefully. He visited all the towns. As he had done in the other areas, he talked about the local needs, showed them examples of plans of what their town would be like. He explained the economic potential of each town and showed how they would achieve development. By the time he finished touring all the towns there was no doubt that he had the people on his side. If the people would vote in the numbers that attended the rallies, Chimwanga, despite his best efforts, would never manage to rig the elections.

The third phase was campaigning in the rural areas. The strategy here was different. Moses strolled to the podium and addressed the people in their local languages. This was now typical of his campaigns; he began by addressing their needs of which he had a list drawn by the delegates from the conference and observations he noted as he went out on business. He even read about the history of the village and the area and the people loved him. He showed a video or pictures of a village and town with similar geographical features from abroad and contrasted the development. Then he ended with a list of strategies on how they should start to improve their village or town, starting with the things they could do without huge sums of money. His local party committees were asked to lead on these projects and in all the places he had visited, people joined in to work on various projects.

Delilah became his number one admirer, keen to learn and ask questions. She had long realised that Moses had unique combinations of character. He was a learned man, hard worker, eloquent speaker, loving and understanding yet assertive, strong but calm. Even at his most vulnerable, these qualities carried him through remarkably well. Perhaps the most potent weapon was his ability to communicate with all types of people. Artistic oratory with intellectual spices were overwhelming for his audiences. He was even getting better at it with every rally. When he spoke with international leaders he was full of confidence and strategic. When he spoke to the unemployed, he spoke with reassurance. She therefore made studying him and his tactics a personal private project.

"Why are you running these projects around the country now? Wouldn't it be a good idea to wait until you become president?" Delilah asked as they were waiting to leave Chimwanga's town where people were so excited and had just launched one of the projects.

"Because I am not driven by popularity but service. I also want to give people belief that they can change and change begins with them. In addition, I want to harness the communal spirit; it will be the radar guiding this country during my presidency."

"Is that the reason you do not give a lot of money to the political activists like other politicians?"

"Yes, I will give them sufficient money to survive on because hungry people will not do a good job, but free money is part of a false economy. Instead, I will give money for projects to benefit many people. Besides, I want people to support the movement and buy into its values, not to buy support which is also false political capital."

"When and how did you learn all these languages?"

"Delilah, you remind me of my six-year-old boy, he asks interesting questions! I began learning when I decided I would enter politics. The reason why Chimwanga's current strategy is not working is because he does not understand people. I do. For many years our country was ruled by divide and rule along tribal loyalties and the legacy you know – wars, suspicions, tensions and underdevelopment. I want to show people that we should value our languages and cultures but we should value the human being most. We shouldn't be divided because we speak different languages. Remember God did not breathe into a language but man. Our value is in what we are as human beings in spite of your language, culture or colour of skin."

"You have not answered the other question, Sir? How did you learn?"

"Let us leave that for another day, the campaign is still long."

There had been rumours recently that President Chimwanga had brought in Mercenaries from another despot to assassinate Moses. He had no faith in his own security forces who he accused of being sympathetic to Moses.

The next visit was to a large rural town with beautiful surroundings. The land was exceptionally fertile and the undulations in the hills gave the area tranquillity and made it good for retreats. Moses had built a motel on one of the hills giving him beautiful scenery. It was popular with visitors and tourists.

When he landed, people blocked the road to the motel and told him not to go there because they had seen suspicious strangers in the area. His security team advised him to cancel the rally scheduled for that afternoon. He refused. He said he was not giving in to these people. As the security officers were trying to figure out what to do, he walked off to the school opposite the road and knocked on the Headteacher's house. Delilah followed him.

"Can I come in Mr Banda?"

"Yes, Sir, but the house is not clean for important people," Banda explained, rather embarrassed as he cleared his papers. Moses helped pick up the papers from the floor, drew the nearest table chair towards him and sat down.

"Mr Banda, listen carefully, I was on my way to the hotel but I am told there are undesirable people around. Have you seen any strange visitors? And can we sit here for an hour before the rally?"

Mr Banda was suddenly speechless, looked terrified and scared. He pointed at one of the rooms. Moses thought he was being given a room to rest. He stood up, walked to the door and was about to open the door when Delilah dived and pushed him down away from the door and drugged him out of the house. He walked out, stretched his suit and was immediately surrounded by his security team and driven away. Delilah did not recall what happened.

Banda was dragged out with his two-year-old child and the house was surrounded. Poor Banda did not know that the men who hired a room in his house were mercenaries hired to kill the candidate. They hired the room because it was overlooking the venue of the rally and gave them a good view.

In the ensuing gun fight, General Kalwiji was slightly wounded but the two men were killed. The rumours were confirmed.

The rally would go ahead, insisted Moses. Seven other mercenaries were found in the motel and arrested. The rally was attended by many people. The man who was told he had walked into death had renewed vigour. He began his speech taunting President Chimwanga:

"President Chimwanga, Sir, your foreign soldiers are here; eight are dead and two are attending my rally in chains."

Unexpectedly, he asked the security men to bring the arrested men forward. He asked them why they wanted to kill him. They could not afford to lie in front of the large crowd.

"Ladies and gentlemen, you heard with your ears, they were hired from the north and promised to be paid millions. Take them away and let them be locked up. Be careful with such men, they must be well trained."

The rally went ahead as planned; he showed them pictures of a similar town in Norway and showed what it would look like if they developed that area. He visited some of the projects, people had done then he left for the day.

"Sir, you are not scared, why?" asked Delilah.

"Thank you for saving my life, Delilah. I did not plan to go to that house, it was instinctive."

"You were in the lion's mouth, Sir," Delilah said.

The telephone rang – it was General Kalwiji.

"General, thank you for saving my life; how are you feeling?"

"Sir, please do not enter any more houses."

"Yes, Sir. How are you?"

"I am fine, Sir. Fine, only a grazing on my forehead."

"Are you sure, can I fly you out to the hospital? I can't afford to lose you."

"No, Sir, this is nothing. I am back to work planning for the next battle. Chimwanga is still going strong."

"Well, the old cliché, the last kicks of a dying horse. Thanks general, I shall see you soon."

Another phone call. This time it was Rachel. She had remained behind because of the children.

"Hi darling, how are you feeling? Are you alright? Why didn't you call or ask Delilah to call? I have just seen the shoot out on the news."

"Sorry mum, I was busy with the rally."

"Stubborn man, who will look after these children? What happened?"

"Delilah was there, she dragged me out of the room! What would I do without the women in my life? Here is Delilah, she will tell you everything."

Delilah narrated the full story like an article for an evening paper, receiving much gratitude from Rachel who thanked her profusely for saving the father of her children.

"Hey darling, take care, I shall be home soon; I am alive to die another day."

After the second assassination attempt, Moses' followers forced him to postpone a few rallies and made him rest for a while. Meanwhile, all newspapers were full of praise for his courage and bravery. *The Citizen Chronicle* focussed more on the projects he was initiating and how they were already changing the attitudes and lives of the people. Much of the campaign money went into the projects and the people seemed to appreciate this more than individual gifts. The fact that he could speak almost all the major languages was a big bonus. But this was not an accident; he planned it and worked at it. This was a long term project that caught everybody by surprise, especially the government.

Many international observers were setting up for the Election Day. Moses had yet a few more rallies to attend. One would be in his home district and the last one in the capital city on the eve of the Election Day.

Chapter Ten

CHIMWANGA and Absalom had hardly done any campaigning. Chimwanga's popularity had plummeted and the invincibility and fear he held over people had evaporated. It was unthinkable not long ago that the people of Lubanda would be so brave as to challenge the President. They were scared of going out and when they did only a few people turned up. He even attempted a rally in his hometown but people refused to attend. The few that attended told him off for putting them in danger with his record. If a new government came to power and behaved like him, they would all be dead. He had disgraced the clan and the tribe because other tribes would never trust them. He stormed out of the meeting angrily and complained of being betrayed.

Absalom went to his constituency and he too was not welcomed by his supporters. He was called a traitor and he left before he could address a single rally. It appeared there were now very few places for them to hide or run to. This was a people's revolution of a kind unseen before. With every day that went by, the people felt confident to overhaul the regime they hated. Hon. Katooka was reported to have frozen all the accounts he managed on behalf of President Chimwanga and had told him the money would be returned to the people.

President Chimwanga had two cards left, one to rig the elections, the other being to attempt once again to kill Moses. The first may not work because nobody might be ready and willing to do the rigging for him. They would give it another try to eliminate him anyway. The primary strategy was still to throw the opposition in disarray by killing Moses. They could not understand how Moses had managed to escape all the traps that were set for him. The next target would be the rally in Moses' home district.

For the next attempt, President Chimwanga contacted all the people that had killed for him before and told them if they did not stop Moses, he would hang them all for their crimes when he became president. To survive, they should stop him. They planned to ambush him on his way home after the rally. They guessed he would travel by road to greet people who were already anxiously waiting for him in the outlying villages.

The last chance to stop Moses or lose power arrived. These men were more afraid than loyal and this made them determined. They provided them with everything that they wanted. Moses' Special protection force of volunteers had been made aware of vehicles missing from the barracks and some activity going on around Absalom's farm. They alerted the protection network of an impending attack. They did not know what form it would take and who was still supporting President Chimwanga. They suspected that since he had tried a bomb and failed, snipers and failed, he might try an ambush. They suggested Moses fly back to the city after the rally but Moses thought going by road would enable him to campaign along the road and meet those who were waiting for him. He did not want to disappoint any of his supporters.

The new hit squad set off at dusk in four land rovers and a jeep. Unfortunately, in their reckless rush, one of the front vehicles hit a buffalo (one of a herd of buffalo) crossing the road and overturned killing three men and badly injured two. They had no time to lose so they left the injured and dead to wait for a backup from Absalom.

Meanwhile, Moses' nephew, a medical doctor, had promised to join him on the campaign that day but he had a long list of operations to finish. After the shift he decided to join him anyway and meet him. He had not been allowed to join these campaigns because Moses believed some members of the family should stay away in case he died. On the way he was the first to come across the accident involving an army vehicle. He stopped to help any victims. As he gathered the papers and belongings of the victims, he noticed the picture of Moses in a folder. He looked around and saw identical folders with identical content. He opened one and found a detailed and chilling account of the plot; he immediately left the scene. He had the presence of mind to take photographs of the vehicle, the dead people and the two injured men.

After driving away from the scene, he stopped and called to alert Moses of his find. Moses told him to immediately go back to the city and look after his family in case they decided to attack the farm as well. The doctor turned back and sped to the capital. When he reached the scene of the accident again, he took the two injured men with him to the hospital. He gave them Valium in case they woke up. "This Geneva Convention is stupid, how can I save men who were going to kill my uncle? God, for my kindness please preserve my Moses," he prayed.

He drove straight to the hospital and left them. He told the hospital that he found them on the road but he carried all the folders.

In the village the rally was well attended; men and women came from all the surrounding villages and sang and danced as though they had already won the elections. After all, Moses was their child. The fact that one of them was about to become a president filled them with great pride. It was a carnival in traditional African style.

General Kalwiji and his unit devised a plan; instead of fighting because they did not know how big the threat was, they decided to hide. They sent more men to guard Rachel. They decided to leave Delilah in the village but took her suitcase full of dresses. Although Delilah was not happy to remain behind, she agreed to join them the following day.

"Please look after my clothes in the suitcase."

"Sorry mum, you may never wear these again," General Kalwiji dismissed the protestations laughing.

"Now we shall all go into the car but three miles away, we shall come out and walk into the bush. We saw a farmer's shelter at the fields and we shall go there for the night. We shall change into Delilah's dresses after we have left the village," General Kalwiji told the group.

They said their goodbyes and left. Moses and his entourage got into the car but when they reached the outskirts of the village they stopped, switched off the lights and got out, leaving the driver in the car. They told him to continue on the journey until the next big village but advised him to be careful and do all he could to stay alive. General Kalwiji got effigies of Moses from the boot and placed them at the back of the car. Then they told the driver to proceed.

"Sir, tell my children I love them," said the driver in a quivering voice.

"Don't go!" whispered Moses.

"No, Sir, I will go for your sake and I am not scared of death," he replied as he drove off.

"Don't worry Sir, he was my driver. He is a brave and skilled man and will handle any situation," the General assured Moses.

Deep into the forest they shared Delilah's clothes but Moses refused to wear a dress. The general explained that it was a disguise so they could confuse the enemy. He was having none of it. The bodyguard ripped a blouse and tied it to Moses' head. They followed a path into the woods and then into a maize field where there was an open shelter. They all looked funny in their disguise. They secretly sent a message back to Delilah to tell the local party chairman that they were still around in that area and they disclosed their whereabouts to him.

Six miles away the driver entered the woods and suddenly a duiker ran across the road and he swerved the car to the side of the road. Without warning he heard gunshots and being a former soldier he dived to the other side of the car and exited through the passenger door. There were more bursts of gunshots. A bullet ripped through his left leg but he managed to crawl away and hide behind the nearest big tree. The assailants continued firing at the car ceasing only when the engine began to smoke and crackle. They jumped into their cars and sped away. The driver was able to read one number plate as they left. He slowly crawled his way to the nearest village about three miles away and took refuge in one of the houses in the village.

Moses sat quietly, thinking. General Kalwiji who ripped up two skirts to make one in order to fit his waist sent two of the men to look for the driver. Half way to the scene the driver rang and told them he was injured in the leg and gave a description of where he was. They found him and gave him a lift back to the shelter.

Around midnight the President announced the death of Moses. He ordered flags to fly at half mask and he declared a one-week period of national morning. He did not tell Moses' wife or his Cabinet.

The country was shocked. Rachel told the followers to be calm and she said she would not start crying until she saw his body. The nation would be informed once they got concrete information. In the village, the Party Chairman and Delilah sneaked away to the field to bring medicine for the injured man and tea. When they arrived at the shelter Delilah almost spilled whatever she carried in a fit of laughter. Seeing all the men in her clothes was hilarious. She still laughs uncontrollably whenever she recalled the incident of that night.

They were airlifted secretly in the morning to Moses' farm. There were doctors at hand to treat the driver. Delilah continued to enjoy the fun as she asked for clothes to wear because her clothes had been ripped by the men.

Rumours surfaced that Moses was alive. Absalom and Chimwanga were embarrassed and scared when it was confirmed Moses was alive and well. For the first time, they realised the power they had abused was no longer theirs. In the afternoon, Moses held a press conference at his farm. He told the people what had happened and asked them to spend the day in thanksgiving to God for preserving him yet again. In the next few days, *The Citizen Chronicle* published the details of the plot from the papers found at the scene of the accident. The evidence from the injured hit squad taken to the hospital and those who carried out the assassination attempt was so overwhelming that it could not be denied. The police were compelled to arrest Absalom on the orders of the fired generals who felt that they had to keep order or the country would be ungovernable. Chimwanga intervened; he was bailed out and put on house arrest. Moses insisted that the elections must go ahead and Chimwanga be kept in office to protect the constitution.

Chapter Eleven

MOSES SAT IN HIS OFFICE withdrawn from the activity and joy outside, deep in thought. He wondered how many of these attacks he would have to survive. He stood up, walked to a hidden filing cabinet and took out a notebook. It was a register of names he had been compiling over the years, of people who had been killed by the current president or whose deaths had been linked to Chimwanga's dirty tricks. By a stroke of sheer luck, and perhaps because of forthright judgements and thinking, he had so far been spared the fate of Makobo, Musachi, Chishika and Mulumendo who had all previously tried to challenge President Chimwanga and were annihilated, not allowed to fulfil their dreams. These were leaders who could have changed the country, yet the tyrant exterminated them in cold blood to enable him to remain in power. Somehow, here he was, still alive although unlike the others, he had experienced the mourning of his own death.

He was grateful to all those who did *something* to save his life. He thought of the ambush the previous night near his home in which an innocent Asian businessman who drove a car that was similar to his was badly injured and the other failed ambush in the central region. He had been out campaigning and at the end of the day he was getting into the car when a small boy ran to him and put a paper in his hand. Many people were pressing on him and touching him so he could not remember the boy's face.

When he opened the piece of paper, there were three words written on it: "DO NOT TRAVEL." He stopped the car, told General Kalwiji and both agreed not to travel. He learnt later that the message came from a supporter who worked in the secret service office, one hundred miles away from the village where he got the note. He remembered the story behind the note clearly.

The message came from a woman in the city. The woman was semi illiterate, having dropped out of school because she needed a job to support her siblings left orphaned by AIDS. On that day Moses was campaigning in the central region. Muyokela was carrying out her duty cleaning offices near the Commander of the Intelligence Service when she noticed a note that had slipped off the table. Aware of the cameras and surveillance equipment in the building, she swept the note along until she reached a blind corner behind the filing cabinets. She scooped up the rubbish and took the piece of paper, evading the monitoring security cameras.

She read the paper, which said:

"Ambush target X as he leaves the town at junction F. Target car, drive into it from the side road to appear like an accident. Do not mess it up."

The note may have fallen as someone was rushing away. She guessed the X must be Moses. The woman quickly finished cleaning her portion of the premises and ran home. She called her cousin who lived near the venue of the rally in the central region.

The woman's story and her commitment to save his life were remarkable. "These are the real heroes of change," Moses muttered to himself. Ordinary people and the heroic service of the Special Secret Service helped to keep him alive. All he had was an ambition to save Lubanda; an ambition long conceived but nurtured by fortune, misfortune and smart thinking.

He thought of the final rally, the grand finale mass rally coming at midday. His mind wandered from the speech to the management of the event and safety for the people. What was in store for him today? How many people would come? What else was Chimwanga planning? How about the safety of all the people who were coming? He walked to the window, gazing into the far distance or into his soul...

Rachel's voice brought him back.
"Hi honey, how is the speech coming along? How are the children?"
"They are fine."
"I don't want them to go to the stadium in case of trouble. However, there will be many families so we shall take them with us. Please listen to whatever General Kalwiji advises you to do."
"What do you think Chimwanga and Absalom will be doing today?"
"Plotting their next attack."
"I think today they will be scared of the people. It will be foolish for them to attack me openly because the people will defend me or riot."
"I think they will drink themselves to bed to avoid watching us."
"Darling, whatever they choose to do, God is with you. I brought you tea."

As he sipped his tea he remembered the last trip he took with Mary. It was at the end of the semester, after the severe asthma attack that nearly killed him. Mary had decided to take him out on holiday to Tennessee. Mary had long realised that Moses was interested in politics. She loved the way he came alive when talking about politics. She also discovered that he knew more about Martin Luther King Jr. than herself. He must have read more about him. In one of their many discussions about politics, Moses said what he liked best about Martin Luther King Jr was the sincerity of his convictions. He often referred to him as one of the black people's greatest leaders. Another man who received this honour was Nelson Mandela. So on this occasion Mary thought a visit to the spot where Martin Luther King Jr was shot would be a good idea. Romance was put aside as they approached Lorraine Motel. Moses stopped.

"Mary, this is where the leader was short, am I right?"

She nodded. "I'm sorry, I wanted to surprise you," said Mary in a quivering voice.

"Please don't apologise, I am grateful, will forever be grateful."

"How did you recognise this place?"

He did not wait to answer the question. He walked straight to the spot where the true leader was shot, oblivious of all those who were there including Mary. He stood on the spot silently for several minutes. Mary who had followed him hardly said a word. Suddenly, he turned to Mary. "The dream did not end here," he said. "The dream will not end here. The dream shall end at God's court of justice." He grabbed Mary, hugged her as never before, looked into her eyes, and kissed her. Mary wrote an account of this event in her diary of which a copy was given to him after her funeral. According to Mary, he displayed very strong emotions of anger and defiance.

Whether Moses was visiting Lorraine Motel or some other shrine of political resistance, he finally came back. He stood up, straightened his suit and said to himself, "The fight is not over. We shall fight to win, not to die. Many have died for the cause but the cause does not die. Every generation has a duty to provide leadership for the cause until justice is secured at God's court of justice." Whether it was Martin Luther King Jr, Mary or Abel's spirit that visited him, we shall never know. Moses with a bright face and a determined look in his eyes, was ready for the next and final fight for freedom from Chimwanga.

Chapter Twelve

THE STREETS OF LUBINDI, the capital city of Lubanda, were overflowing with people. Like a herd of buffalo, the peopled trouped to the stadium and other places designated for them to participate in the rally. They moved the whole morning, sending tremors to Chimwanga's heart and lungs. This was not an ordinary rally; it was a consummation of the people's movement. Movement for change, movement to dismiss Chimwanga and movement for the future of Lubanda. There were people shouting, others singing, children crying, car horns blowing and many talking and laughing. The air was full of overwhelming excitement and optimism.

It had been like this since dawn. In a show of support, the people had been trouping to either the stadium or a viewing post set up for this event. The rally was due to start in two hours and everyone was rushing to one of the many places where they could watch the big screen and listen to their leader's speech. Moses and his team had been planning for this event for a long time. He had identified open fields where people could gather to listen to the speech while watching a big screen. Apart from the main arena, all other viewing posts around the city were located either in open football grounds or other large open spaces. He had also ordered several vans carrying big mobile screens that could broadcast the speech across many places in the city. These were now deployed in all the viewing posts. All but the public television stations were enlisted to cover the event live.

Although the planning for this event was meticulous, there was still nervousness in the candidate's team. Chimwanga, though weakened, might try something that would harm the people. The last desperate kicks of a near dead regime. This was the day to carry out the plan and they hoped it would work perfectly well. Moses had considered the security implications seriously in case the incumbent president and his government decided to attack the people. He had worked out a secret plan with the police chief. Many people did not seem to mind about security concerns, they were prepared to fight or die for change. Defiance that had been building since Moses entered the presidential race. Many people flocked to the stadium where the main event was taking place. It was a carnival-like atmosphere, good natured and peaceful. It was not a day to wear the colours of Chimwanga's party which had been distributed over the years and worn proudly by his true supporters and many forced supporters. Mr Kamawu relied on the conversations he had with the police chief for the success of the rally. The latter promised to keep an eye on the movements of Absalom. Moses had been holding meetings with the most senior policeman for weeks before to try and win his support so that there was no violence across the city. Perhaps recognising the tide of change, he co-operated with Moses. He was confident that the police chief favourably considered his requests because all the suggestions had been incorporated in the plan they agreed upon.

Moses sat in his office making the final touches to the speech. This was the largest audience he had ever addressed and it was the defining moment. He had no problem in presenting himself as a statesman. Considering his age, inexperience and the weight of expectation he carried, this was the time to convince those who doubted and to inspire all his supporters to vote confidently. A lot hinged on this speech. Even a man who rarely doubted himself would be nervous on this big stage. Over the years he had been thinking of addressing the whole nation and here he was, on the verge of making history. He was confident of success. He had been preparing for this speech for some time. He knew it would have to inspire the people, give them a clear vision and assure them of better things to come.

They must feel the change. The serenity in his room was broken by a soft knock on the door.

"Come in Rachel, is everything okay?"

"Yes, everything is fine thank you. They say people are excited and looking forward to seeing you and it is now time – the hour has come for you to speak and make your final appeal to the country. I know you have been waiting for this hour for a long time and everyone is behind you. People have been praying for you all night and trusting that the event will pass peacefully. Let's go."

"You look stunningly beautiful, Rachel!" Moses said as he sprang from his chair and walked to meet Rachel across the room. Rachel noticed he was more relaxed and could feel the energy both in his arms and his voice. He sat down for his meal with a smile. Rachel had never known what happened to Moses in that room.

"How do you feel?" asked Rachel.

"Great. I am very fine," Moses replied.

"Have you had time to rehearse the speech?"

"I suppose over the years, yes, not today. I did more reflections."

"Is there anything I can do for you?"

"Pray for peace and look after the children; ultimately, you are all that I have."

"You have the whole country with you!"

"And the spirits of the dead in heaven!"

Holding Rachel's hand, they knelt down and prayed. Then he stood up and walked slowly along the corridor touching each picture of his heroes hanging on the wall. He reached the last two pictures; one was his Dad's and he whispered, "Thank you Dad for all you have done and taught me."

The last picture was of Professor Elijah Kamona. He said, "You started it all. It's time, let us go." With energy in his voice, he took down the picture and put it in his briefcase.

His security team were waiting in the sitting room. After half an hour of briefing and final arrangements, it was time to go. "General Kalwiji, make sure Abel and his sisters are safe!" Just as he was about to step out, general Kalwiji pulled him back in and closed the door.

"Sorry Sir, there have been shootings and we should wait for further instructions," the General said. "We have to be cautious. Please wait here until I come back." After an hour, he returned. "It is you nemesis Absalom, Sir. He wanted to leave his house with a gun but he was restrained. His gun went off in the scuffle with security but no one has been hurt. I have been told he has been locked up. The police do not think there is any threat."

Finally, the party was ready to leave. As soon as Moses stepped out, he looked at the two hundred people waiting for him like a general calling his men to arms. They cheered and screamed and he waved at them. The more he waved the louder they replied. He motioned for silence and said, "The hour ladies and gentlemen has come, it is time." This was only a rally but not an inauguration, perhaps a rehearsal for it. However, it was more important than the inauguration because it had potential to break the spine of what Moses was now calling the 'people's revolution.'

He was escorted to his car sandwiched between several cars in front and several behind. The convoy started off for the stadium. All along the route people were singing and dancing. The Lubandans love their song and dance. Here happiness does not depend on the size of the bank account but the feeling of the heart. It is the natural expression of joy that embodies the purpose for life. These poor people were living more fulfilled lives than millionaires caught up in the pursuit of riches. Moses believed that if he enhanced their lives a little bit with some life comforts like piped water and electricity, the soul of the nation would be healthier.

The twenty minutes journey from his house to the stadium took almost one and half hours as people pushed and screamed and lined the streets waving. It wasn't possible to drive at any higher speed. When he finally got to the stadium the big crowd went wild, not only those that were at the stadium but all those who were able to see him on the screens across the city and country – they all screamed and shouted. You could not mistake the fact that the man was making history and that it was his day. The level of jubilation and excitement had never been seen in Lubindi before.

Mr Kamawu's Special Forces had become a well organised force with volunteers from all forces. They covered strategic places and relayed information to the stadium. Just before Moses left his house, they had delivered an important note from the head of the army. It read:

"Good luck, Sir, the country is behind you."

The Special Forces did not take things for granted. They deployed men in his street.

One man was absent and could not witness the historic revolution – President Chimwanga. Chimwanga had been going round the country to campaign but was having little luck. The former compelling aura of fear around him was gone. A few hundred attended his rallies, possibly out of sympathy and respect, but his grip had certainly been much loosened. On this last day of campaigning, he chose to go on a state visit to the southern state. The incumbent there had been in power for many years. He had held fake elections, rigged them and continued to rule. People had given up on change. They did not know what living in a well-run, independent country meant. They knew a lot more about a despot who had amassed powers beyond removal. Chimwanga chose to visit. There were rumours he had gone for advice on how to either rig the election or secure support for a military fight. What was obvious was that the switch of allegiance in Lubanda would not be easy to fight. The people had made up their minds and the momentum was strong. He would have to kill more than half the population to secure himself another term in office. This time round, it was more than an ordinary vote, it was a revolution. Whatever Chimwanga chose to do, he would have to fight.

The moment everyone had been waiting for had arrived; Moses was introduced for the last time as a candidate to the nation. Deafening noise erupted across the city, echoes of which returned from the rest of the country.

He stood up and greeted the crowd in all the major languages of Lubanda. The crowd loved it.

"Let us first send our opponents a message…" On the screen appeared handwriting:

Mene, Mene, Tekel, Upharsin.

"Have you weighed the government of Mr Chimwanga and found it wanting?"

The crowd replied spontaneously, "YES!"

"Wanting in our freedoms?"

"Yes!"

"Wanting in providing for our health care?"

"Yes!"

"Wanting in providing for our children's education?"

"Yes!"

"Wanting in running the economy?"
"Yes!"
"Wanting in governing Lubanda?"
"YEEES!"

"The days of the present government are numbered," declared Moses. "Ladies and gentlemen, I would like to show you what we are capable of doing together."

The screen lit up with projects people had been doing all over the country initiated by DPPL and popularly known as the People's Projects. A range of projects from cleaning up communal places such as local markets, repairing failing clinics and even providing water pipes to villages. The showcase video featured unique projects from all districts – much to the delight of his audience.

"Countrymen, if we have been able to do all these projects together with little or no money, is it possible to do more with all our resources?"

"Yes!" shouted the crowd.

"Now let me show you what the power of your vote can achieve if you vote wisely on Monday."

Once again the screen lit up with the worst parts of the capital city, comparing it to major cities in the world. There were photographs of what the major cities of the world used to look like in the early nineteenth century and what they looked like in the twenty-first century. The audience fell silent. Development in Lubanda was not only possible but waiting to happen. Then they were shown examples of transformations that could happen in the major districts. They were showed examples of what good schools and modern hospitals should look like. Moses explained how he was going to fund his proposals and the number of years it would take him to achieve those goals. He explained what people can do to make individual progress, what contributions they can make as a community to develop their areas, what the business community would do to help advance prosperity and what the government would do to develop the country. Finally, he unveiled what he thought the future Lubindi should look like. The artist's impression was breath-taking.

Now that there was a visual definition for development to help those trapped in their local experience to understand that life can be better and to assure them that things do not have to be as they are, the flame of hope was burning brightly for Lubanda. The crowd burst into a praise song shouting his now familiar nickname of "Teacher! Teacher! Teacher!"

"Ladies and gentlemen, this is what we call development, improving our infrastructure and enhancing our comfort. Improving life now and laying a foundation for the unborn descendants, using our strengths and working on our weaknesses. Together as a community, complementing our gifts and talents, we shall move forward.

"It is pathetic that our African leaders' vision starts and ends with them; it ends in their pockets, it ends in their stomachs, it ends in their families and it ends in self-glorification. They do not think about the hungry man in the street looking for a job, or the one toiling in the village to look after his family, or the woman trekking with a calabash of water on her head or any others as worthy of a good life too. They do not even think about the future of their children and grandchildren, what a society they will live in, what opportunities they will have. They do not think about what the country will be in the 22nd or 23rd century. For them it is immediate self-gratification and indulgence. Are you surprised then that there has been no development? A vote for them is a vote of self-denial; it is a surrender of your hopes, and it is a vote for doom.

"True leadership is a service. A service to make life better for all. True leadership will give you an opportunity to make progress: to build a decent house, provide food beyond a survival morsel, to provide education to learn and innovate, to help you to be better tomorrow than you are today. True leadership is like a shepherd, showing and providing green pastures for all the citizens.

"That is what you shall get from DPPL. I shall lead a responsible government creating a society for you and your children's enjoyment. We shall spend our resources wisely and create not only jobs but wealth for all."

He went on to give evidence of mismanagement and money that had been stolen by the present government and where it could have improved the lives of the people. The details Delilah's uncle provided were good ammunition for Moses. This was not good music for Chimwanga's supporters if they were listening.

"Countrymen, we shall work together to establish a constitution that will not be amended every day on the behest of the sitting president or be dismissed at will to serve the ruling party's interests. The Lubanda Constitution is the beacon of society. We shall restore it as the founding agreement of our nation state. Today the oath of office for the president is useless because he and his party members do not uphold and defend the constitution. The greatest tragedy is our helplessness or inability to remove them from power if they violate the constitution. There is only one thing I shall ask to change in the constitution – to have two seven-year periods. The president shall have the powers to call elections in the last two years of the seven-year term. We shall strengthen the constitution so no madman or woman shall remain in office messing things up.

"Let us also remember that there are more than 1.3 billion black people across the globe but we all seem to be struggling economically and politically. Mired in poverty, deprivation and destined for a similar fate. Surely, is there nothing we can do? It seems the whole race is stuck somewhere. I am aware the shackles and wounds of slavery and oppression run deep but is there something that we can do for ourselves? We need to look first, within; at our systems, cultures and beliefs. If there are practices that prevent us from acquiring political, economic and social progress, we should evolve, modify or change these obstacles. Secondly, we need to look without, to systems that have delivered development and political stability. We should adapt systems that have worked for others to our own context; otherwise the status quo will continue to keep us at the bottom of the ethnic pile – poor, pitiful and even enslaved.

"Countrymen and women, a law to prevent and eradicate political violence shall be enacted. Any party contesting power through violence would be banned. The law should also hold leaders of political parties responsible for maintaining political sanity. All sections of society, civil, political and traditional shall be mobilised and given various responsibilities to prevent violence. We shall all learn to 'disagree in peace'.

"Finally, I shall labour to restore the dignity of the Lubandan, dignity that was stolen by slave traders, stolen by colonialism, stolen by poverty and stolen by incompetent leadership. In my government and country all of you are and shall be valued. You are all important and valuable like any other soul on earth, be they presidents or kings and queens. No Lubandan shall be paraded in front of a camera and humiliated for a sympathetic donation. No law- abiding Lubandan shall be beaten with sticks like dogs for staging a peaceful demonstration.

"Will you come with me to the promised land?"

It was not clear whether the ground or walls shook but whatever it was, the answer to the question shook the hearts. He appealed to them to be peaceful and responsible. He asked them to use the following day, Sunday, to reflect and pray for peace and to turn up on Monday in large numbers to vote. "If all of you vote, Chimwanga won't manage to rig himself into power. If he hires troops from the southern state we shall fight until the last Lubandan sings the national anthem on his deathbed. Be vigilant!"

Mr Kamawu had unleashed an unstoppable whirlwind of change. As the people walked and drove home, they knew it was a new dawn. They were impressed by the vision they had been given; the echoes of unity and the clear model of political stability. Only one more ritual was needed: casting the vote.

Chimwanga was a man who was never willing to go quietly. The arrest of Absalom had shaken his resolve. He did not understand why Moses had been allowed to get as far as he had. Like most dictators, they never seem to know when their time was up.

He called in the few friends who were stuck with him and knew that they would be in trouble with a change of the regime. They sat in the room, some dozing off in their chairs.

"You sleepy bastards, this is why this idiot will hang you all on Tuesday! All you have been doing is sleeping while this fool has been walking on your heads. Did you see the details he showed the people? Who gave it to him? Did you see the number of people who attended his rally? He has bewitched the nation – we must stop him. I have just fired the police chief for allowing the rally. I have also fired the head of intelligence for not disrupting his speech. I am going to fire you all for being hopeless idiots."

The minister for home affairs stood up and started walking away.

"Where do you think you are going?"

"I am going home Mr President."

"The meeting has not started yet."

"But the insults have. You have been insulting us all these years and you are still insulting us. Even at this hour when you need us the most you are still insulting us. I do not care whether you fire me or not. It is all over. Mr President, you are in trouble."

"I am sorry Hon. Minister. I am upset with the situation. Did you see the handwriting on the screen telling me that my days are numbered? He should not insult me like that. We need to do something."

"Sorry Mr President, there is nothing you can do now. You have been campaigning but people have ignored you. You have tried to kill him on many occasions but you have failed. As we speak, there are thousands of people around his farm guarding him. The foreign embassies are all behind him. It will also be difficult to rig the elections because all his supporters will be there. It is all over."

Chimwanga lost his temper and went into a fit of anger. He hurled a newspaper at the Interior Minister while hollering incoherently. The man was cursing and throwing things, attacking his ministers physically. They called in his wife to calm him down. He kept shouting: "Kill him, kill him, kill him! I am the President! Kill him."

Not knowing whether the President had gone berserk or not, the ministers left the room one by one, shaking their heads; one was even crying. "It is not easy to tell the emperor that he is naked," whispered the senior minister as he walked out of the room and closed the door behind him.

On Sunday, the day before the elections, there was calm. Many churches were praying for peaceful elections and transfer of power. News from the presidential palace was not good. There were rumours of the president trying to commit suicide, others reporting he had gone mad. One source reported that the first lady had been beaten badly and had fled.

Nobody was coming forward to verify the rumours. The public had very little sympathy for him and the few supporters he had were hardly making any impact on the elections. People thought the arrest of Absalom was the biggest blow to the President. There was no doubt that he felt isolated and was sure that the country had turned against him – a thought he found difficult to entertain.

Very early Monday morning, the country stirred into activity. People woke up at dawn and started queuing at polling stations. No other election had energised everyone like this one. The old, the middle-aged and the young all trooped to the polling stations. They peacefully lined up in long queues waiting to get their chance to cast their vote. Neighbours assisted each other by looking after the children or transporting elderly voters.

Those who voted joyously went home full of pride and satisfaction for a job well done. One ninety-one-year-old woman broke down as she cast her vote. She told of how Chimwanga had killed her husband, two sons and two nephews who campaigned for the last candidate who challenged him. She said she had come to vote as the only thing she can physically do to honour her fallen family.

Folks could not understand how Chimwanga had been rendered so helpless. It was clear from exit polls that those who voted for him were very few. He was understood to have gone to the polling station near him and cast his vote almost secretly. As the day went by, he was reported to be irritable and occasionally shouting and insulting people but looking exhausted.

Moses' camp was more jubilant. He went to his polling station with his family and hundreds of supporters. There were cameramen and women taking photos every way he turned. Women were dancing, in the tradition of Lubandans celebrating a marriage. As he walked back to his residence supporters shouted and waved at him.

"Will I get a job?" someone shouted.

"Not only will you get a job but your children, grandchildren and great grandchildren as well," shouted Moses back to the cheers from onlookers.

"Please do not imprison me," pleaded a tramp standing nearby.

"Prison is for criminals and unrepentant people! Be good and your country will be good to you," came back the answer from their future president.

In spite of the optimism, people were still nervous. What will Chimwanga do? Rig the results, send the army in, and declare a state of emergency as he did fifteen years before? Perhaps he will still try to assassinate Moses. There were more rumours about him going to seek help from the other despots in the region.

Far-fetched as these conspiracy theories were, no one expected Chimwanga to go quietly. It was understood that the reason he was not causing much trouble was because the army had withdrawn their support for him. The truth was that like every brutal dictator, their days were indeed numbered. Not only did the armed forces withdraw their support but many of his supporters too.

There was little to show for his many years in office. The list of abuses of power exposed was beyond belief for many people. Revelations about stolen millions and the misuses of power had been revealed by Moses for all to see. Thanks to his sources, the President could not refute what was being revealed. The most shocking was the money he spent on a villa on an island in the Caribbean bought through a loyal white friend of his. Moses had told them that that money alone would be sufficient to run the health service for two years. Lists of people killed by the regime and details about how they died popped up everywhere on the Internet.

The beautiful African sunset in all its glory with stunning array of colours was marking a historical end. The red background blending with pink, yellow and green appeared to be announcing the end not of an era but the bloodshed and the shooting red rays above the darkening horizon left behind memories of sorrow that had paid for such a peaceful election. As voting came to a close and counting started, distant drums of the spirits invoked melodies of celebrations not to be witnessed for many centuries to come. The announcements were formal rituals of the obvious. It was clear that if the results were going any other way other than the way of change that would be a signal to war.

Chimwanga was too drunk to follow the proceedings. His wife was worried he would do harm to himself. He never cared to listen to any results. A few of his remaining loyal friends either joined in the drinking or sat quietly like mourners. At four o'clock in the morning the country was confident the tyrant was gone. Chimwanga's sleeping friends were awakened by a commotion in the presidential living quarters. They rushed to find the drunken president and his wife fighting over a gun. She screamed for help because Chimwanga was attempting to shoot himself.

The night had been eventful for many people in different ways. In a little village in the western part of the country the villagers gathered together outside a small house around a bonfire watching the only television in the village. In their midst were the Sambondu family who had travelled, as Peter Sambondu did every election year, to vote in the constituency of his birth. He often claimed he was keeping the tradition of the Sambondus. However, this election was special; the potential removal of a tyrant and his first cousin was standing as a member of parliament. Maybe one day he would be the one standing. Another reason for being here was that he had come with his son, daughter and a heavily pregnant wife who was due to deliver any time. They discussed the possibility of her delivering on the night of the elections. One thing was sure; they would not go to the local district hospital a few miles down the road. When they visited a relative who was admitted there, the hospital was not good. They wondered how patients could be admitted to a place so unhygienic you would not like to touch anything let alone sleep on the bug infested mattresses. The smell of people and drugs nauseated visitors. The strips of bed coverings had barely been washed since they were donated to the hospital several years ago and were full of stains and holes. This would not be an appropriate reception for the Sambondu baby.

"In a civilised country this hospital would have been closed down a long time ago. There is very high mortality, everything is filthy and apart from the hearts of the nurses, all was rotten," declared Joyce Sambondu as she declined the option.

Instead they would have to travel thirty-five miles away to a mission hospital where standards were better. The best option would be to go back to the capital to a private hospital. Peter's grandmother was not impressed with the farce of driving several miles to look for a hospital for the birth of a child.

"I was not born in a hospital, neither were many of my parents and grandparents. We were born in the village with village midwives. Look at me, am I different?" she asked her rather ashamed audience.

"Before the white man came and brought shame upon all that we believed in and did, we had our own people doing these jobs. The skills are sadly all gone with them to the grave. They should have retrained them and supported them. But like anything about the black man, it was all labelled as bad."

Nobody dared challenge "*nkaka*" (grandma) when she was in this mood.

When the first election results were announced, the whole village roared and clapped.

Joyce had retired to bed early because she was feeling tired from the long drive.

When the clapping died down, Peter's five-year-old asked grandma:

"How do babies know it is time to be born? Do they hear a bell, a voice or someone shakes them up?"

Grandma was not expecting such a question and said calmly, "It is time to go to bed. Let us talk about it tomorrow, shall we?"

Another set of results and more jumping, shouting and dancing. No need to guess who had won the parliamentary seat!

"Peter, Peter, Peter, please come quickly!" shouted Joyce from the bedroom of their small village house. They had built this house a few years ago because each time they had come home there was nowhere to sleep.

"Let us go to the hospital now, the baby is coming."

"Are we going to make it to the hospital?" inquired Peter.

"I don't know, but we have to go."

Peter called for help and their first plan was put in action. They left the children but took with them Peter's sister. Joyce demanded the radio be turned off. Peter could not understand the demands brought about by labour pains and dutifully respected the wishes of his wife; after all, nature had let him off the hook. He only sowed the seeds and someone else had to carry the burden for up to nine months plus hours of anguish in the last lap.

"Have you decided on the name?" asked Peter's sister.

"Moses," shouted both Joyce and Peter simultaneously.

"If she is a girl?" the sister asked.

She immediately realised that thought was not welcome. Peter quickly changed the subject and joined in a muted shout as he drove past jubilant crowds who thought Moses was going on a celebration drive. A few profanities from Joyce reminded Peter there were more serious matters to attend to. Restraining from the joy outside was not easy. On this occasion, he was willing to tolerate the vulgarities of a woman in labour but every now and again jumped along in his driver's seat to join in the celebrations outside. He did not require a radio for now the cheers of the gathering crowds were enough to tell him what was happening.

The mission hospital was alerted to the coming patient and was waiting ready to receive her. They quickly rushed to the car with covers to afford her some privacy and rushed her into the maternity ward straight away. In less than fifteen minutes the baby made its exit from God's secret factory.

The Doctor said, "Congratulations, you have a baby boy."

"Moses!" Joyce and Peter shouted at the same time.

Everyone joined in the celebrations. They had lost count of the number of MPs their party had won. Peter rang friends to tell them the news of the new born baby and in exchange they updated him on the election results. He had missed the moment his cousin's seat was announced. It was not a surprise but an historical moment.

Chapter Thirteen

AT FIVE O'CLOCK in the morning, the whole country was glued to the television, radio or mobile phone for the official announcement. The chief returning officers stood up to officially declare the results:

"Ladies and gentlemen, according to the powers accorded to me by article seven of the constitution of Lubanda, I am here to announce the final results of the presidential elections. I therefore declare that Mr. Moses Kamawu has been duly elected as the next president of the Republic of Lubanda with 90% of the total votes cast. Congratulations, Sir."

The whole country burst into more jubilation and dancing and singing. Moses, the President-elect stood up at his headquarters to make a few remarks as all successful candidates do.

"Countrymen, thank you. Thank you for the victory; it is the victory of the people for the people. Thank you for your confidence. I honour all those who died fighting for change but never to see this day. May their spirits join in the celebrations. Thank you to you all. The real work begins now!

"You have voted for change and change you will get. You have voted for change, and you and your children shall feel the change. You have voted for change, for a different direction of the country, change for the health of the nation, change for economic progress, change for education for all our children.

"You have voted for a new vision. A vision for progress, a vision for jobs, a vision for excellence, a vision for our destiny. You have voted for yourselves, you have voted for your children and you have voted for your grandchildren and their children.

"You have voted for change because you want to move forward instead of backward, you have voted to be makers, not mere consumers, and you have voted to be respected rather than objects of abuse, shame, laughter and pity.

"Countrymen and countrywomen, together we shall deliver the change. I want us all to look back on this day with no regret but gratitude to heaven above for having taken part in a momentous event. The years ahead will be momentous but I am convinced they will bring comfort and satisfaction so we all can live like many other people around the world and give hope to our neighbours, near and far...

"Thank you for your vote, it is a vote of confidence and I invite you on this journey of change.

"God bless you all."

Before his victory speech, he had a brief telephone conversation with the incumbent President who congratulated him and wished him well. Moses thought the conversation was subdued so he kept it brief and tried to be cordial. Moses informed him about the date for inauguration and that he had two weeks to wind down.

People continued celebrating but Moses slipped into his office at home. He opened the drawers and took out the campaign folder, made some entries and put it away in a secured cabinet behind him. He reached out for another folder titled 'Inauguration'. In it were all the plans and details of how the inauguration would be organised. It was another elaborate and meticulous plan. The first day's itinerary swung into 'operation inauguration.'

First, a meeting took place with all the defence chiefs on the day of the election, to assess their loyalty and explain what he was going to do so there would be no power vacuum. The inauguration would take place in exactly two weeks and he would be sworn in at half past one exactly. In the meantime, the transition team would be deployed to all government ministries and departments. He had a list of security issues and concerns for the nation. He also had a list of invited dignitaries. On top of this list were Mary's parents. A meeting of the shadow cabinet was scheduled for the evening to brief them. In the night he would review the cabinet appointments he had been secretly making.

He had a list of regional leaders to invite and letters would have to be sent the following day. He looked at the invitation template and made adjustments. During the two weeks he would visit every district to thank the people and talk to them.

Everything in the file was arranged in steps with actions outlined. His secretary often remarked that she has never worked under such a highly organised regime. Somehow he found the time to research and plan in spite of his heavy schedule.

Moses sat in his study at 2:00 a.m. with a folder in front of him. He had been working since 18.00 p.m. after the meeting with the intelligence chiefs. The meeting had gone very well. They spoke respectfully with genuine loyalty. His mind was at peace and the briefing assured him all was under control. What was keeping him awake was the cabinet. Most posts had been filled already.

"I brought you coffee and my new recipe cake, darling. How is it going?"

She was used to him working late nights most days. He rarely went to bed early. Before the politics it was business. He had a routine, a day specifically set to spend time with Rachel. Every day he would spend time with the children for at least an hour. Otherwise, he would be in the office working.

"Sit down, please. I was actually intending to call you. I am missing Professor Solomon Mayuka, the party VP. He is a very intelligent man and respected by the party. I would count on him to keep an eye on things. Unfortunately, the doctors called me again today to tell me that his condition is getting worse. The cancer was detected late and they do not want me to send him to a specialist hospital abroad."

"Who then will you appoint as your Vice President?"

"Tell me what do you think of Yudas Kayumba Mwale?"

"He is arrogant. Since he took over from me as Secretary General, people have regularly complained about the way he talks to them," Rachel said. "One more thing, I think he resents you or is more than a little jealousy of you."

"Why do you say that?" he asked curiously.

"I am sure you know this already; he often tries to challenge you and he is never happy in your company. He looks at you with an evil look. Is this the man you can trust with that position? Sometimes I think you made a mistake asking him to join you."

"Thanks Rachel, those are accurate assessments. I did not make a mistake; he is a very intelligent man and a good economist. I want strong candidates whether they like me or not," explained Moses. "There has always been an undercurrent rivalry between him and me," he smiled and continued, "At university he always complained I was the first choice for prettier girls. I know I was!"

Rachel, with a queer flash of jealousy in her eyes, mumbled and remonstrated a little and said, "You're mine now, remember!"

Moses remembered one of the incidents in which he differed with Yudas. Yudas felt that Moses was pro-West, especially regarding America, and he would end up pandering to the Western leaders. He also felt that Moses was feeding into the narrative that black people cannot do anything for themselves without the so-called white saviour. Moses thought this was the mistake the founding fathers of independence in Africa had made. At independence, they resented the West and went for the ideology of the East led by communist Russia. Unfortunately, the ideology and social context of Africa did not match and the experiment ended in a catastrophic failure. Secondly, Yudas was missing the point that the history of any developed country showed that development came from innovations within the country and borrowing technologies and systems that worked elsewhere. He would work to take advantage of learning from successful models and people and adapt the systems to the needs of Lubanda. He would not reject the good systems from the West just because of the bitterness of colonialism. He would evolve his own systems within the framework of good reason.

After a long discussion, Moses concluded that Yudas and him had some fundamental ideological differences. He wanted what worked while Yudas was less clear of the practical implications of what he wanted to achieve.

"Rachel, what do you think of Uncle Mazombu?"

"I think he has done well as your spokesman but surely, you're not intending to appoint him to the post of Vice President, are you? It will not be good to have Kamawu for President and Vice President." She continued after a moment of reflection: "By the way, a few people have said Uncle gets too close to women so you might have an embarrassing scandal – but one thing to note is that he is very loyal to you and is completely devoted.

"Listen," she added, "whoever you decide to appoint, you shall have my full support, except Delilah." With that she left the office darting away like a model on stage.

Delilah had proved the greatest asset of the team. She, like Moses, often thought ahead and planned everything meticulously. Delilah appeared to have understood Moses more than anybody. She was also a very keen student of his. She was a loyal disciple and hardly left his side and the *Citizen Chronicle* contributed to the landslide election results. But she was not elected to any post in the party and she was not an MP. He could appoint her as a special elected MP but how would the party and the country respond? He sat turning over these points again and again in his mind.

In one private conversation, Moses told Delilah a secret to be guarded.

This was not the time for her, was it?

Over the previous six months, Moses had toured all the constituencies and had private meetings with each prospective Member of Parliament. He had the curriculum vitae of each candidate and from their private discussions he gathered information about their suitability for jobs in the new government.

Some blew their chances away. One man Moses was considering for a ministerial post blew his chance for a cabinet office. When he met Moses, the later asked him what he thought of the education system.

"Rotten, Sir! That is why we are voting for you."

"What changes do you want to see in education?"

"We want you to take charge, Sir."

"If you were a minister of education, what would you do?"

"I would kick the current regional education officer out. He is useless."

"What type of education do you think our children should get?"

"Anything but the current system."

"Thank you very much for the meal and I am looking forward to the elections."

Those who had intelligent conversations and passed the three mark test – visionary, intelligent and passionate – went down into a special file and these were the ones to be appointed to ministerial jobs.

The other criteria of the new government were tribal balancing. Every principal tribal group would be represented in Cabinet. Although he would reduce the cabinet portfolios, there would be enough posts to achieve a balance. Inclusion of all and balancing representation, ability and skills would be cardinal values of the new government.

By the day of the election, many of his shadow cabinet would transfer to their respective substantive posts. Sadly, the Vice President fell seriously ill ten days before the elections. He was a respected man who could have done the job very well. Conspiracy theories implicated Yudas because he wanted to be the Vice President. This opened up a vacancy unexpectedly. The two posts that caused him sleepless nights were the Defence Minister and the Vice President. Two people, the Secretary General Yudas and his uncle Mazombu were aspiring for the post of a Vice Presidency. There was notable dislike and friction between Uncle Mazombu and Yudas. The latter would be a natural choice but Rachel's assessment of him was worrying.

The room was full of journalists who had come to listen to the President-elect announce his Cabinet. There had been speculations in the morning papers that Yudas had not been appointed and that there was a falling out with the President. The President did not tell anyone including Rachel but he had telephoned to tell Yudas that he was appointing him as the Minister of Finance. It appeared the conversation did not go well but Moses told him off and gave him ten minutes to accept the post or be dropped completely. He must have mentioned this to someone who informed the press.

The list was read methodically; people were most interested in who was to fill the post of Vice President. When the President announced that the position of Minister of Defence would go to Uncle Mazombu and that Yudas would become the Minister of Finance, the room broke into consternation. Finally, the President announce in his usual confident manner:

"I have decided to appoint Miss Delilah Banda Mashidika as my Vice President."

The appointment of the Vice President generated the most controversy both in the home, party and media. It was apparent that no one including the First Lady had any idea of the President's decision. It is believed Delilah was informed an hour before the announcement that she was going to be in the cabinet but the post was not mentioned. Both Yudas and Uncle Mazombu were stunned. However, during the campaign no one could argue that she put in the most work and she was a talented communicator and strategist. Conspiracy theories began spreading.

The rest of the cabinet was impressive; very educated men and women, high flyers in their fields, excellent regional and tribal representations. All were excited except Yudas who hardly smiled or clapped at the announcement of Delilah. Although Uncle Mazombu was always suspicious of Delilah, he had unflinching confidence and loyalty in Moses and soon moved on. The country was happy and trusted their President. Perhaps the only person truly begrudging was Yudas.

The days leading to the inauguration ceremony were busy and stressful. Moses decided that his team should take full responsibility in order to learn how to organise such events but working in consultation with all relevant government departments. Many heads of state had been invited. All logistics were in the inauguration plan Moses had long been preparing. The Special Force had not been disbanded yet and was drafted in to work with the national security team, now firmly in the hands of the President-elect, to help control the crowds. This aspect was very well taken care of. Moses struck a deal with the transport providers who generously offered to transport people free of charge as a contribution to the celebrations. In fact, all businesses joined in the feel good factor and contributed "something" for free.

People started streaming into the arena the day before and by 6.00 am, the place was full. All the overflow areas demarcated were also filling fast. By nine, all was in place and ready for the historical event. In the stand sitting next to his parents were special visitors, Mary's parents that had flown in two days before, specially invited to attend the ceremony.

On Monday, 5 September 2086, at 1.30 p.m., Mr Moses Kamawu said the words everyone had been waiting to hear:

"I Moses Kabwibu Kamawu, do solemnly swear that I will faithfully execute the Office of President of Lubanda, and I shall, to the best of my ability, preserve, protect and defend and uphold the Constitution of the Republic of Lubanda."

"Congratulations, Mr President," said the most senior judge in the land. "You may address the nation."

The crowd had gone wild as usual, shouting, screaming and jumping for joy, with simultaneous bursts of songs. After a long standing ovation from all present, he motioned to them for silence.

"Thank you Mr. Judge. Invited guests, dignitaries, ladies and gentlemen; fellow countrymen and women, thank you for being here with me. Before I give a short speech, I would like all Lubandans to please stand up. You have sworn me in office today but I do not want to undertake this journey alone. It will not be fair, will it?"

"No!" screamed the crowd.

"So wherever you are, in your homes watching on television, listening to the radio or walking on the street, I invite you to go with me on this journey and take a pledge of loyalty to Lubanda.

"Please raise your right hand and repeat after me and where I mention my name, say your name…" An example quickly flashes on the screen.

"I… do pledge to obey the laws of Lubanda, to do all I can to develop Lubanda and to use my vote to remove incompetent leaders from power and to offer whatever I can to develop Lubanda. So help me God."

Much more energetic cheering…

"I haven't seen that before," whispered the British Ambassador to his wife. "It is new, I suppose!"

"He has just sworn in the whole country," whispered the American Ambassador.

"Thank you to everyone who's taken the pledge. It means you and I are all responsible for the destiny of this country. Great nations are built with a vision beyond periodic leadership. There are things leaders can do and things the ordinary citizens can contribute to the development and wellbeing of the nation. You and I are a team.

"Ladies and gentlemen, fellow Lubandans, I am proud and humbled to stand before you. I am proud of you for realising that the country needs to change and you voted for change and change you shall get under my leadership and government. There will be change around you but progress will also demand change from within you.

"I am humbled to stand before you because you have placed hope in me, trust in me and the future of Lubanda in me. My prayer to God is that I live up to your expectations. It was not long ago that few people in the country knew who I was but today I know all of you as my family. I can pledge to you that I shall do my very best. You may not understand all the policies I shall promote but I hope you shall understand my intent to develop this beloved country.

"Today I would like to outline the fundamental framework of your next government. First, you have elected me to govern and govern I shall do. This country has for long been drifting like a raft on the sea with no defined direction but the waves of corruption, self-interest, tribalism, nepotism, and dire mismanagement. We have drifted to nowhere. My government shall provide leadership and a well-defined course of progress for Lubanda. My government shall uphold the rule of law and I expect all of you to live by and respect the laws of this country. We shall strengthen democratic institutions and develop and enhance systems of governance. As you all know, the Lubanda of today is marginally different from the Lubanda of the 20th century, the 19th century and the centuries before. This must change.

"Secondly, my government shall move the country forward down the path of development. We shall move the country forward in all areas of human endeavour and we shall move individuals up, to actualisation. Lubandans should aim to reach beyond their current horizons of knowledge, space and experience.

"Thirdly, my government shall restore dignity stolen by slavery, colonialism, and media lynching. We shall restore national and individual pride.

"Fourthly, my government shall promote unity; unity of the nation, unity of purpose and unity of will.

"Finally, we shall seek to protect what is Lubandan, its people, culture, values, borders, resources, and our space. Yes, we shall protect the land and soil of Lubanda as well. We shall pursue the path of harmony and peace with all our neighbours and robustly defend ourselves in the face of aggression and provocation.

"We shall achieve all these through a proper plan. We shall eagerly learn from those who have successfully travelled down the path of development. We shall reorganise to remove obstacles to progress. To achieve these goals, we may be required to make changes as individuals, as a community and as a country.

"Countrymen and women, I want us to build a nation. We shall build a great nation. A nation that will be proud and respected in the world. A nation whose children shall not die from hunger or be paraded in western media as objects of pity and a nation whose older people and senior citizens shall be respected and well looked after. A nation with strong economy where there will be a job for everyone. A nation where there shall be good healthcare for all. A nation whose schools shall nurture intellect, creativity and innovation. A nation where there is hope for all.

"We shall build a nation that shall soar above other nations. We shall build a nation that shall change people's lives. A nation powerful enough to defend itself but that will cherish peace with all our neighbours.

"In the coming week you will get details of what we all shall have to do to lift this country from its current position, rebuild and move forward down the path to development. The five pillars to progress will enable us to achieve progress and development.

"Thank you all and God bless you and our beloved nation Lubanda."

The celebrations went on deep into the night with the whole country taking part except his opponents who appeared to have dispersed into oblivion. This was the first Christmas of the year. One wondered whether there would be money left for the real Christmas. Although no count was made for the number of chickens, goats, sheep and cattle slaughtered that day, thousands were certainly offered to the shrines of pure joy and ecstasy. The air waves were filled with beating drums, beautiful melodies of jubilation. This was the climax of the celebrations that had been going on since the Election Day.

Moses' family and friends and the cabinet except Yudas were gathered at the farm after the party for the invited foreign dignitaries. They sang, danced and danced again and again until their bodies ached. Eyes were on Delilah who was having a good time but making sure she kept her distance from the Kamawus. Those who could not dance gathered around grannies for sweet old stories of the brave warriors of Lubanda. By coincidence or design, they told these stories with great enthusiasm and storytelling mastery.

Moses' grandmother was not worried about telling some embarrassing tales of his childhood. She told them how he beat a tall bully in school and how he came home with torn clothes. The children enjoyed these heroic stories more than the television. Rachel made sure any woman passing by or dancing with the President did not cross the red line. Sly and innocuous glances were enough to scare romantic opportunists.

The carnival at the farm did not prevent the New President from sneaking into his office to write a speech for his first engagement. People knew he never drank alcohol so the chances were that he would not enjoy the gibberish mouthing of his drunken guests. Even Uncle Mazombu was aware that no misbehaviour would be tolerated. At the party held for foreign dignitaries soon after the inauguration, one neighbouring president was saved from embarrassment by his wife when it was apparent he had finished one bottle of whisky and started flirting with the stunningly dressed waitresses. Moses had seized the opportunity to speak to more foreign dignitaries and extracted commitments and promises for supporting his government. The creditors who were all too eager to work with this young educated leader promised to review the debt of the country. They all appeared to have been charmed into offering some form of support to the new President.

During all the partying, there was time set aside for special guests, Mary's parents. In an exclusive VIP guest wing, Moses and his family sat for a meal with his special visitors. They sat round the table with the girls sitting next to the visitors and Abel between Rachel and Moses. In spite of the fact that they had met for a short time, the children had warmed to them. They called them grandma and granddad. They had gone to shop with Rachel and the girls the day before and they felt very welcome indeed. After the sweet course was served, Rachel conveniently left them together. It was the only time Moses had to talk to them in a relaxed way. He talked about the places he visited with Mary and some of the discussions they had. You could feel the loss in his voice. Mary's mum handed him a small envelope she had been carrying for years in her handbag. It was a collection of special moments he shared with Mary before she died. Moses stood up, embraced both and thanked them for bringing the photos. "I was not sure whether they would cause offence especially to Rachel but I thought you should have them," Mary's mum said with a tear in her eye.

"Thanks mum, I appreciate it. Mary is part of my life. Death robbed me of two of the closest people that I have ever kwon: Abel and Mary. I am where I am because of them. They are alive in my heart. I know they are not here to join us in celebrating my victory in person but their spirits are always present with me. They must be celebrating where they are, I know they have met. No one will ever take them away from my heart."

Moses shared with them some of the struggles, how he had escaped death on a number of occasions. Mary's Dad told him how proud they were of him. They had been following the elections from the first time he rang to tell them he was standing for elections. Quiet moments, tears and embraces; bonds were renewed and life must go on.

Moses' loyalty to Mary was beyond ordinary friendship. One winter season, there had been a severe snowfall in Boston. A week before the end of year examinations, Mary arrived for the lecture early; somehow she had made her way through the traffic chaos. She was the first to arrive. This was unusual because the person who always arrived first in the group was Moses. Thirty minutes later, Moses had not arrived. She thought there might be a problem. She left the lecture theatre before the lecture started, apologised to the lecturer who she met in the door and ran to Moses' flat. After frantic knocking on the door, she dived in her bag for the key. She opened the door and found Moses lying face down on the floor in front of the bathroom door in his pyjamas. Mary threw down all her books and bags, dived to the lifeless body and turned him up. He was still warm. She grabbed his inhaler that had fallen a few centimetres from his right hand and started pumping it into his nostrils, alternating with CPR motions. After several attempts and shouts for help, he coughed. The neighbour joined her and called 911 for help. By this time Moses had started breathing. She sat by Moses' bed for the next five days, looking after him and revising for her exams. She contacted all his lecturers to discuss his exams, rang Lubanda to tell his parents and sat vigil. On the day she was writing her exams she called her mum who came to relieve her. After five days, Moses began breathing unaided. Doctors said it was a severe asthma attack. If Mary had not found him, he would probably have died within an hour. It was therefore a friendship of life.

At 5 a.m. the following day the President woke up to prepare for security briefings. Unlike the lot snoring all over the farm houses, he was up early, strong and fresh, ready for the day's work. The meeting with the security was a new arrangement he had agreed with the security forces, especially with so many foreign leaders in the country. This was a new practice for the forces as the previous president never bothered at all. The security forces were very happy with the way the events of the inauguration day were organised and the clarity of instructions given. The Head of the Army was most complimentary and was heard shouting, "It is a new dawn!"

A new dawn indeed it was; the joy and happiness in the land was unprecedented in the history of Lubanda. Many wondered whether he would deliver and fulfil all the people's hopes. Others did not care how much was achieved; removing Chimwanga was a big achievement in itself. The beginning of an era never imagined even a year ago. They all had to get used to new ways of doing things and they were keen to play their part. After all, they all swore to work with him.

Part II

Chapter Fourteen

THE FIRST DAY in the office started with the swearing in of ministers in the morning followed by the first Cabinet meeting in the afternoon. As the Cabinet posed for an official photograph, you could not mistake the joy in their hearts translated through their broad smiles. Far from being uncomfortable, Delilah stood next to the President confidently adding a feminine exuberance. Looking rather dejected in the back row, without a smile, was Yudas.

The first Cabinet meeting was the next most important event that would chime the bells of change and set the tone of authority. All the ministers were seated fifteen minutes before the President. In came the first bodyguard. He opened and held the door for the President who walked majestically into the room to a long standing ovation. He stood by the large presidential chair and bowed in response to the now cheering and shouting ministers. The bodyguard pulled out the chair and the new President sat down motioning everyone to do the same.

"Good afternoon and congratulations, ladies and gentlemen, for making the first cabinet." They all sat up and listened like a class of primary school pupils. "I am delighted to be working with each one of you because I know you are exceptional individuals. You may not agree with all my decisions but together we shall deliver the change for which the people have elected us. I wish to thank you all for your effort and sacrifices that enabled us to achieve power. Power is important and if used wisely and effectively can yield many good things. As we have seen in the recent past, if power is misused, it can bring utter ruin to a nation."

"Where are the praise singers, Sir?" shouted one minister.

"I shall not have praise singers; we shall leave that to chiefs."

"How about a choir, Sir?"

"Neither shall I have a choir, Hon. Minister, we are civil servants who should work to earn praise."

The mood was jovial and friendly.

"Mr. President, I think I am the oldest man at sixty and I should say once again, congratulations, Sir. As you can see, this is one of the best days of our lives."

"So far," one minister interjected to more applause and laughing.

The first agenda item was the ministerial code of conduct. It was read, explained and all ministers accepted it. The second item was the manifesto. They were reminded that the manifesto should guide whatever they were doing in their ministry or constituency. They were issued with summary copies of aspects of the manifesto their departments must deliver. They were then advised that no new projects should be started until after the national review reports were published and priority lists drawn, a process that would take six to nine months. The President asked all ministers to audit skills, projects and their ministerial budgets and present a report about the state of their respective ministries. This activity would be more of an investigation, with much research and planning ahead. They were told to present a written report of their findings to the cabinet in three months with weekly updates to the president himself.

Secondly, they were asked to present a seven-year development plan for their departments. An ad hoc committee, chaired by the Vice President, was announced to lead on the writing of the national development plan to be delivered in exactly six months. The President would announce the plan to the country shortly after. Various issues of protocols and training for all ministers were discussed. Finally the President announced a special committee to review corruption. The head of the inquiry would be one of the most respected judges assisted by a special team reporting directly to the President. The public would be asked to report instances and practice of corruption and theft of public property or funds covering the period of the previous government.

The President explained that once all the reports and plans had come in, the government would take three months to put together a seven-year national development plan. It was therefore very important that ministers gave the audit and planning serious priority. The national plan would be an enhancement of the party plan but informed by the actual state of the country.

"As you may realise ladies and gentlemen, the country will not be waiting for your plan for six months, the normal functions of government will continue. I will be making changes slowly to fit our vision and address the needs of the nation. We have to hit the ground running. Be honest with the people but be wise. To help you in communicating with the public, I have appointed a government spokesperson. Minister Mazombu in addition to his ministerial duties will continue to be the spokesperson. The first few months will be difficult for everyone but there are enough brains and wisdom in this room to effectively tackle all the problems we have. Please talk to one another and to me if you need to clarify your thinking or need support. You will no doubt make some mistakes; if you do, be honest to the people of Lubanda."

A list of immediate issues of concern was presented and discussed. One of the biggest problems of the new government was the national finances. The country was technically bankrupt. The budget did not exist nor were any fiscal rules followed in the day-to-day running of the country. The previous president had usurped all the monetary powers from the right people and departments. President Kamawu had been investigating and collecting information about the state of the economy for a long time, more so since the elections two weeks ago. He had formed a special task force led by Mr Yudas Kayumba Mwale, now the Minister of Finance. A twelve months emergency plan was drawn and presented to the Cabinet. Minister Mwale ably explained the situation and the Cabinet passed the plan unanimously. An amendment to the law would be presented to Parliament in five days' time for approval. Up to this point, not many realised the essence of the emergency plan.

President Kamawu then told the ministers that during the emergency period, the government would not spend more than it earned and that he would tell the people himself. This would make their jobs tough but it would be a steep learning curve for the leaders and the people.

"Excuse me, Sir, how can we run the government without money? I mean, how possibly can we do anything?"

"Honourable Minister, thank you for your intelligent question. We need to start somewhere in order to move forward. There will be very little money so you'll have to be wise as to how you use it. For example, I have suspended all trips abroad except to the regional heads of states and the UN. I will go with a small group of people and will use ordinary passenger planes. So we all have to make sacrifices. Keep your spirits up. We shall start by doing that which requires little or no money. Changes must start today."

The five-hour meeting was concluded with an invitation to a presidential dinner for the ministers and their families at a local top hotel. They sang the national anthem with gratitude for being in the team.

"I wish the President would donate the party money to my ministry," grumbled Dr Joy Lombe, the minister of Health who seemed most worried. "How can I run the hospitals, let alone heal the sick, without money?"

"That is why I appointed you Minister, Lombe, and I am glad you have started thinking about it. Please come to my office tomorrow morning so we can talk about it." Rather embarrassed and not having expected the President to hear her, she accepted the invitation with a smile. She did not know whether it was an order or a request. Yudas, with a rare smile on his face, came by and assured her there would be enough money to pay for medicines and staff. They were joined by Minister of Defence Mazombu who was usually in good spirits especially around ladies.

"Are you both coming to the party?" Minister Mazombu asked.

"Of course, yes," said Yudas excitedly, "with my wife and children."

"I think he wants us to bond," said Joy "But it will be costly."

"Do not worry, Joy, I am told the President is paying for the dinner from his private resources."

The ministers were generally buoyant after the first meeting. Although not quite what they were expecting, almost all the ministers were pleased with their President. He was calm, knowledgeable, reflective and decisive. He patiently allowed everyone to contribute and was sharp at tying the gold threads together. A number of ministers were worried about the economy but the emergency plan was reassuring although they were not sure what the lack of money meant for their work. The President was clearly in control and within a short time he already had a working knowledge and insights into all the government machinery.

The family dinner lifted the spirits of the team as the President called his Cabinet. The food was a blend of a traditional and modern menu. The wives very happily chatting away and the noisy children made the atmosphere friendly. Everyone was on their best behaviour. The President took time to meet every family and he was introduced to all the families. Rachel, as the first lady, was immaculate and in command. Delilah kept her distance but had constructive conversations with the families.

The longest conversation was between Yudas' wife and the President. Yudas did not seem to mind. She had heard much about him and greeted him on many occasions but this was the first time she had spoken to him beyond a greeting. They spoke about politics and family. Yudas' wife was as impressed and pleased as all the other families. Yudas himself was in good spirits, joking and talking to more people than he usually did. Joy appeared to be nervous, perhaps because of her outburst, but when the President came to her table, she was reassured there was no offence caused; at least, no strain of anger could be detected from the President.

There were no speeches except a short welcome message and a goodbye from the President. The President left an hour earlier than the rest. Allowing the five-hour family time was the consummation of the team but the real magic of this strategic event was in the lasting impression on the ministers' spouses which Moses would benefit from for years to come.

The first week was the busiest of any new president. He had to make time for visitors, meetings, family, telephone calls with other leaders, review state secrets and work on implementing his plan; he hardly had time for his lunch.

People noticed that he wanted to simply be called Mr President and not "His Excellency the President of Lubanda."

This was left for appropriate ceremonial events. The public were stopped from escorting him to the airport and there were no praise singers. "I am not here to build a cult but to work," he would remind them. He even refused to move into the presidential palace until after renovations and upgrading. This was estimated to take five years but he did not seem to worry about it. He promised to save money for the building work every year until he had saved up enough money for the reconstruction. All these small changes reminded people he would do things differently.

The country was told that a special team was assembled to look into the ministry of finance and the Bank of Lubanda. Preliminary forensic analyses by local and foreign experts had been carried out to understand the scale of the national finances. This report was most worrying. The country was utterly bankrupt. Every economic indicator was in negative territory and the country had borrowed one hundred and ten percent of the GDP. This was worse than first thought. A full report was still to be presented in due course.

The President told the nation that the government had declared a national financial emergency. The citizens were informed about the implications of this situation. The government would not spend more than it was getting from its income streams and that to get things to change, this would take time and people should understand. Yet the President was still upbeat about the future. The job was hard but the process would go ahead. People wondered how he would deliver on the promises he made with such empty coffers but they were willing to give him all the time he needed; after all, they were living through the worst of times. He told them that after the review, he would present an 'Emancipation Plan.' The media code named it 'the Moses Marshall Plan.' Everybody's expectations were now fixed on the Moses Emancipation Plan.

Chapter Fifteen

PRESIDENT KAMAWU had long decided that there would be no meaningful change in Lubanda unless fundamental changes were made to the thinking paradigm of the people, the institutions and the social, economic and government systems. So he prioritised this as emergency.

Democracy to him was the best option of governance but the cultural context dictated the quality of democracy. He believed democracy had a different meaning to the ordinary people, therefore, they did not fully understand the processes of full democracy. To them, democracy was listening to speeches and voting. To the journalist it was freedom of speech. It meant far more than that for it to work. Democracy was about power, but who actually got the power?

He was convinced democracy was an excellent concept that gave people an opportunity to choose their leaders and government. There were elements of democracy in the traditional society. The chiefs broadly consulted with senior village leaders although they were largely authoritarian. However, human society is not a level playing field. Even in the most primitive of societies, differences in abilities, opportunities and mischief soon evolve into the weak and strong, those who eventually acquire power and those who are led. In the 21st Century democracy is a tool used by the rich and powerful to acquire power to perpetuate the status quo. Those who have money and those who control wealth and the media are the real power holders and brokers. The uneducated are masses coerced to vote, often against their own interests. In America, money and racial supremacy determine governments.

At least there is an opportunity for the people to listen to their candidates directly. This helps to downplay the influence of the media. In Britain, the strongest power broker is the media, since the politicians have very little opportunities to speak directly to the people except through the media. Therefore the powerful media align and promote the leader they like. In Africa, ignorance and illiteracy compound the difficulties of true democracy.

The concept of democracy is therefore distorted by money, media, ignorance and lies. However, it is still the best option to choose a government. What was needed were systems to minimise what he called the nemesis of democracy – money, media and greed. To do this there was a need to create and enhance strong institutions and educate the people to be custodians of democracy. Throughout history there have been men and women of strong political convictions that came into politics to make a difference. Political conviction should be elevated above the financially powerful who needed power as a toy for status or a tool for more financial acquisitions. He therefore set out to strengthen structures in the armed forces, police and other government systems. He started by cleansing the personal stipulations added to the constitution by his predecessors to enhance absolute power. Power should be spread and not concentrated in a single individual. He decided to make the constitution sacred, never to be changed and manipulated at the pleasure and will of successive governments. Sacrosanct procedures would be set to preserve it. A committee was set up to examine the original founding constitution of Lubanda, examine the amendments that had been made since, review the constitutions of the most politically stable countries in the world and make longstanding amendments to the Lubandan constitution so it can withstand the test of time. The committee included visits abroad and consulting with experts.

At the core of the reforms was the need to balance the government powers between the executive, judiciary, and legislature. The other aspect would be how to prevent the misuse of power, how to remove a president when they acted in disregard of the constitution and how to maintain unity of the state of Lubanda. He understood that disillusionment was precipitated by exclusion from power and its benefits; this had been the cause of many civil wars on the continent. He was determined to remove the legacy of tribal suspicion and rivalry in order to build a true nation state where every citizen felt proud to belong.

To implement an economic programme that worked, the rule of law was paramount. This required reviewing laws that promoted personal gain for the administrations, sorting out the police force and educating the public. Unfortunately, this move forced an unprecedented purge of the police force. There was a need for retraining and rebranding the whole force at every level. He would have to raise their salaries but at the right time. The ongoing inquiry resulted in many of the police officers being fired or resigning for abuse of their authority.

The President sent all ministers across the nation to explain to the people the importance of abiding by the law and why it was the responsibility of every citizen and not only the government to build a strong nation. The nation was more important than the individual. After the three months of ministerial reviews, officers were sent abroad to study systems that worked well and came with ideas to adapt. Experts were brought in from abroad to train civil servants where upskilling was identified as a need. The emphasis was put on discipline replicating tested systems that worked and learning from experts.

Unfortunately, this exercise proved more expensive than he had planned. With the emergency plan, there was no room for overspending and there was very little money for running government. He suspended services that were not essential and pressed ahead with the reorganisation.

On the 25th day of the sixth month of his term, all reviews and plans were submitted to the President, on time. The work appears to have taken a toll on him. He had been personally involved at every stage. He was looking thinner than when he came into office; he had hardly rested and rarely ate well. He probably slept a few hours a day. According to his plan, on the 31st of the sixth month he would deliver a state of the nation address in which he would announce all changes including the much anticipated Emancipation Plan.

Four days before the big speech a mini tragedy struck: the President had a severe attack of Asthma that sent the nation into a panic mode. There was fear and concern when the news was announced. All religious faith groups held mass prayers. Fortunately, although this was the worst attack in years, it was not as severe as the last attack that nearly killed him in the USA. Doctors forced him to rest for at least four days in bed but his strength to deliver the all-important state of the nation address was uncertain.

Chapter Sixteen

THE DAY OF THE EMANCIPATION PLAN came with great expectations for this poor country. The media were excited, as they always normally were, frantically asking bewildered people, even those with very little political acumen to predict what was in the President's most significant speech. Large screens, televisions, radios, computers and all types of wearable gadgets were switched on from six in the morning even when the event was scheduled to start at 1.30 pm. Most if not all of the President's important events started at 1.30 pm. It is rumoured that this was the time his brother Abel died. Whatever the reason, he religiously stuck to this schedule.

The unemployed were hopeful jobs were coming their way. The poor keenly awaited anything, possibly everything that may be thrown at them. The civil servants wanted more money for their pockets and a little more to help them deliver services more efficiently. Like the poor, businessmen and women wanted all and everything that brought profit. Yet this was not a budget but a plan. They had taken to heart what their President had been telling them for six months: "Failure to plan is planning to fail. A nation without a good plan is a failed state."

The speech was to be delivered in Parliament, in front of parliamentarians, and invited dignitaries but with each Lubandan outside the real audience. Some said the President regarded this to be more important than the opening of parliament. It was to be delivered with much pomp, for a President who preferred modesty as a virtue.

The Lubandan Parliament was itself not grand compared to some of the buildings President Kamawu had visited in Europe and America. Set on the hillside of the capital city, Lubindi, its colonial pillars made it an imposing structure. By the standard of Lubanda, a decent structure: simple design, neglected much of the past half century. It had seen contradictions of not only character but style from its past and certainly present members. In Chimwanga's government there were members who slept almost in every session; bored by dull, incoherent long rambling speeches from people who hardly knew their subjects. There had also been heated moments when bums never touched the benches but floated like peacocks eager to gain the speakers' attention to be appointed and to make their point. The current speaker, a woman of great integrity, had stamped her authority and her sharp wit often shamed the men into harassed loyalty. She often reminded them that the intensity and passion of their feelings and arguments were reflected by their opponents, so there was a need to show respect for every member and to disagree with honour.

The President arrived at 1.00 pm, leaving enough time for the pomp and ceremony before rising to speak. As his motorcade weaved through the narrow streets of Lubindi, he could almost feel the thickness of the weight of expectation but his assuring smile seemed to calm all including himself. Before he stepped out of the car, the praise singers surrounded him, showering him with praise. It was the only time he permitted them to indulge themselves in this traditional ritual which he had adamantly confined to very few occasions. One led him to the hall following just behind the Speaker. This time the President was definitely enjoying it. The praise singer bellowed out a poem to which T.S. Elliot would have given full marks, at the very least, for the enthusiastic style of delivery:

> Here comes the conqueror of Goliath,
> The man among men,
> The doctor who heals the sickness of the mind,
> The man whose feet have trodden distant lands,
> Lands of the white man,
> Lands of milk and honey,
> Stolen from African lands,
> The man among men,
> The leader of Lubanda,
> Hear ye him today,
> He speaks with the voice of wisdom,
> He speaks the words of all Lubanda ancestral wisdom,
> He beats the drum of hope,
> Hope for the living and the unborn,
> Hear ye him today and all days,
> Hear ye him today and all days.

As everyone rose to a standing ovation, the mood grew pre-emptively celebratory. The stage was set for one of the most important speeches ever delivered in Lubanda. As he stood to speak, there was expectant and reverent silence, not only in the room but across the vast expanse of the country.

At exactly 1:30 pm, the President stood to speak. He began by outlining the state of the country he had inherited, the broken systems, corrupt policemen, disgraced judges, unemployment, and poor educational and health services. For each he gave a case study.

"People have for long occupied the seats of power without realising its purpose in bringing good to Lubandans. The previous government of Lubanda was all but *magogu*."

He outlined some of the causes of the situation.

"At independence we did not make a proper transition from a tribal system to a nation state administration. Therefore, the tribal mind-set was transferred to the nation state administration, with dire consequences. The leaders thought the post of a president was like a paramount chief of all paramount chiefs. This was complicated by the importation of ideologies from abroad that people did not fully understand. Communist and socialist ideological policies implemented by men with capitalist tastes became a breeding ground for political ill and unimaginable incompetence.

"The other precipitating factor was that newly independent countries did not make proper transition from rural subsistence economy to a modern national and global economy. Through the little tastes of modern life, they were easily tamed into consumer reservoirs. Those charged with managing the economy had a rudimentary understanding of economic systems. As a result of this situation, the economies of the independent African states were disorganised and stagnated. That is the reason why so many years after independence, the Lubandan is still caught up in a struggle for basic needs, survival and hardly ever engages in activities to take them beyond food, shelter and clothing, actualisation activities that inspire innovation and academic excellence.

"My government will tackle these fundamental challenges and move this country forward down the path of development. I therefore have the pleasure to present our plan for advancing the country."

He lifted the seven volumes sitting in front and presented them to the speaker of the house. In it were detailed lists of development projects for every ward, district and region sectioned into seven-year development periods. This according to the president was the blueprint foundation for development in Lubanda. Some of the projects may not be completed in his term in office but they would one day be completed. The presentation of the volumes was done simultaneously with the official launch of the online version. People would click on their wards and towns and see visual plans of the changes that would come when the projects were completed. He told his audience that good living involved people enjoying good healthy food, enjoying freedoms and being happy. "We see these demonstrated in the Garden of Eden. They are God-given attributes and essential to all Lubandans.

"This is but the first step; how are we going to make these changes a reality with an empty and overdrawn account?" He went on to remind his audience that after the Second World War the European countries were provided an opportunity to rebuild their economies through the Marshall Plan. "I am presenting to you an Emancipation Plan for Lubanda."

He went on to outline his plans to help him and the people realise the development plan. The government will be an agent of development. The government would be the guarantor and sponsor of projects and initiatives that would empower the people to make fundamental transitions to help Lubandans to acquire skills and knowledge to participate effectively in the world economy and advance in development; lifting themselves out of poverty. The government would offer capital to individuals and companies through loans and grants. These loans, unlike schemes that were tried elsewhere, would be properly managed by an autonomous agent answerable to Parliament.

Any citizen with an idea for business would seek a loan from the state or the state will guarantee a loan from the bank. Initially, the state would own 51% and the owner could redeem the rest of the shares over a period providing capital for business. He told them that this plan couldn't be executed by loans from abroad for a number of reasons. Donations and aid from abroad had been ineffectual in the past because the donors did not fully understand the context and fundamental predicaments of the African society. NGOs and Aid did not tackle fundamental issues. First, they focused on alleviating the current pain but not the underlying causes. Secondly, the cultural and ideological perspectives of the donating countries and organisations lacked understanding of the prevailing historical and social contexts of Lubanda. Donors set conditions that made sense to Western countries whose mind-set and social and economic equilibriums did not apply to an African state. For example, austerity had a different impact in an economy that gives generous welfare to its citizens as compared to those where governmental handouts do not exist. In addition, those giving aid attached strings that undermined their objectives. Lubanda had borrowed over and above its GDP and had no capacity to borrow further. The interest on the loans was like a stone around the neck of the country slowly drowning it in poverty for centuries to come and an underclass status. He also hated the donor culture that had evolved and made the people believe they were incapable of doing anything for themselves, becoming beggars and not doers. He absolutely hated television adverts that paraded black people like incapable animals, even though the intent to stir the conscience of a philanthropist may have been benign.

The Emancipation Plan would be executed with local resources, ingenuity, grants, knowledge and skills from individuals and countries that show a willingness to be partners within the framework set up by the government. The key outcome would be results of progress and development. Development would come, not by models of development drawn up by people sitting in overseas offices offering doctorate theories of development but by models designed by Lubandans who understand all aspects of Lubandan life, and could use this culture alongside knowledge and models from those who had succeeded.

Firstly, he would start with what the country already had – its strengths. He had enough labour. He would establish citizen labour loans; the citizens lend their labour to the government at the going rates. The people could voluntarily sign up to one of the projects running at the time in their locality. They will then lend their labour to the state. The state would issue them with loan accounts that would be redeemed with a small amount of interest paid over time as and when the government gets the money to settle labour loans. The national budget would create a fund that would gradually settle these loans. The country would owe its citizens. This is not forced labour but giving people an opportunity to receive an income in their lifetime.

Secondly, he told them that he had created citizen development bonds, CDB. Private Citizens and organisations with extra cash would buy these bonds and decide which projects their money should go to. These would be redeemed flexibly with very low interest rates. Qualified fund managers would oversee the administration of the government funds with the whole process remaining transparent. No dime would go to any government department unless they were a client.

Thirdly, they had identified many individuals who had stolen from the state through corrupt practices or embezzlement. He was going to give them an amnesty to refund what they had stolen. The money should be collected through transfers or the new Anti-Corruption Bureau. "Please note that I disbanded the ineffectual anti-corruption commission I found because a commission set up by corrupt leaders to fight corruption does not work. The money collected will go to the projects fund. This is for citizens who owe their country. After the three months amnesty, we shall take the individuals to court and charge them interest. Individuals who failed to comply shall have their assets frozen or ceased by the state.

"I am also pleased to report that we have reclaimed the property Chimwanga bought in the Caribbean and taken possession of it. We have added it to the list of state assets and we are making money out of it.

"The plan will not work without knowledge and skills. Local skills will be utilised to increase the skill base of the community as a whole. Therefore, education, research and innovation will be prioritised by the government. There will be a skills drive in the course of the current Parliament to further increase and diversify the skills base. The other area that will be prioritised is the enhancement and restructuring of relevant administrative and economic systems.

"The poor, ignorant villager ushered into a ruthless world economy will never make progress on his own. They have very little idea about the money economy. My government will educate its rural citizens in understanding the money economy and equipping them to participate effectively with skills that can pass to the next generation. They should know why buying a traditional cloth made in China is making them poorer and the Chinese merchant richer. Besides, why shouldn't Lubandans make their own clothes?

"The culture and attitudes of poverty will need to change in order to move forward.

"In the development plan are what I call vanity projects. These are projects that will offer a unique character to this nation and its successive generations. They are aspirational and may take centuries to complete but at least we shall make a genuine start. In the pursuit of a good life, happiness and the defence of freedom, there is after all, room for aesthetic indulgence.

"Finally, ladies and gentlemen," he said as he wound up his speech, "we cannot progress with the current constitution that has been tempered by personal interests and rendering the government inefficient."

He took out a copy of the revised constitution, explained parts he wanted to highlight and presented it to the speaker. "I am giving the country three months to debate these proposals and we shall hold a referendum on the last day of my ninth month in office. If you approve them the programme shall commence on the first day of the tenth month. I commend the Emancipation Plan to the people of Lubanda."

There was cheering across the land. The vision for the country was clear and here was the plan. The people had a say and not just a blindfolded endorsement. They liked the loans even if they did not know what or how it was going to work. Economists like Yudas were not fully convinced because there was no economic theory for what the president was proposing. Governments, after all, are not good at running business. In addition, too much of the government's hand in the economy through the initiatives announced had the capacity to harm as much as help the economy. However, there were many too who felt strongly that a new and clear path was needed to give a shot at development. Some argued that many good initiatives had not worked because of poor leadership. Moses had the credentials strong enough to pull this off. Meanwhile, Yudas would have to wait for his term in office to ditch these plans. In the Cabinet the President told him to either accept the plan with reservations or leave if he felt too strongly about the ideas. "You have to try new things provided you have the courage and the brains," Moses admonished those who disagreed with him.

The three months that followed passed quickly with passionate debates, meetings and mass mobilization campaigns. Some people did not agree with the extension of the life of Parliament after elections from five to seven years with flexibility for the President to call elections after the first five years of the running parliament. Many agreed with the creation of a second chamber of eminent persons, two thirds of whom would be elected by the principle tribes and one third elected by each region to regulate the power of the executive. They liked too the rare grounds on which the police and defence forces could disobey the president, if he acted against the constitution. The president had clear grounds on which he would be impeached by a two thirds majority in both houses; the Parliament and the House of Ndunas. The clause that the constitution shall not be changed but only amended would give it stability. All in all, they felt it was brilliant.

With few voices of dissent, the Emancipation Plan was approved by over ninety percent of the votes. On the first day of the tenth month, he signed the plan into law and the reign of the real president had truly commenced.

By a stroke of fortune and prudence, the next few months were like a miracle to Lubanda. Almost overnight, the day the Emancipation Plan and the constitution were signed, unemployment appeared to be solved. Millions of Lubandans signed up to the projects in their local areas. Projects in the seven-year plan were initiated. They were happy to work and be owed by the state and were happy to pass on the loans to their children if the state did not pay them in their lifetime. Some converted their loans into CDB bonds. Fortunately, they did not have to wait long to start getting paid.

The citizen development bond was very successful. Many wealthy and ordinary citizens including Lubandan registered companies bought bonds and the government had more than ten billion dollars to invest. By gentle coercion, the corruption recovery agency had recovered billions in money and assets surrendered to the state. The food production programmes had helped to boost food surplus. In fact, in almost all parts of the country, silos became the first projects to be completed. This helped to drop prices of food imports. Foreign companies were lining up to invest and other organisations and governments were happy to offer grants towards the Emancipation plan. A law had been enacted that foreign investment would require local partnership. He could not have wished for a better start to his reign, which seemed almost perfect. But alas, just as all was going so well, a potential disaster struck.

Chapter Seventeen

ON THE LAST DAY of the fifteenth month of President Kamawu's reign, personal news created a nightmare for the President. The news broke in the prime time 6.00 pm news that Delilah was pregnant. The newscaster appeared to be unsure whether to announce that the President's favourite disciple was going to have a baby. Her sigh at the end of that item summed up the mood of the public. Although out of respect the media did not mention the President, but speculation and suspicion was obvious on everyone's lips.

Yudas was in the lounge sipping whisky when he heard the news that Delilah was pregnant. He leaped out of the chair for joy and danced up and down – Shaka Zulu would have been proud of him. He smiled, laughed and clapped as though he had just been elected president.

He called his wife: "This is the moment I have been waiting for! I knew it would come."

As he lay in bed that night, he hatched his plan. He would tell the media what he thought had been happening: "President Kamawu had been living a life of infidelity, not what you would expect from a role model like him. He is a disgrace and both he and Delilah should be impeached. Only a fool will not realise why he, Yudas, was not given the Vice Presidency. He wanted a concubine. I am told he leaves the office late – do you want answers for this too! I will tell Rachel what he has been doing and she will roast him! This is a God-given chance.

"I knew one day I shall be president of Lubanda. Poor Moses, it takes a long time to build but only a few minutes to destroy. It will take him years to gather the smithereens of his reputation."

It could not have happened at a worse time in the week. The following day, the President had his weekly press conference, an opportunity for the media to interrogate his innocence or sniff out his guilty secret. The day after he was hosting a state visit of his closest ally in the region. You would not like a distinguished guest to be embarrassed by revelations of David's sin. As he walked to the lectern, there was indefensible harshness in the room. The journalists were not sure whether they should ask questions about the pregnancy or not. They respected him so much that they feared antagonising him; they felt their questions would make them unpopular with the people of Lubanda and were certain to be regarded almost as instigators of treason intended to spoil the shoots of good times. Others feared that the President might respond in a way that would embarrass them; he had built up a reputation for dealing ruthlessly yet graciously with the media.

However, the President walked calmly to the lectern; if there was trouble in his heart, his eyes or body did not show it. He briefed them about the new projects and the progress the country was making on the various projects. He talked about the visiting head of state and what they hope to accomplish during the visit. When he finished, one journalist could not resist the chance to ask him about the elephant in the room.

"Sir, we hear the Vice President is expecting a child."

"The President of Lubanda doses not seek to be a spokesman for private circumstances of its members, he replied, but added, "We shall always be delighted with any Lubandan born."

The innocence in his voice invited no further interrogations. At home Rachel was not as considerate. She lost it and took the President to task.

"Are you by any chance involved with Delilah?"

The President stopped whatever he was doing, looked at Rachel in disbelief, then shock with visible revulsion.

"Darling, never ever ask me that question again."

"But… but…"

"No but, if you think I have been promiscuous, you should not be in this house."

The subject was never mentioned again in the Kamawu home until the birth of the baby. Unfortunately, Rachel was badly hurt with the rumours circulating that the President had impregnated Delilah. Yudas told her his rehearsed version of the story. She was withdrawn and rarely ventured out. The President understood the situation but he acted as though the world had gone bonkers and he was the only sane soul lingering upon the planet. There was no hint of concern in his words or actions at all.

The social media went mad with speculations, suggesting names and sending congratulatory messages. What was clear was the lack of condemnation of the President. Far from condemnation, the people seemed to accept it as a small stumble on a social pothole. His cabinet colleagues were more worried about the rumours. His close associates were reporting that he did not want to comment on the rumours because he did not want to elevate the discussion or beg for trust, only earn it.

Both Delilah and President Kamawu acted normally. Delilah went ahead with her businesses as though nothing had happened. Her usual infectious and exuberant personality was hard to ignore and encouraged forgiveness. She was often seen stroking the prince or princess swimming in her womb. In the official engagements the President always addressed her formally as he had done ever since he had first met her. The President knew his character was now questionable and Rachel was devastated but he had resolved not to say a word until the baby was born.

Nine months was a long wait; eventually there was a report that Delilah had had a baby boy she named Moses and the President publicly congratulated her on the birth of her son. When the name was announced, Rachel stood up and became hysterical, walking round the house, cursing. To her this was the confirmation she was waiting for. She knew Delilah loved the President, from the way she always flirted with him but the name of the child must have a deeper meaning. She tried to call the President but he was in a meeting. She spoke with her mum who immediately drove to her house. This was clearly unbearable for her.

As more information emerged about Delilah's baby in the day, it was clear something was amiss. The journalists gathered at the hospital began receiving news that the child was possibly not the President's because he was white! Others began reporting that he was an albino.

Rachel did not need to be convinced it was her husband's son, and she had no time or room to think otherwise. When the President walked in she began sobbing on her mother's lap.

"Good evening mum, who has died?"

"Nobody Son, it is Delilah's newborn baby."

"What has happened to the baby?"

Nobody would answer him; they all looked embarrassed.

He walked past them and went to his office. He realised Rachel might have had a nervous breakdown. He changed into casual clothes and went to walk with his son Abel in the orchard. While the President was in the orchard, someone rang Rachel to tell her that the child was not the President's because he was of mixed race. Rachel's mum could not wait to look the President in the eye; she slipped out and sped away to her home. Although the information came from her cousin who was a nurse at the hospital, Rachel would still not believe.

Yudas was right. Everyone is wrong. She decided to visit Delilah. She carried a card, flowers and a cake.

Delilah was so pleased to see her. She let her hold the baby and they talked and laughed. Rachel analysed the boy's face for any clues to prove her hypothesis. As she left the hospital, a cloud of guilt descended upon her. She was now fearful of facing him but she had to do it.

"How is Delilah and the baby?"

"They are both very well and looking terrific. She was pleased to see me." She asked: "Why did you not tell me nine months ago?"

"Tell you what?"

"That you had nothing to do with her pregnancy?"

"Was I in court?"

"No."

"Do you think a President should go around apologising for people's imaginations?"

"No," she said with a quivering voice.

"Right, if a wife decides to lose trust and confidence in her husband that is her decision. I do not have to plead for trust and honour, I earn it."

Rachel realised her apology was so inadequate and feeble that she could not talk to him about it again. It was her turn to earn and restore his respect for her.

Two days later Delilah emerged from the Lubanda private hospital, presented the child to the public and thanked them for their support. The public realised that the boy was of mixed heritage.

Those who realised their suspicions were unfounded walked with guilt in their eyes. One woman who stood by the President was his PA Kashimbi. She had consistently told Rachel and whoever cared to listen that they were wrong because he was a man of principles and integrity. At no time did she suspect a relationship between the President and Delilah. She knew that Delilah loved and respected the President because of his leadership qualities, in the same way that they all loved and respected him.

Far from being damaged, the President came out of the misunderstanding more revered by his admirers and supporters. The real casualty of this episode was the Minister of Finance, Yudas Kayumba Mwale.

The following day there was a special Cabinet meeting attended by everyone except Yudas. The President who rarely showed any emotions walked in as usual and sat down. Everyone was asking where the Minister of Finance had gone.

"Ladies and gentlemen, I wish to announce that I have relieved Hon Yudas Kayumba Mwale of his responsibilities as the Minister of Finance with immediate effect. I called to inform him last night and I would be announcing a reshuffle this afternoon."

They all gasped and looked alarmed.

"Why has he been dropped, Sir?" asked Hon. Mazombu.

"Mr Mwale has been briefing the media about my assumed extramarital relationship with Ms Delilah. He secretly offered support to my wife. He is the person who has been responsible for all the misinformation and lies that have been spread about me. I cannot work with colleagues who undermine me or other leaders for their own political ambitions. I know that some of you had secret discussions with him and I will be talking to individuals privately."

The meeting proceeded in an atmosphere of fear and guilt. Some ministers who had conversations with Yudas about their suspicions of a love relationship between the President and the Vice President could hardly look at the President.

That was the second minister to be fired. The first was Hon. Kawayawaya. Six months after the elections Mr Kawayawaya called on the President to introduce a potential Italian investor called Palmiro. When they walked into the President's office, he had already carried out research on him and whatever he found out was not good news.

After introductions, Palmiro had walked into a merciless interview.

"Mr. Palmiro, tell me about your investment profile," the President prompted.

Mr Palmiro fumbled an incoherent answer.

"Will you please tell me about your proposed project?"

"We are looking for one thousand hectares of land to build a food processing plant."

"Can I have a look at your business plan?"

"I do not have one, Sir."

"You are coming to the President to ask for so much land yet you do not have a business plan?"

Mr Kawayawaya who was listening most of the time explained that he had approved the land application and that he would ask Palmiro to present a business plan. Mr Palmiro then stood up and placed a large envelope on the President's table.

The President called his security officer and ordered him to open the envelope. It contained US $20,000 in cash.

"Mr. Palmiro, what is this for?"

"It is a gift, Sir."

"Whose gift, mine or the nation? This is your business, going round corrupting leaders. Is this the value of one thousand hectors of land?"

They both realised the gesture had misfired. Mr Kawayawaya tried to speak but he was told to shut up. He had never seen the President so angry.

"How much did he give you?

"Sir?"

"Tell me, how much did he buy you for?"

"$10,000 Sir."

"Mr Kawayawaya, you have disappointed me. I had so much confidence in you but I am sorry to say you have no place in my government with immediate effect. Thank you for your services to this point. I would like you to go on air and apologise to the people of Lubanda for your actions. Meanwhile, you will be escorted to the office to collect your personal belongings.

"As for you Mr Palmiro, the application has been cancelled; you and your money will be taken to the police where they will deal with you according to the laws of Lubanda."

Security officers were called and escorted both men out of the office. Later that evening Hon Kawayawaya apologised to the nation and sadly committed suicide a couple of days later.

Hon. Yudas was not asked to apologise to the nation because of the personal nature of the problem but it is strongly rumoured that he received a dressing down for his mischief. The President was well aware of Yudas' mischievous activities and ambitions. He even knew how he danced in his house upon hearing Delilah was pregnant and vowed to nail down both the President and Delilah so he could take over the government. The President was also aware of his contacts with fired policemen and some people from the previous government. He even played telephone conversations in which he spoke to the First Lady giving her information about the President's movements and private meetings with Delilah.

It was reported that he hardly spoke after the President revealed these activities. When the President told him he had betrayed his personal trust and was forthwith fired from his ministerial position, he broke down. Unfortunately, his tears did not save his job. As it turned out, this was not the last of Hon. Yudas Kayumba Mwale.

Chapter Eighteen

CHIMWANGA'S TRIAL was the first major test of the new constitution. At midnight the President received a call from five members of his cabinet who wanted to talk to him. They had been discussing the upcoming trial since the last cabinet meeting and so they decided to have an audience with the President.

"Good evening lady and gentlemen, what brings you here so late in the night?"

"Sir, we do not think the trial should go ahead. Chimwanga will feast on it and attack you and the government. You should ring the judge to cancel or postpone the trial," said the spokesman of the group.

"I understand your concerns, they are genuine and it is possible he will do so. However, interfering in the judicial process is undermining the independence of the judiciary. The judges must act without the influence of the President, Parliament, Government or the media. I will not undermine one of the most important pillars of a true democracy."

"What will you do if he says things embarrassing to you or the Government?" asked one of the ministers.

"We need to help the public to understand the rule of law and the independence of the courts as custodians of the law. Allowing this man to stand trial is not a sign of weakness. I am sure the public is mature enough to understand the rumblings of a fallen tyranny."

"Have you had a word with the judge, Sir?"

"About what?"

"About the court appearance of Chimwanga."

"I am not interested in talking to judges about court cases. None of the ministers or government officials must ever speak to the judges to influence judgements."

"This may be a mistake, Sir?" said the only lady in the group.

"A mistake will be to interfere with the judiciary. A true democracy survives on the rule of law and there should never be any complicity. My government will protect this institution. Never again shall we have arbitrary actions by the President."

After three hours of discussion, the ministers realised this was a different era. He lectured to them about the importance of protecting the independence of the courts to the point where they thought the President was too idealistic.

The court session was as dramatic as expected. Mr Chimawanga walked in to jeers from the waiting curious crowd.

"Can you confirm your name, Sir?" said the judge.

"Don't be silly, everybody in here knows all about me," shouted the unimpressed former president.

"Will you please confirm your name, these are court procedures," said the Judge.

"My name is Chimwanga."

"Full names please."

"You idiots, don't mess up with me. I am not a common man. Do you understand?"

"I am charging you with contempt of court. You must know we are in a different era, Sir. The days are gone when you could insult and run the courts with your incompetent judges. In the new Lubanda everyone is equal before the law. Everyone is treated equally under the law. All behaviour by paupers or millionaires, the rich or powerful shall conform to the same Lubandan law," the angry judge told him.

"What is this weak young president of yours teaching you?"

"He is teaching us how a democracy works and how a government works."

"And me, didn't I teach you anything?"

"Perhaps you showed us how not to govern."

"So he is teaching you how to try a former president?"

"He is teaching us how to be true guardians of the law and democracy."

"I deserve to be respected."

"You deserve to respect this court, Sir."

"Have you forgotten that it is me who appointed your father a permanent secretary so as to be able to educate you?"

"If my father were standing in that dock like you, I would do the same," said the Judge.

"Because you are an idiot!" shouted Chimwanga.

"Lock him up for seven days for contempt of court. The court is adjourned for seven days. He should come from jail straight back to court. No bail. See you in a week's time," said the Judge and walked out.

Chimwanga's seven days in prison were a joy for the policemen who threw him in the same cells common prisoners spend their time. The few supporters he had appeared to have deserted him except for Matthew Kapoya who visited him loyally every day. After serving the seven days, he came back to court humbler. He now fully understood what he seemed not to have realised for two years that he was powerless.

He sat quietly as the two thousand and fourteen counts of abuse of power, murder and embezzlement of public funds were read. Cases spanning a period of thirty years. Occasionally he looked up, sighed and gazed at the Judge. The taming of the tyrant. The stage was set for his undignified ordeal.

Many months had been spent gathering information relating to his misdeeds. When the trial started in earnest the public were more interested in knowing what he had been doing than the process. They had never seen a former leader so tamed. The real message of the trial was that in Lubanda aspiring to be a true democracy, no one shall be above the law no matter what his or her status was.

"Mr Chimwanga," the prosecutor began.

"Call me President Chimwanga!" he shouted.

"I am sorry, you are no longer president," the prosecutor replied.

"That's what you think, wishful thinking. When this boy fails and you all turn to me, you will be the first..." He made a cut throat sign.

"Behave yourself and answer the questions Mr Chimwanga, don't threaten anyone in my court," ordered the Judge. "Mr Chimwanga, at the last election you had one hundred and ten million dollars in your Lubanda Barclays account; tell the court how you accumulated this amount."

"Why are you asking me, your President took it away from me? It was my money. As president I owned everything in Lubanda. I owned the judges because I appointed them. I enjoyed firing them as well. There was no one who had power over me. I owned everything in Lubanda. I even owned you, do you understand? So how can I fail to get one hundred million? What is your problem?" Chimwanga grumbled angrily.

"The problem is that you got the money from the loan the country was given for treating patients during the outbreak of measles and cholera and you put it into your personal account. As a result five thousand children died. How did you feel when these children were dying?"

"Children always die. Children will always die. Even as we speak children are dying in Lubanda."

"You were so heartless you couldn't be sad about so many children dying while you enjoyed the money which was meant for their medicine. Why didn't you buy medicines, Mr Chimwanga? Is it true that you used half of this money for your daughter's wedding?"

"She was the daughter of a president and deserved the wedding."

"While other people's children deserved death? Mr Chimwanga, you were too greedy to save lives?"

"Presidents everywhere enjoy themselves, why would you ask me such questions?"

"I ask you because you were a stealing President; you stole from the most vulnerable people for your private benefit. You stole public funds. You were possessed by an evil spirit of greed, violence and wilful ignorance."

"Objection, your honour," interjected the defence lawyer. "You cannot call my client a thief before the court finds him guilty."

"Objection, declined. It is a line of questioning," said the judge.

"Let us move on to another account," the prosecutor said as he cleared his throat. "All your budgets ran out six months after they were announced. Please tell the court why this was happening."

"Ask the finance ministers."

"You had no part in it? Is it not true that you were ordering departments to deposit the money into your numerous accounts sometimes late in the night? I have a record of the times you rang the manager of the Lubanda commercial bank and asked for a transfer of five million dollars from the education account into your son's account in Switzerland. Can you tell the court please, tell the court about this transaction?"

"Why don't you ask the manager instead of me?"

"He will have his turn to tell his tale to the court, this is your turn."

"Nonsense."

"Mr Chimwanga, this is not nonsense; taking money from the treasury and spending it on your leisure and personal expenses is a serious matter. That is why the government ran out of money, borrowed perpetually and went broke. That is not the bank manager's fault; it was the president's responsibility. You did this throughout your time in office."

"So what? I was the president so I enjoyed myself."

"You were an incompetent president, Sir. Is it true that at one time you attended a meeting of heads of state and they were talking about GDP. You turned to your so-called adviser and said, 'This GDP is a very strong man. What country does he rule?' To which your adviser replied, 'He rules all countries.' Your reply was, 'He doesn't rule my country and if he shows up I shall cut his throat.' Is that true Mr Chimwanga?"

"Objection," interjected the defence lawyer.

"What are you going to get out of this?" asked Chimawanga.

"Justice for the people of Lubanda," replied the prosecutor, and continued: "Mr Chimwanga, let us move to your wife's holiday that led to the closure of the electricity company in which the government had shares. Did you ask for twenty million dollars for your wife's holiday and your birthday party?"

"I was not the manager of the company."

"Mr Chimawanga, I have all the information here and the people will testify. Did you order them to transfer fifty million into your account in Switzerland?"

"I cannot comment on private dealings."

"I am sorry, sir, they are no longer private. Did you?"

"It was a loan."

"When did you pay it back?"

"The company went into administration."

"So you paid back the loan by ordering the closure of the company?"

"Do you have evidence?"

"Yes, it is all here, even the minutes of the meetings you held and a recording of your order."

"One more thing Mr Chimwanga; is it true that in your last year in office you fired the finance minister, the professor, who you told off for refusing to give you and your henchmen pay rises from government loans?"

"Listen, presidents always fire people. Your young man has done the same so what is my crime?"

"Your crime is that the minister in question refused to award you an increase. You demanded an increment or you would fire him before he presented the budget. It was impossible for him to do it because he was a principled man. He tried to explain to you but you wouldn't listen. You personally called Lubanda broadcasting to inform them that you had fired the minister of finance for stealing public funds. Is that not true? You were running your government like *magogu* Mr Chimwanga. Please tell the court how many such increments you received from the treasury?"

"Who stopped you from becoming a politician to enjoy power and wealth?"

"Answer the question Mr Chimawanga, how many arbitrary increments did you receive?"

"Enough to buy a coffin for you and your father."

"I have no further questions, your honour."

The summation of the first part was very damning. In closing the prosecutor did not have kind words.

"Mr Chimwanga was a manipulative and greedy man. He behaved like one possessed with an evil spirit of greediness; he was so drunk with power that he did not know its boundaries and he used it to amass wealth at the expense of the people of Lubanda. Possessed by a spirit of violence and a sense of impunity, he sacked and even killed or jailed people who stood in his way. He had a complete lack of understanding of the economy and how it works. Your honour, Mr Chimwanga is guilty on every single account of financial embezzlement and I recommend that he should be jailed for life for causing so much misery for the people of Lubanda. An unrepentant arrogant tyrant does not deserve to tread the streets of free citizens; neither does he deserve any clemency."

Mr Chimwanga had grown wary of attending these unending court sessions. At every appearance, there was a new case and more evidence. He grew very angry with each session. Unfortunately, this was but the beginning. The prosecution had arranged that they would start with cases of embezzlement of funds, followed by cases of general abuse of power and end up with cases of attempted murder and political killings. This was a long journey for Chimwanga. As he sat through the summation of the first part of his trial, he came up with a plan.

Up until now former president Chimawanga had been placed under house arrest for abuse of power, awaiting court appearances. President Kamawu did not want to humiliate him but to let the due process of the law have the final word. The news of Yudas' dismissal was a gift to Chimwanga. Although he had taken to drink and had grown physically weak as a result, he felt strong enough to make another shot at the post he so dearly cherished and missed.

His plan was to trick Yudas into fighting the President. He would offer to support him to mount a coup. Once this was done, he would kill Yudas before he was sworn in and assume power. Although Yudas had no previous dealings with Chimwanga, his injured ego persuaded him to take up his offer of support. What started as clandestine contacts soon became open friendship. He would be seen driving to the former president's residence and staying there for hours.

Chimwanga who was now reinvigorated hatched out a master plan. He contacted his former sympathisers, policemen who had been fired and his other dark network of cells that lay dormant. The President was due to fly out for a two-day meeting. They would mount a surprise attack on the broadcasting house and take it over. Chimwanga even contacted his despot friend from the southern state who did not like the progress going on in Lubanda. He promised to give financial and military support.

Clandestine conversations between the men became a little open in their homes. Mwale's wife became uncomfortable with her husband's plans and contacts with Chimwanga. When she tried to dissuade him, he beat her up. She had secretly become a staunch supporter of the President since the first family party the President threw for his cabinet and they had a conversation. She, like Delilah and many others, had seen something unique in the man and would not allow anybody to harm him. She was determined to do something. Lubanda was more important than the ambitions of his husband.

Although he was aware of their contacts through the security forces, the President thought Yudas was not so evil. His private and official security personnel warned him of the imminent attack. With information from within the enemy camp, he planned his defence. On the day of his trip, he flew out as usual at the officially scheduled time. He circled the country and landed in a rural aerodrome. He drove back to the capital city in an unmarked vehicle and went straight to the presidential palace where he worked but did not live. Security was beefed up at all the key installations.

At 03.00 am the Yudas – Chimwanga operation was set in motion. Chimwanga, who had tricked Yudas to go to the broadcasting house in order for him to occupy the presidential palace, was the first to die in a gun battle. His convoy of rebels was ambushed by the army shortly after starting off from a secret location in the outskirts of the capital. Yudas, changed his mind at the last minute and refused to lead the assault on the broadcasting house, fearing for his life. Those who went never reached the gates; they all perished in a separate security operation. A foreign helicopter was captured at the border and all the soldiers who came in from the south were arrested. The storm of discontent was over before it began in earnest.

Yudas and a few supporters were arrested and locked up. At five in the morning, the President made a rare early morning announcement informing the nation about the foiled coup attempt and that President Chimwanga, one of the architects, had sadly lost his life in a gun battle. He appealed for calm and told Lubadans to go about their business as usual but to be vigilant. Little did he know they would gather round his house and the presidential palace instead of going about their business. They were infuriated by the foreign involvement and many demanded to be enlisted to go and fight.

The foreign involvement sparked an unprecedented response. Internationally, all regional leaders condemned the President of the Southern State. They offered moral and military support to President Kamawu. The Southern State was also suspended from the regional grouping.

In the Southern State itself, the people saw their leader's interference as a self-defence action because he was scared of the progress taking place in Lubanda, thinking it would spark louder demands for change. The opposition took advantage by mobilising protests against the government. The southern state military blamed their president for the arrested soldiers, a move that inspired mass demonstrations.

In Lubanda, there was anger at both Chimwanga and Yudas. The Lubandans who did not believe the coup had failed mobilised into people's militias and thousands stood in vigil around their President's house and office. Villagers near borders joined the army to reinforce patrols. They saw this as an attack not only on their President but the whole country which they had to defend. Young men and women lined up at the barracks demanding guns and military training. They only calmed down after the President assured them there was no danger to him or the country. He even flew out to attend the meeting as a demonstration to the public that all was under control. Although they blamed him for going soft on Chimawanga who they thought should have been locked up in a maximum security prison or hanged the day after the elections, they respected his judgements with a gentle censure.

The uprising in the neighbouring state was more than a victory for Lubanda. The coup had after all been successful, except for a wrong man, President Kamawu. With both the battle and war won and all arch rivals taking themselves out of the scene, Lubanda entered a long period of peace, tranquillity and economic progress.

Chapter Nineteen

"**M**OSES! It is time for supper, can you please tell everybody to come to the table."
Family life had changed over the past two and half years since the new government came to power. The number of middle class citizens had dramatically increased.

"How was school…?"

"It was good, Dad. We had so many things to do as usual."

"What did you do?"

"We played football, rugby and tennis. The teacher said I was very good at tennis. Can I join a club?"

"That's okay," said Dad. "We shall look for a good club for you. Do you know where some of your friends go?"

"I'll find out Dad."

"How about you, how was school?"

"Alright, I suppose."

"What happened?"

"I did not get my maths class work right and the teacher was not happy."

"Do not be upset about it, we shall look at it together before you go to sleep."

"I played with my friends. We made cars, played with cars. I…I painted and spilt the paint all over. Look at my clothes, they're dirty."

"Don't worry; your mum will put that in the washing machine. Come on, finish your food so we can go to bed."

After supper mum took two of the children to bed while dad stayed to go over the maths homework before taking their second child to bed. Sambondu watched his son drift away into sleep as he read the last phrase, "...lived happily ever after." He tucked him in, kissed him on the forehead and slowly walked out of the room, dimmed the lights and closed the door gently behind him.

After all the children went to bed, mum and dad sat down for coffee. "Juggling family commitments and work can be difficult but things seem to be working well so far. So much has changed in the two years, you cannot believe we are the same people."

This had become a ritual for Peter whenever he managed to come home early from work. Between him and his wife Joyce, they took turns to read for their youngest child and listen to the older ones read to them. This had become a ritual not only for them but for all Lubandans. Part of the education law required parents to read and/or listen to their children between the ages of two and twelve read. The President was reported to have insisted on this because he believed it would help the intellectual development of Lubandans. The President bought a citizen development bond, CDB to kick start the programme.

Some people were skeptical because they thought it was such a crazy idea to implement when nearly half of the adult population was either illiterate or semi-illiterate. The programme began by acknowledging that reading to children was not a new concept. For centuries the African child sat around the fire in the evening to listen to their grandparents and other older people tell them stories. Stories such as how the clever little hare split her lip laughing at the elephant and the hippopotamus locked in a tug of war challenge the hare initiated. He had gone to each one of them secretly to challenge them to a tug of war contest. Both were convinced they would certainly win and the two giants took on the challenge. On the day of the contest, he gave them each the end of the same rope, telling them to start pulling when the rope moved.

The hare then rushed to the middle of the rope where neither the elephant nor the hippopotamus would see him, tapped the rope and the two giants started pulling, much to the hare's pleasure. Such stories with themes of courage, intelligence, moral responsibility and love built not only character and vocabulary but also creativity.

The bedtime story reading programme, which was part of the literacy strategy, identified and trained reading champions in every village. Parents who could not read asked neighbours who were encouraged to read. A small appreciation allowance was paid to the reading champions. Schoolchildren who were able to read began reading to their siblings or other children in the home or village. After a few years, the reading programme had become accepted as part of the new culture. These home initiatives complemented school activities that taught personal discipline and organization, held as essential ingredients of successful people.

There was another reason Peter had come home early, to prepare for a two-week family holiday in his home village. It had been five years since they last visited home. In fact, they last visited when their young son named Moses was born on that dramatic night of election. Their holiday was part of the birthday celebrations. They planned to spend time with family, visit the hospital where their son was born and help out with programmes going on in the village. The actual birthday party would take place in the capital and coincide with the five year celebrations of President Kamawu's election. Friends and relatives agreed to join the Sambondus at their new home in Lubindi, the capital city for joint celebrations.

The Sambondus were now the symbol of the emancipation age. Joyce Sambondu was a hospital matron. Since she was nominated to lead a group of nurses on a study tour to some of the best hospitals in Europe and the USA, she had done well for herself. The government realised that the country had local skills such as nurses but these needed to be improved to match international standards. They came up with a programme of sending their best skilled workers to the best institutions and organisations to learn best practices. Unlike similar feeble attempts in the past by the governments before Chimwanga's, this was well organised and resourced. A department headed by a Deputy Permanent Secretary in the Ministry of Development was solely charged with this responsibility. Study tours involved observations, lectures, reflections, discussions by the teams and hands on practical work. At the end, they were given a month to sit with experts in the field and develop plans to improve the current practice of their institutions in Lubanda. The programme was well funded by grants and government resources. Upon arrival, the plans were reviewed with senior management and implemented.

Joyce was one of the first to go on these study tours. As a team leader, she came back with a comprehensive plan for turning a government hospital into a world class health facility. The board decided the plan must be implemented in full and they chose her hospital to start the implementation. Since then, she had visited the hospitals abroad bringing back expertise and contributing to Lubanda's first world class hospital. Even the President came to this hospital for his medical check-ups. The government had started implementing the plans in every hospital in the country. There were now fewer patients being sent abroad for medication. There was talk that Joyce should be promoted to a national office to overlook the changes they were making but the board would like her to complete all the phases of the plan. However, to keep her happy, she received a special salary for the extra work she did.

Peter Sambondu initially trained as a primary school teacher. He decided to change career by studying electronics by correspondence. When he finished the course he joined Phillips electronic company repairing gadgets. He proved to be exceptionally good. Coincidentally, the government decided to train electronic engineers. The President personally took charge of the programme for training engineers and he kept a close eye on this project. Ironically, it was not education or health that received the biggest budget, it was engineering. Many citizen CDBs were pledged towards engineering so it was a flagship programme. Five years on, the country had increased the number of engineers by half. The clever move was to sponsor all those with relevant diploma qualifications and degrees to undertake two years practical industrial training abroad. The next push was for electronic engineers.

Peter won a sponsorship to Germany and did a one-year practical training course in the USA. Upon his return, the company reimbursed the government by redeeming a few CDB bonds they bought, and promoted him to divisional manager. The increases to the household income for Joyce and Peter allowed them life comforts. They were able to send their children to private schools, buy a big new house and expensive cars. Peter and Joyce felt a debt of gratitude to both the nation and President Kamawu.

Joyce had so far formed a charity for traditional midwifery skills. Since her ordeal five years ago when she nearly gave birth in the car, she decided to revisit the traditional midwifery skills and bring them in line with the 21st century. Her goal was to recognise the talent and skills and use them whenever it was possible to complement modern practice especially in emergency situations. Her charity has since trained and developed a data base of people with these skills all over the country.

Peter was recently elected as the Chairman of the students "Idea clubs." This is an offshoot of the President's programme of think tanks. Every college and university had a think tank grant to facilitate philosophical discussion. Given his own experience of a think tank at the university, he studied this movement for his Ph. D. programme. He was intrigued by the Bilderberg Group, a secret group whose deliberations impact on the whole world. In primary and secondary schools the little think tanks were called idea clubs. Children were encouraged to join and there were different activities for them. These activities ranged from practical skills to discussions and debates. The President explained the reasons behind this initiative:

"Every man's practical activity starts in the mind, with an idea. Success and failure nestle in the mind. Many of our political parties lack a foundation. Think tanks will enable young people and adults to research, analyse, and debate ideas. This will be a strong philosophical basis for our democracy and progress."

In addition Peter was also a member of the ruling party's own think tank. They were independent and once in a year met with the President and his Cabinet to discuss government policies. In their last meeting the Minister of Mines was so animated that the President threw him out of the meeting. The reason for his agitation was that the think tank tore his policies apart and accused him of being a traitor. He has since apologised to the group and is considering some of their viable proposals.

The two weeks holiday was therefore a welcome rest for both Peter and Joyce. The past five years have been so busy that they hardly had enough quality time together as a family. It was also an opportunity to see what was going on in the countryside. They had heard many reports of the transformation taking place but they had't had an opportunity to see for themselves.

Chapter Twenty

PETER AND JOYCE had never had such a pleasurable scenic drive to the village. The new road, half completed, had been re-sited, giving gorgeous scenery of the plains. The remaining scattered herds of elephants, kudus and deer chasing one another was better than watching television animal documentaries. The blossoming green plants formed canopies below the savannah-equatorial trees. The singing birds reminded Peter of his childhood days when he would go hunting with his late father. On good days, they chased and killed at least a deer and a bush baby. It was his responsibility to carry the carcass while his dad would carry a piece of bark full of honey.

He fondly remembered these days with nostalgia. The excitement in the village when they arrived made him feel good, a satisfying feeling of accomplishment. Unfortunately, he could not go hunting in the same way with his two sons. At least he could take them fishing one day, a promise he never fulfilled on every trip to the village.

Something else made this journey special; the countryside was being transformed much quicker than they both imagined. The new road under construction would reduce the travelling time by half, from five hours to two and half hours. Many folk from the towns were travelling to this part of the world more frequently as a result. Already the part that had been tarred had made a long journey a pleasure. There were nice lay-bys, with nice circular concrete chairs and tables. The bus stops in the villages had grown with farmers' markets where they sold their produce at reduced prices.

There were also small silos in areas with major concentrations of people. This was the first project undertaken by the citizen loans. The government provided money for materials and engineers and the local people supplied labour loans. Fortunately for them, they started getting paid before the projects were finished because the government had secured funding. Now there was no staple food wasted. The President banned food exports for the first three years. He told the country to only sell surplus when the country had enough food reserves. In order to make farmers happy, they were all paid on time. The food policies were based on knowledge, skill and mechanisation. There was widespread training and education programmes for all subsistence farmers. Many of these were carried out with commercial farmers who were paid to work with local farmers in their locality or adopt farmers in a different part of the country who they visited and invited for hands-on practice in commercial farming. As part of the Emancipation programme, the government bought a tractor for every ten small villages. The government would start recovering the costs through a percentage of the produce in the second year of the programme. The government provided implements while the villagers put money together to purchase fuel and pay the allowances for the drivers. Once the full cost was recovered, the machinery would be handed to the people. Some villages decided to redeem part of their citizen loans to pay back for the tractors.

The result of all these initiatives was increased food production and security for Lubanda. Nobody saw this coming so fast. The people were buying into government policies with complete trust and commitment. These were surely good days for Lubanda.

They arrived home at dusk to ululations and much excitement. Peter's mum had been to their home in Lubindi several times travelling by bus to help out with the children, especially when he was out studying. For many of the relatives, they were seeing them for the first time in five years. Nobody minded the long drive; all they wanted were the stories from town and experiences from overseas. It was surely a long night.

The first day was pretty much spent in the previous night. Peter and Joyce woke up at two in the afternoon. There was much noise in the village and when they peeped through the window, they saw a police van, and queues. They quickly dressed up and rushed out of the house only to find a mobile bank truck. People were depositing and withdrawing money from the ATM machines and the teller by the side of the van. They had no idea about this part of modern village life.

They looked for their children only to find them playing a version of Monopoly. The village boys were certainly good at it because they had a lot of monopoly money. The monopoly they were playing was different from the standard game. It was an adapted version. Instead of buying houses there were common items found in the village like oxen. Peter was most intrigued and asked about the mobile banks and new monopoly games.

They knew the President wanted the villagers to learn the financial systems. They could not participate fully in the global economy without knowing the banking system. He introduced the mobile bank that enabled people to open accounts. What Peter and Joyce did not know was how it worked. Uncle Josiah was surprised they were not so well informed about these changes. He explained that the monopoly game was part of the programme. Villagers were given sets of the game and asked to play. They learnt basic financial skills. Players could bank the money they made with the banker. That is why it differed from the standard monopoly game. The next steps were free courses about banking and financial management. This was to explain the systems beyond the transactions they were already doing.

By the time the real accounts were opened, everyone was enlightened.

The van left at 05.00 pm. It all made sense; instead of building banks, the mobile van would fulfil this purpose until there was a need to construct buildings. This was not the only change from Peter's childhood days.

At dusk after supper, the children gathered to listen to *Nkaka* tell stories. This part was familiar. Their children listened to a number of stories. One story they remembered and loved well was how the villagers killed an ogre.

"Once upon a time," Nkaka said as she started every story in the same way. "There was a family with two daughters. The younger was very beautiful but the elder one was lame in the leg. A handsome man came round to marry the younger sister. She insisted on going with her sister. One day the girl left her sister in one of the shelters and went to the fields. Whilst she was away, the ogre came home without transforming himself. He started bragging about how he would kill them. After a while he left and went away. When the wife came back, the sister told her they should flee because the handsome man was after all an ogre.

"They ran home and narrated the story. The villagers came up with a plan to deal with him. They dug a ten-foot deep pit, put spears in the bottom sticking upwards and covered it with a mat. Supporting the mat were pounding sticks laid across the pit. As expected the handsome ogre followed his wife and they offered him the mat. One by one the girls came to pull out the pounding sticks, sending him down the pit and onto the spears." The children loved the songs that came with each story. The story teller ended with the moral of the story: no disabled person is useless and team work is important for success.

The two weeks passed very fast. They made repairs to their house and visited the hospital where their youngest son was born. Joyce offered a refresher course to the maternity ward nurses, which was much appreciated by the hospital. Peter had taken the children fishing, the highlight of their visit. It was just as well they reserved days for rest because this was more of a working holiday.

Peter was busy packing for the return trip on the following day when Uncle Josiah called him over. Uncle Josiah was the only surviving brother of Peter's mother. He always bore an air of the lion of the tribe. He was a respected man in the area. People found him intelligent and wise. In spite of Peter's status, he always gave him respect.

"Please sit down, I hope I am not interrupting your packing, but there is still time," said Uncle Josiah.

"I still have a few things to do but it's fine," replied Peter.

"As you may have heard on the news six months ago, I had the privilege of shaking the hands of the President."

"What do you think of him?"

"He is a clever man, patient and astute."

"I heard he came to launch a programme ten miles away. Is that the time you met him?"

"That's right. I have not called you to tell you I shook the hands of the great man," Uncle Josiah said adjusting his posture leaning towards Peter, "It is what happened that I want to share with you.

"All headmen in the area were called to a series of business meetings. The first meeting was on a Thursday. We were ferried to the school in the morning and given very good breakfast. On the first day we were taught about business – what is business, how it works and types of business. Businessmen in the area were invited to tell us about their experiences."

"Did people understand all this?" asked the puzzled Peter.

"Yes, it was explained simply with pictures and in our languages," answered Uncle Josiah with a proud grin.

"Wait, that wasn't the end. On Friday they came again, picked us up and dropped us at the school. We were taught how to run a business. We were told that by spending money buying goods in shops made in China and other countries we were making the Chinese rich and Lubanda poor."

He grabbed a file of papers and showed it to Peter. He explained some of the financial literacy lessons he had learned.

"On Saturday the President came. For the first time we were told why we were learning these lessons. He explained that the people of Lubanda will never be lifted out of poverty by donations and aid. They should lift themselves out. What they needed were the skills and knowledge to do so. We were largely a consuming nation but we should be a selling nation as well. He went on to announce that the government was launching a programme called Family Loans. Lubandans were already organised and had large extended families. This was a system that he wanted to use. We had been chosen as headmen because we already look after the families and villages. A sum of two billion lindi had been secured as part of the Emancipation Programme. He did not expect every business to succeed but he did expect fifty percent to do so. If that was realised, it would pay for the fifty percent loss. There were two major problems with family business, trust and hard work. The government would nurture every business started under this scheme. The scheme would run for a limited time and the government would sell its shares. He believed that although some Lubandans were running businesses, it was a small number. The government did not run businesses but it was important to give the people a starting base. Details of how it would work were given to us in a booklet."

"Will this work?" asked Peter.

"Yes, I think it will. That brings us to my last point; Peter, I would like you and your cousin to join us to start a family business. Will you? We have ideas but we need the support of you and your cousin because you are more informed than us. If you do not empower your relatives, they will always depend on you for assistance, but if you do, the responsibility shoulders will be widened."

"Uncle, this is a very good programme, I shall think about it and will get back to you. I need to read about how it will work and what we should do. I have a lot of work for my company so we need to analyse all aspects. Thank you for discussing this with me."

As he walked to his house, Peter had mixed emotions; he understood why the President had launched the scheme but he was not sure the batch of nephews and nieces in the village could run a business. Running a business requires lots of time, a commodity he surely didn't have. In spite of the misgivings, somewhere in his mind, he was convinced it was a thrilling opportunity.

Driving back to the city was faster because the last half of the road was already tarred. The children were tired and fast asleep.

"Joyce, what do you think of the transformation going on in the rural areas?" asked Peter.

"Amazing. I never imagined five years ago that I would ever see the progress we have seen; things were going nowhere," replied Joyce.

"What do you think has made a difference?" asked Peter.

"Leadership, leadership, leadership!" screamed Joyce.

"So that means the vote does make a difference? I am so proud I voted sensibly!" said Peter with a smile.

"If we still had Chimwanga, we would be locked up in the dark ages," said Joyce.

"Now Joyce, what do you think of the Family Loans and businesses?" asked Peter.

"To be honest, I think it is a good idea. You could one day be running your own multi- million lindi business." said Joyce.

"Uncle Josiah is excited about it. You should see him talk about it. Whatever they did to him, he is hooked to the idea," said Peter as the pulled into their garage.

"Children, we have arrived home!" shouted Peter.

Sleepy bodies half opened their eyes and drifted off again.

"Come on, we have arrived! Let us go in so we can start preparing for the birthday party tomorrow," shouted Peter again.

This was more than a birthday party. It was a birthday party for the young Moses, a party to mark the 5th year rule of President Kamawu and a housewarming party.

As visitors arrived, Peter took them around the house. It was a new house they had recently bought.

"Welcome to the Sambondus," Peter would say as he greeted his visitors who stood in the doorway admiring the reception hall. The reception hall merged into a large family room. On the left was a door leading to the kitchen and down beyond the family lounge were a few steps leading to a sunken large second lounge. Adjacent to the main sitting room was a bar. All the main bedrooms were on the first floor. In addition to the five bedrooms was a big study. By the standards of Lubindi, it was a very big house but this was one of many such houses the new Lubandan middle class were building or buying. Perhaps it is wrong to call them a middle class because the class system is atypical to Africa. Instead, we should call them wealthy Lubadans.

"This is the kitchen," said Joyce to her friend Kashimbi.

"My goodness, this is a beautiful kitchen. There is a table in the corner with five chairs and a very nice cooker!"

"How many bedrooms?" asked the overwhelmed Kashimbi.

"Five," said Joyce, "all en-suite."

"This must have cost you a fortune. What was the mortgage?" asked Kashimbi.

"No mortgage on it. We saved money when I was promoted and we saved all Peter's salary when he was studying abroad."

"You must be rich people," said Kashimbi with a touch of jealousy.

"No, we are not rich but comfortable," replied Joyce, rather embarrassed. "With a saving plan, everyone can build a big house like this one."

"I do not think I can afford it," said Kashimbi.

"Yes, you can. The problem is that we were brought up with the poor man's culture and habits. You get the money and buy, and buy, and buy. We buy things we do not need. Look at your cars; we have only two cheap cars to move us around," said Joyce.

"You are right, I think it is a mind-set," said Kashimbi.

"A poor mind-set likes luxury you cannot afford, comparing yourself with others to appear rich, filling wardrobes with clothes you do not wear and borrowing without thinking of the implications. Kashimbi, we need to change and start valuing money."

Peter and Joyce repeated these conversations with a dozen friends and relatives who admired their house and dared to ask.

By 14.00hrs the party was in full swing, the fathers busy on the barbeque roasting meat and serving themselves. A new way of doing things in modern Lubanda. As everyone settled to eat and drink, the mothers were busy on the bouncing castles and others playing games with children. There were activities for everyone, family games, discussions and whisky for others.

The gathering was a professional representation of Lubanda; doctors, nurses, bankers, engineers, teachers, businessmen and women. It was a snapshot of Kamawu's Lubanda.

The men soon gathered in the lounge and left the women looking after the children who were enjoying themselves. The President was addressing the nation to mark five years of his rule. The message was short, thanking the people for what they had achieved and promising them that together they will achieve more.

"Let us toast to the President's healthy and continued leadership," said Peter.

"Peter, what do you think of our Lubanda?" asked one of the guests.

"What do you mean?"

"How do you compare Lubanda today and where it was five years ago?"

"I owe all that I have to the President. As you know, Lubanda is a different country now. From the rural areas to towns, people are not only happy; they feel free and are full of life. We have never seen this before in the history of this country. As you know, I recently visited my ancestral home and what I saw makes me proud to see and marvel at how much has changed. The question is why we didn't do this at independence?" asked Peter.

"Because of leadership," said one half drunk man. "I think a country has to be lucky to get a true leader. South Africa had Mandela, the Americans had Lincoln and we have Kamawu. My fear is that when he goes, we shall slip back to those frogs."

"Yes, we did not have capable leaders, think of the imbecile Chimwanga."

"I did not know the difference between a real leader and an idiot until President Kamawu came along. I think people now know the qualities of good leaders and the constitution will protect us in future," said another.

"Yet we believed the *magogu*! Playing to be leaders," uttered a voice in the corner. Political passion and gratitude combined with whisky can be a melodious blend to spark off wit and humour.

"We were all fools; we chose to do nothing about those semi-illiterates."

"No, we weren't fools, we were ignorant."

"What is your favourite scheme?" someone asked.

"The skills training scheme! We had so many skilled people that were retired and forgotten yet the President has mobilised them, recognized them and has asked them to contribute by passing on their skills and knowledge. This reservoir of skills has played an important role in our development. We should not forget the various training programmes that have raised the level of skills to the 21st century."

"I love the constitution," said a dozing man. "I also like the land reform. Foreigners were buying us out of our land but now I know my great, great grandchildren shall have land."

Moses' government had instituted radical land reforms. Lease for foreigners had been reduced to thirty years and five hectares except for commercial farmers. Naturalisation rules had been altered to prevent future invasion. Moses believed land was the most precious commodity Lubadans had and must never be given away. He believed a poor Lubandan with land was far better off than a poor person with no land.

"You have forgotten the 49% ownership of our mines. Previous presidents handed over our wealth but the buying of the shares back gives us a portion of our own wealth. By the way the emancipation of the institutions of learning to world class status is a priceless investment for any developing nation."

"The vanity projects will be exciting, judging by the new presidential palace. I am told this will be the feature of the new presidential term. He wanted to complete the palace first. It is rumoured that companies will be given tax breaks if they embarked on spectacular buildings."

"Family loans, although they are just starting, I believe they will inspire entrepreneurship and generate businesses that will sustain economic momentum," shouted Peter.

"Every single one of them," said a female voice. "The problem with men is that they do not see the whole picture. It is a package. There is more to come."

"What do you think is in the president's bag of Emancipation schemes?"

"At one meeting he talked about personal actualisation. People should be seen to move from seekers of basic needs to pursue their full potential. Watch this space."

"Scientific research. We shall be the first African state to put a man on the moon!"

"Remember, he has often said in his first term of office, he will build systems and if elected again, he will then consolidate the systems. He is waiting for economic growth to spur development. That is a man with a vision and knows both the path he is travelling on and the destination," said another female voice. "By the way, it is not so much a matter of having money that has moved us forward, it is having brains."

"I love this President, please God bless him with many more years," said the guest who appeared to be snoring in the corner. "I am happy our policemen now wear boots and carry authority."

By 22.00hrs all the visitors were gone to take their children to bed. Peter was worried about a few who had drunk one too many and that they might not drive safely but hoped their wives would insist on driving them home. As Peter and Joyce put the children to bed and locked up the house, there was satisfaction on their faces. It was a good party and everyone enjoyed themselves. They retired to bed and Joyce heard Peter repeating to himself, "It takes a real president to move the country forward, I owe all I have to him. It is leadership." These were his words as he drifted off to sleep.

Peter arrived at work early; it was his first day back from a three weeks holiday. He was known to be the most hardworking worker. This was the reason the company did not allow the government to keep him after his training.

On his desk to his left was a pile of letters waiting for him. Next to the pile was one letter deliberately positioned to attract his attention. He wondered what it was. He picked it up but before he could open it, his boss walked in.

"Good morning Peter, it's good to see you. Did you have a good holiday?"

"Good morning, Sir. Yes, I had a lovely time with family and friends."

"Can I please talk to you in my office?"

"Sure."

"Things have gone well since you left. We kept the most important work for you."

"I have seen the pending pile! It sure will keep me busy for days."

"Peter, the board met two weeks ago and they decided to appoint you Deputy CEO for the company." He picked up a letter from his drawer and gave it to the beaming Peter.

"Thank you very much, Sir. I owe you a lot."

"Peter, you do not owe me anything, it was the Board's decision. They have been following your contributions to the company for many years now and they are convinced just as I am that you are the deserving candidate. By the way, you are the first Deputy CEO to be appointed from within the company. I'm sure you will also be the first Lubandan CEO to be appointment when I retire next year."

The temptation to ring Joyce and tell her was great but he decided against it until he got back home. Naturally, he could not resist feeling good. Soon after the meeting with the CEO, an email was sent to all employees announcing the new appointment.

The office became so busy that he forgot the other letter on the table; he even slipped it under the pile as people walked in and out to congratulate him. At the end of the day when the office was once again quiet with most workers gone, he remembered he had a letter which according to the way it was placed on the table was important but he could not find it.

He searched the drawers, the folders on the table and even the rubbish basket. Finally, he searched the pile and there it was under the pile of letters. He opened it and realised why it was placed apart from the others.

Dear Mr Peter Sambondu,

The President has been pleased with your contributions to the country through your patronage of the idea clubs in schools. He is therefore pleased to invite you and your family to join him for supper on Friday.

Please, contact the office to confirm your attendance and security clearance.

Yours sincerely,
Chief of staff

"Double blessing or a curse?" He sat rather confused with all these good things coming to him. He wondered whether the two developments were related. Did the President ask the company to promote him, or was it a sweet coincidence. "Which one should I tell Joyce first?"

The evening meal was normal to all but Peter. He was unusually full of smiles. The little Moses asked, "Dad, you look happy, how was work today?"

"It was fine, sonny, very fine. I found a lot of work waiting for me."

"I did not realise you would be so happy to get back to work," interjected Joyce.

"Okay – listen everyone; on Friday evening we are going to have supper away, guess with who?"

"Uncle,"

"No."

"Your boss."

"No. The President!"

The stunned family could not believe they would get to meet the President. They discussed why he had been invited: a job offer, just a meal, or trouble?

"Now listen up everyone, that was part A. Here is part B – I have been appointed the Deputy CEO of Phillips."

"What!" screamed everyone.

"Now this deserves a party to celebrate."

"Yeah, another party!" shouted the children.

"Congratulations and here is a kiss for a start," said the excited Joyce.

Peter and Joyce spoke late into the night, rang a few friends and embraced for joy again and again. It was too good to be true.

Friday came by very quickly for Peter and the family. He spent the week trying to understand the scope and responsibilities of his new post. He was a very popular appointment; he received congratulatory cards and good wishes from every employee. The outgoing Deputy CEO offered to spend the following month handing over and mentoring him.

They were all dressed smartly as they pulled up at the gate. Peter and his family had long been supporters but they had never been inside the house. The President was still living in his house, five years after he had been elected. He was on record that he would move once the new State Palace was completed. This would not happen before the next election. Much work had been done and those who had seen the inside of the Palace said it was just as spectacular as the outrageous outside designs. For now, he was more than comfortable in his own house.

The President was standing on his verandah when they pulled into the car park. He came to meet them down the stairs, shook hands and took them up into the lounge. It was a big room with very expensive furniture. The room was twice the size of his lounge. Rachel joined them, embracing the youngest boy. Peter introduced everyone ending with the young Moses.

"This is Moses, he is five years old."

"When were you born?" the President asked.

"2086."

"That is the year I was elected!"

"Yes, Sir," said the excited Peter.

"Hence the name, Sir," added Joyce who did not wish to be left out.

"You are a special guest here," said the President.

"He has so many children named after him; he has decided to hold a party with them shortly. Letters have been sent and maybe yours is in the post," said Rachel.

"It was not my idea, it was hers!" said the laughing President. "May I please invite you straight to the table?"

The family soon settled to a delicious meal. The President listened to personal stories from his guests but hardly said much about himself or any member of his family. It appeared to be taboo to discuss their personal experiences. The President was such a keen listener that you would think he remembered everything he heard. They talked about political issues and he looked happiest when talking about the progress Lubandans were making. After the meal Peter was invited to what looked like a boardroom.

"Mr Sambondu, thank you very much for the work you do with the Idea Clubs. I am getting very good reports about the progress the young people are making."

"Thank you Sir. We have very committed people writing booklets and teachers are enthusiastic about the clubs."

"I am thinking of establishing a Lubanda Academy of Scholars and a Lubanda Scholars University. It will be a secondary school and a university. A special test shall be offered to all children in the last year of primary school and those who pass shall be selected to go to this school. The school shall specialise in engineering, economics, mathematics and sciences. There will be another selection exam at the end of secondary school in addition to exams taken during the course of their secondary school. The highest achievers in each school in the country shall also be offered the test that will save as admission to the new university. The idea is to nurture the most intelligent children in Lubanda. What do you think?"

"It is a brilliant idea, Sir. I know many years ago special schools were established but because of undue political influence the standards fell back and soon they became ordinary schools. If given genuine autonomy, the schools will thrive."

"Thank you Mr Sambondu. I would like to assemble a team of three people to lead on this project refining the ideas, drawing up programmes of study and planning for the university. I would like you to lead on this project and ultimately, to head the university."

"Thank you for kindly thinking of me Sir, I am delighted with the project. The only problem is that I have just taken up a new post at work."

"I know, and that is good so that you can gain more skills to transfer to this job. This project will be implemented in the second year of my presidency if I am re-elected. We have two years to prepare. When the program starts both the university and school will start. I have appointed the other two to full-time positions but I would like you to be the chairman to steer the project. I would expect you to resign and take up full responsibility after the next election."

"I certainly would be happy and honoured to be involved with this important project."

"Thank you Mr Sambondu, I am aware you have a big responsibility as a Deputy CEO but I want the best men to build this a nation. I am convinced you will understand the project and will steer it to a glorious success. You will receive a letter from my office next week."

"Thank you, Sir."

The Sambondus spent another hour discussing politics, especially their experiences in the village recently. After three hours they said their goodbyes. Driving back home, the family were very joyful. At home Peter told Joyce that he had been offered another job.

"Did you take it?"

"I had no option and I think it will be good for the country."

"You are mad, how will you do two jobs?"

"Mad, I know. How do I do two jobs? I will have to figure it out."

"No more cutting of family time, you know!"

"I'm afraid that is likely."

"Good luck."

"I will be a chairman to provide strategic guidance but will resign my current job to go and establish a new university."

"So you will be a chancellor?"

"I think a vice-chancellor."

"Why don't you go right away?"

"Loyalty and money. I am sure the government will not match my current conditions but I also need to see the company through the current leadership changes."

The man with two jobs was yet to have another. Three months after his meal with the President, his CEO was taken ill and the Board asked him to act. Doing two jobs was very hard but Peter the superman excelled in all.

PART III

Chapter Twenty-One

PRESIDENT KAMAWU had made very few trips abroad in five years. He was often asked about his non-engagement at this level and his standard explanation was that "Poor people are weak and no one listens to them or takes them serious. If you are powerful in some way you would be listened to even if what you say is not special."

However, the previous year he had been nominated the Chairman of the African Union and his address caused discomfort to his audience. Below is part of what he said:

"As world power has shifted, so has been the occupation of Africa. First Arabs with their trading skills were involved in stealing and buying black people and trading them as slaves. Then came the trans-Atlantic slave trade, which apart from physical degradation, stole the dignity of the black person. Championed by Lynch's philosophy, the black person has never recovered from indignity.

"Colonisation and divide and rule plundered resources, entrenched divisions resulting in civil wars that continue to ravage Africa today.

"Power shifted to America from Britain. America enjoyed the enslavement of black people as much as Britain. The conscience of American supremacy meant that their engagement with Africa was low profile. The champions of freedom hardly feature in any advocacy role for freedom during the colonial occupation of Africa. Black men including those in their backyard did not deserve freedom. Freedom is all in the colour of the skin.

"Towards the end of the Cold War and the beginning of the 21st century a number of things happened: Implosion of capitalist greed signified a changing of monetary number system from thousands and millions to billions and trillions. A stroke of Chinese genius and Arab ingenuity positioned themselves as influential powers. The Arabs used their oil money to buy large chunks of the western economy and skills; so did the Chinese who lent money to western governments and bought a lot of the western companies. The pursuit of cheap labour to acquire trillions of profit by western companies took manufacturing to the Chinese who benefited from their skills and export income and hence had become a very strong economic powerhouse indeed. I know you guessed it right; this led to the Chinese occupation of Africa in order to extract resources for their internal Chinese development.

"The Russians gave a gift of their AK-47 weapon to the Africans who have used it for many years to slaughter themselves. Perhaps inspired by traditions of tribal wars and lack of coherent nation states, ruled by presidents who saw themselves as the Chief of all Chiefs with no good understanding of democratic rule, it was inevitable that civil wars with Russian arms would plague the continent. Africa is littered with Russian AK47 corpses and skeletons. The other gift the Russians gave the newly independent states in Africa was ideological confusion: most of colonial Africa had western influence and pseudo western systems. Traditional sub systems were a mishmash of autocratic and in some instances tyrannical rule through chiefs and communalism. Russians spread communism, not fully grasped and often confused with communalism. Since this ideology was spread by remote propaganda rather than occupation, it did not grow deep roots. However, the ruthless practice of Stalin and Lenin were appealing to most post-colonial African leaders who evolved systems of exclusion and self-interest.

"The end product in Africa was a mishmash of political, social and economic systems that lacked vision, direction and lack of good governance. Systems with no respect for human dignity that had no value for life, systems that promoted self-indulgence and corruption, systems for destruction rather than construction, systems that have continued to hold back progress and make the African continue to languish at the bottom of the ethnic pile. Systems of doom.

"Ladies and gentlemen, this has been illustrated more clearly in our dear country of Lubanda in the past thirty years as it slid into an abyss under President Chimwanga. This is what led to the virtual collapse of the health institutions, schools and rule of law. If you have basic financial literacy you would have seen that it is all not because of lack of money but lack of knowledge, will and ideology, leadership and sound management. This is what my Party and leadership is providing to the nation.

"Ladies and gentlemen, there are things we can do for ourselves as leaders, there are things those we lead can do themselves to develop and there are things the world can do to help Africa. We need to emancipate ourselves from degradation, ridicule, disease and poverty. Clasping bowls like Oliver Twist asking for some more from others will not take this continent anywhere but throw us back again and again into slavery, colonialism and eventual annihilation. The catastrophe is that as we come to the end of this century, Africa is still very weak. The whole continent can even be overrun by a few bands of criminals with warped minds, ideologies or fortune seekers. As African leaders we should begin to see beyond ourselves, our generations to protect our continent for our people for centuries to come. I fear that the second coming of Jesus will be too late to find a single African walking on the continent of Africa.

"My government has embarked on this journey; it is hard but with the will and resolve of an African warrior, not to kill a brother or sister but to overcome survival odds, we can move this continent forward."

He said he was encouraged by the response to his address and the conversations he had with both African political and business leaders. He had forged alliances with some of those who at a point in the past were dismissive of his policies and plans. Some commentators argued that the impact he made convinced him he had acquired the power he needed which would make people listen; that made him decide to go and address the UN general Assembly this year. Whatever it is that has changed his attitude, this year we shall hear him address the UN General Assembly for the first time.

After five years of hard work, the President was going abroad for four weeks. Initially, he was going to attend the U.N. General Assembly for the first time and then proceed to Harvard University to receive an honorary degree. However, the cabinet prevailed upon him to take a long overdue well deserved holiday. He was now going to spend two weeks holiday in the Bahamas, with no official engagements; so they thought.

On the day of his departure, the whole Cabinet and the well-wishers gathered at the airport to see him off. He tried to stop this tradition but he was not succeeding because followers turned up without invitation. Behind his medical team, and the family, he turned every few steps to wave until he was finally on the plane. In his address to the nation, he asked the nation to support Delilah and the ministers. As the plane took off the escorting party stood, waved, and waved, until the plane disappeared in the distance before they dispersed.

It had been raining most of the day and eighteen hours felt like ten in the evening. It was dark and cold. Most of the prisoners were preparing to go to bed. Suddenly, there was coughing and screaming in the cell in the middle of the jail. All the prisoners in this prison were very unscrupulous; murderers or other violent people. Everyone knew the noise was coming from what was dubbed cell no 1 – Absalom's cell.

The prison warders rushed to the cell. Absalom was sick and had collapsed when the door was opened. They carried him to the gates. An ambulance was called and in the company of two armed guards, he was taken to the hospital. He was almost a forgotten man but it appeared he was not finished. He was admitted to hospital and put in a side ward. The doctors suggested that he should not be chained to allow the free flow of blood.

At midnight, one of the security prison warders guarding him walked out quietly to go to the toilet. The other was dozing heavily in the chair. Absalom came out of bed slowly, removed the intravenous drip and grabbed the gun from the prisoner warder. A short struggle and a bang woke everyone up in the hospital. The prisoner warder lay in a pool of blood as Absalom dashed out of the room and leaped out through the window. By the time the other warder ran to the side ward and gave chase, Absalom had already vanished into the darkness.

The Vice President was awakened an hour later to be told that Absalom had escaped from prison. The first night without President Kamawu was turning out to be eventful. A man hunt to capture the escaped prisoner was immediately launched.

The trip to the Bahamas was comfortable; there was ample room in the hired private plane. Apart from his personal security, doctor and three accredited journalists, the plane was empty. They had not been on holiday as a family for five years. Without Delilah's insistence, he would have delayed this one as well. The Cabinet led by the Vice President realised that he was looking tired and frail. He had been working so hard for five years. The family had been on holiday every year but without him. This outing which coincided with other programmes had come at the right time.

After a long bath in the Jacuzzi and a game of chess, they slept like babies – only to be awakened at eight o'clock by a phone call from Lubanda.

"Delilah, you wanted me to come on holiday, now you are chasing me up!"

"Good morning, Sir, I am sorry to disturb you but there is a situation I can't deal with alone."

"What has happened?"

"Absalom has escaped from prison."

"I don't care how he did it but capture him quickly before he causes trouble. Let the security find out whether he acted alone or he had help. Please Delilah don't panic, we shall apprehend him."

"Yes, Sir, the public are out in full force."

"Good, keep me informed if there is a significant development. Or do you want me to cut my holiday short?"

"No, Sir."

He sat quietly for a while, stood up and went for a shower. Rachel who woke up earlier and had gone out walking with the children came in to find him deep in thought.

"What is the matter?"

"Absalom has escaped from jail."

"Is he causing trouble?"

"Making people anxious. I think he wants to cause trouble. He knew I was out of the country and he thinks he will get away with it. I have confidence in the people of Lubanda."

"Should we cut short the holiday?"
"No, we won't."

Absalom had been imprisoned for life for his murderous activities. His uncle was unable to save him and his trial had been a public spectacle. It was reported that although his uncle relied on him, he was privately scared of him. There were very few people who sympathised with him. In fact, his sentencing was viewed as a public victory. Now five years on, he had become a public enemy once more. Both the government and the people were not sure whether this was an opportunistic escape or a carefully planned one with assistance from his allies. He certainly was aware the President was going out of the country for a month, therefore, an opportune time to escape.

People seemed unconcerned how and why it happened on that specific night; they saw it as an attempt to destabilise the nation. They all vowed to capture or kill him wherever he could be found. In the morning when the news of the great escape was announced, the law enforcement teams were joined in their search by ordinary citizens.

When Absalom left the hospital, he hijacked a motorist and drove to his house. In the confusion that followed, he told his wife to be calm because he had come to take his country back. He changed into the police uniform he always kept in his wardrobe that seemed to be waiting for him for five years. He strolled out of the house and sped away. He was convinced he could organise a rebellion that would overthrow the government.

The President was calm as usual when Delilah, who sounded panicked on the other end, told him what had happened. He reassured Delilah that all would be fine. He spoke to his security team who advised him not to cut short his holiday. He told them that it was a test of the people's will and that it was a storm in a teacup. However, three days passed and the escapee was still at large. Thousands of people volunteered to join the police every day and night to look for him but he was still at large. It was soon established that he acted alone.

Absalom miscalculated both his timing and the national mood. He found it hard to contact those once his friends and confidants. He had managed to evade capture by travelling at night, living rough in barrows under roads and bridges, hiding in the forest dressed in police uniform. After unsuccessfully trying to organise support, he decided to flee the country to seek political asylum. The northern neighbour was his obvious choice of destination.

After walking for nearly a week, evading people, his luck ran out. He walked to within five miles of the northern state. Walking along a deserted forest path he came across a container of honey by the roadside. A honey hunter had been up early harvesting honey. Five miles from home he decided to rest under a shade. He suddenly heard someone walking. He raised his head only to see a policeman with a gun. He was surprised and scared. He had never seen a policeman in these forests. He thought they were policemen looking for Absalom. He decided to lie low but raised his head only to see what was happening.

The policeman stopped by the honey container. He was looking thin and exhausted. He reached out for the honeycomb and munched it hungrily. He reached for another piece. Unfortunately, he did not see the bees on the back and when he put the piece of honeycomb into his mouth, he was stung. He screamed running away from the honey. In this frantic motion of pain, the hat toppled from his head and the hunter recognised him.

The honey hunter snatched the gun left by the calabash and hid it behind a tree while Absalom writhed in pain. He then asked the screaming man what had happened.

"Officer, can I help you?"

"Water, give me some water, you idiot."

He remembered this man was very stubborn and dangerous. He heard on the radio that he had shot a prison warder and a villager who tried to arrest him.

He let him wriggle a little more in pain. He was scratching his tongue wildly.

"You must calm down, Sir."

"You fool, get me some water, will you?"

The villager produced a half bottle of water and put it down at his feet. Absalom rushed forward to get it. As he bent to get the water, the hunter hit him on the back of the head with the handle of his axe, momentarily blacking him out. He reached for fiber ropes and tied his hands.

"Stand up and turn round, Sir!"

"No I won't."

"Yes, you will."

"No I won't."

He fired the gun between his legs and Absalom jumped; he realised he was no longer in control. He trotted in front of the man and at one point he tried to run and another bullet came whizzing a foot away past his head.

"You should release me if you know what is good for you. Do you know who I am?"

"You are a runaway prisoner, a murderer."

"Good. You know that I have a lot of money; release me and I shall give you more money than you will ever dream to have."

"Come on, walk faster. Do you want me to hang you in that big tree?"

"Look, if you come with me across the border, you will be my bodyguard and I shall look after you well."

"It is not your money; you stole it from the people."

"Look, I have houses – I will give you one."

"We shall soon reach my village so do not play games or I shall kill you."

"Do you want to marry my wife? I can give you my sister or daughter, you know."

"You heartless monster, shut up will you!"

There was no more room to make more offers. This poor man was not excited by money or wives. As soon as they reached the village, he called for the security forces to pick him up.

"You will pay for this when I become president," he shouted as they dragged him to the helicopter. "I shall burn your entire village."

It was not long before he was back in his cell, perhaps never to escape again. The cell was reinforced with a few comforts removed and kept under guard. On the way he tried to bribe the captain with everything he could offer but to no avail.

The few days that followed put a cloud on the President's holiday. They were able to do a number of activities but Moses was still tense. On the seventh day there was a call form Delilah.

"Mr. President, enjoy your holiday, the fugitive is back in prison," reported Delilah.

"Thank you very much and well done, Delilah." It was not her fault, Absalom thought, there was a power vacuum. That is the problem of being in prison – you do not know what is going on outside.

"The people caught him, Sir."

"Please, thank all the Lubandans and especially those who risked their lives for the nation; the nation will show them kindness," the President said as he hang up the telephone.

Meanwhile the country had once again something to cheer about, another round of victory: it was after all not a big threat but a criminal doing what criminals do, longing for freedom that they do not deserve.

In that same night President Kamawu had an asthma attack. The weather had changed in the past days and this affected him. The family doctor was hard at work for the next few days. There were signs of full recovery but he was prevented from doing any strenuous tasks.

President Moses Kamawu was sitting under an umbrella on the beach. The sun was shining brightly, nice and warm. He was wearing a pair of shorts which the paparazzi would have feasted on if he were a western leader. The family were enjoying the weather and the water. He was pleased how tall Abel had grown in the past few years. He felt like a man who had been away because he missed out on many family activities including the growing up of children. He loved the idea that Abel was now a lad, serious with schoolwork, intelligent but marginally interested in politics. It is too early to expect a nine-year-old to know much about politics.

He called him and they went out for a walk along the beach, talking, holding hands like lovers and chasing each other. Rachel was happy to see them together because they rarely spent time together although she was concerned about the running around but she was too far to administer any discipline. Abel liked the childhood stories his grandfather told him. He could not imagine the daily long journeys to school. He had never walked to school, neither did his dad and they both appreciated with gratitude that they were beneficiaries of his sacrifice.

"Dad, will you run again for president at the next elections?"

"Yes. You don't want me to stand?"

"I think the people love you so much that you have to stand. I only think they have more of you than we do. You go early and come back home late in the evening."

"To make change happen takes a lot of time, Abel. Do you think people are happier?"

"Yes, they would do anything for you. I don't know what they would do if you resigned."

"I am sure they will find another leader."

"He won't be like you, I think."

"Listen sonny, they will start looking for us, let us go back. I will try to create a bit more time for you, will you be happier?"

"Yes, dad. But I will still love you even if you are too busy to spend time with us. You are helping Lubandans."

"Thank you sonny, I love you too. You are becoming wiser by the day. You need it because you will soon be a man and start making decisions."

"Dad, what is the hardest part of your job?"

"People. Dealing with people. Letting them see what you see."

"But you are good at talking to them."

"I try; otherwise you cannot do this job."

"Dad, I also want to be president."

"That will be good. There have been families with presidents in each century but what dad wants of you is that you become successful whether that includes being a president or not."

"I will be successful like you."

"There are people who have been more successful than me."

"No, you have been more successful than most people."

"So you should be successful in whatever you choose to do."

"I will be president Dad. How can I become successful?"

"Successful people learn skills and sell these skills. You go to school, take a profession and sell the skills of your profession. You can also use your skills to create goods and services to sell. That is the secret of success. Successful people and countries use this formula. That is why I am interested in your grades at school."

"What skills do I need to learn to be president?"

"Love people and your country!"

"I will try."

"Look at that big ship! It must be several miles from the shore."

"Dad, look the girls are coming! They cannot leave us alone."

"Remember you are supposed to love people!"

"Of course I love my sisters, Dad."

"Hullo girls!"

"You left us."

"I am sorry I was talking to your brother."

"We know you love him more than us."

"No, I love all of you but sometimes as men we have to talk about things that are only relevant to men."

"Now, let us all sit down and tell me the nicest things you have enjoyed in the Bahamas."

Just then his mobile phone rang. He withdrew a short distance away and spoke to someone important. After the telephone conversation he told them that he had been invited to attend the gathering of the Caribbean leaders, eliciting much protestation.

"We are on holiday!" the girls shouted simultaneously. "You should not be working. You promised to spend the day with us and do things," they protested.

"The meeting is the day after tomorrow so we shall do a lot tomorrow. Come on, let us go." They ran past Rachel who was resting on one of the reclining chairs.

"You have been with your children, tomorrow is my turn!"

"No, he has promised us. We are doing lots tomorrow," replied the girls in unison.

"He is also my father; I need to be with him."

"He is your husband, not your father, he is my father," screamed the last born holding the father's leg.

"Okay, enough of the fights! Time for supper and scrabble."

Rachel was not pleased either with the official engagement because it obtruded into their holiday time. They were getting used to having him around all the time. When they reached America they would not have much time with him. If he has an engagement he spends time preparing, so this will not be different. However, since he was so excited about the invitation, they reluctantly accepted the obvious.

He came back from the meeting with the Caribbean leaders five hours later than planned. The family had seen part of his address on the television.

"Ladies and gentlemen, brothers and sisters, thank you for inviting me to your important meeting. Thank you for the warm welcome. I'm truly among kith and kin.

"For a long time we have been divided. The architects of divide and rule instituted a tool into our psychological makeup that has and will continue to weaken the black people. During slavery our people were made to hate each other, betray one another out of necessity for survival. Today we are told we are not beautiful or intelligent and fall short of humanity. We believe it, our children believe it and our grandchildren and great grandchildren will believe it. The result is that we do not like ourselves, we do not like those who look like us, and we hate ourselves. Our pride and confidence continues to be stolen. Some black people become embarrassed with the presence of other black people. The legacies of slavery and colonialism have continued to undermine the unity of the black people.

"The result of this conundrum is that we cannot trade with one another, we ignore our own strength in preference for other so-called races and we look down upon our people; psychologically they seek to disassociate with black people, only to be reminded down the road that we are after all black.

"I interrupted my holiday because I am convinced we need to change this situation. Our friends, the so-called white people, have no need to unite because they are not persecuted on the grounds of their colour. Fortune follows wherever they go. We need and we must because we are persecuted because of our skin colour. If we don't, imagine your children or grandchildren or great grandchildren being enslaved. We are not doing enough, using our freedom to insulate the generations to come. I believe the greatest insulation is to give our people knowledge and economic power to help them fight the evils that so often stalk the colour of their skin. With economic and intellectual power we can defend ourselves like the Jews. Let us learn from them, persecuted and yet they thrive. The ideas that brought about slavery and colonialism have not gone away. The economic, political and cultural factors that influenced the slave trade are still here. The doctrine of Willie Lynch of using fear, distrust and envy is still being religiously taught in schools, practised in offices and spread in the media. They are very much alive waiting for an opportune fertile time. Let us remind ourselves about the Willie

Lynch indoctrination method of using fear, distrust and envy to control black slaves:

"'You must pitch the old black male vs the young black and the young black male against the old black male. You must use the dark skin slaves vs the light skin slaves and the light skin slaves against the dark skin slaves. You must use the female vs the male, and the male vs the female. You must also have your white servants distrust all blacks, but it is necessary that your slaves trust and depend on you. They must love, respect and trust only us'."

"So you ask me why we don't trade with each other, it is the Willie Lynch doctrine; why black people are quick to criticize one another or why blacks are not usually employed, it is the Willie lynch doctrine! You ask why black people do not feel good about themselves and feel inadequate? It is the Willie Lynch doctrine.

"The black people are being psychologically lynched daily in the media, in the streets, shops and offices and wherever else their image appears. Brothers and sisters, we the black leaders across the world have power to change this. I would like us to work together for the good of our people. There are millions of black people on this earth yet our fate appears to be predetermined. Many live in poverty even when they are surrounded by white affluence.

"Black people fight individual battles for success, so do all human beings. We fight national battles for progress, so do all nations. But a black man is locked in a lifelong, almost eternal battle for survival, respect and even to exist because of the colour of the skin. For hundreds of years, history is littered with sacrifices and victims of this struggle. In the past five hundred years, this battle has been fought daily. You may excuse my pessimism ladies and gentlemen but I see the situation not changing in the next five hundred years.

"There are forces marshalled against a black person not by their own choice or because they have provoked anyone but simply because of the colour of the skin. Over the centuries, they have made the black man even hate himself. The mind is so corrupted that they are daily brainwashed that they do not deserve privilege and benefit. They have been made to believe that who they are and what they look like is not acceptable; what they do is never good enough.

"I have therefore come to offer you a hand of co-operation and partnership. My country would like to work with your region and all black communities not only to develop our countries economically, but also using our strength in numbers; to bring dignity to the so-called black person. I am here to offer economic, social and political co-operation. I know the areas for each of our countries that we can work together to enhance the lives of our people, including those generations yet to be born."

He went on to talk about the common ancestry that black people share in spite of living in different countries. He told them that he was aware some black people did not want to be associated with Africa because of the many years of negative and degrading images and slights Africans suffered in western media. He said he understood this psychological self-insulation but it would not be long before they are reminded by someone else that they too were black and condemned to the same fate. Then he talked more about working together to restore dignity for all black people. How they all should stand together to support blacks who were abused or attacked as a result of their skin colour through the effective use of diplomatic channels to protest in countries where abuse occurred and develop programmes that inculcated resilience in the young. Finally, he talked about working together to defeat poverty. What impressed his audience was that he had done his homework well; he had identified key strengths and weaknesses of these countries and explained the trading opportunities that would complement and enhance economies of all their peoples. No wonder they all wanted to talk to him.

The personal discussions were private but they loved him even more in the panel discussions that were not televised in which he shared his experiences with them. The insights were great. This meeting was more exciting and intimate than the African Union meeting he attended. It was not surprising that when he said goodbye they all lined up for a group photo and more handshakes that took several more minutes.

Rachel was surprised that he gave a speech because he did not mention it when he was preparing for the visit. He was happy, relaxed and very excited when he walked into his hotel room.

"I'm sorry everyone, I was told it would take me an hour to make a few remarks but as you can see, when you are among your own, you don't see the time pass."

"That was a good speech darling, well done. When did you prepare for it, because you told me you were only going to greet them?"

"A president should always be ready for eventualities!" he said as he walked away smiling broadly like a man on a first date.

"Great work Dad, I enjoyed seeing you on the television," said Abel

"We all enjoyed the visit and so did the gathered leaders," said the bodyguard who was still standing with the President's briefcase.

"So what have you been doing since the speech?" asked Rachel.

"He was having meetings with individual leaders, Mum. They all wanted to talk to him and he wanted to talk to them. He spent hours shaking hands and talking. He had time for each one and I don't know what is in this briefcase, he did a lot of writing as well."

He promised the family that he would make the remaining five days of the holiday memorable and the last five days of the two weeks were indeed fantastic. Rachel who organised the itinerary reserved the best for the last. The boat ride, especially the banana boat, was scary for the girls but they enjoyed their special short ride. The Segway and the horse ride were exciting. Abel was particularly amused to see his dad with a cowboy hat and mum screaming with fear as her horse went wild jumping. The next day they agreed that the girls and Rachel would go for a dolphin swim while Abel and his dad went for fly water sports. Moses and Abel went with their team of security and the doctor. They were all sponsored by the President to join in the fun. When the parties met for lunch, the boys were exhausted. When Rachel inquired what they were doing, they were all breathless. They told her how her husband had won every single race and how dangerously he was racing deep into the ocean. The naughty guard who was left on the beach had made a video that thrilled the girls.

Exhausted as he was, he slumped on the carpet with a newspaper, only to be disturbed by the children.

"Dad, were you naughty when you were young?" one of the girls asked.

"I was a very good boy!" he answered.

"Your grandmum told me you always asked her tough questions," commented Rachel, as she offered him a cup of coffee.

"I don't think asking questions is being naughty!" he protested.

"Dad, tell us a story your grandma told you," requested the youngest child.

"Yes!" they all shouted. "You don't tell us stories."

"Listen, you said grandma, not granddad, you know why?"

"No. Why?" they asked.

"Because men are not good at telling stories! That's why I don't tell you stories."

"Please tell us one that you remember," not giving up to his defence.

"Okay, I will tell you one, only one."

"Yes!" They quickly settled, ready to listen.

"Once upon a time, there had been an unprecedented rainfall, never seen before in two hundred years. The result was widespread flooding that washed away villages, crops and livestock. In one village people saw the waters rising after the river burst its banks. Mothers, fathers, uncles and aunts grabbed their children and made for the only crossing to the higher ground.

"There was a seven-year-old orphan who had no one to grab her hand or to tell her what to do. She instinctively ran with the crowd not understanding much of the turmoil around her. When they reached the crossing point they were almost too late. The stone bridge was under water and most people could not remember where the stones were, and the river was rising fast. When the little girl looked around she saw others carried on their parents' and relatives' shoulders; others were already jumping for joy a hundred metres away on the other side. She knew she had very little chance of surviving. She could not swim and even if she did, she would not be strong enough to overcome the strong current or she will be tired before she reached the dry land.

"A few metres in front of her was a family, a mother who tightly held her ten-year-old son's hand and she seemed to remember where the stone bridge was. The orphan decided to stick with this family, for it was her only chance to try and escape. The mother tightly held the son but the orphan tightly held the reeds by the side.

"She told her son as they waded into the rising waters, 'The stone is on the left, step on it carefully.'

"The orphan made a quick mental note of the stone, quickly calculating the distance between her and the other child and the mother while hanging onto the reeds as the current swept her off her feet.

"'There is a big stone on the right but it feels loose, step on it lightly!' the mother shouted.

"'Yes, Mum. Please hold my hand tightly because I am scared,' the lucky boy moaned.

"The orphan quickly noted the direction and the position of the loose stone. She took in a deep breath and went forward.

"'The current here is very strong, hold my hand! If we manage to go past those reeds we have a good chance of crossing,' the mother cautioned and assured the boy.

"The orphan did not have time to look at the distance; she realised there was danger ahead and if she made it past the point the boy's mother was concerned about, she too would have a chance.

"'Mum, hold me please!' the boy screamed, 'I do not know where to step.'

"'There is a firm stone slightly to the left, step on it and push yourself forward.'

"The orphan reached the spot. 'Surely, this was the most dangerous part of the escape,' she whispered to herself.

"She tried to hold on to the nearby reeds but they too had been uprooted by the power of the water. She had nobody to shout to. She grabbed the tip of another batch of reeds and these appeared to be holding. She then felt for the stone she had heard mentioned, stepped on it and pushed herself forward. She was past the danger point as she heard screams and cries behind her. She kept listening to the directions the mother gave her son.

"'Move quickly, there is an object moving fast fifty metres away on the right, it might be a snake, crocodile or hippo!' the mother shouted.

"The orphan knew there was more danger; she moved quickly behind the mother and son. They jumped onto the fallen tree and leaped to safety. The orphan too jumped onto the log in time to escape the racing crocodile and she too leaped to safety."

The children including Rachel all applauded.

"She was clever," said one of the girls.

"She was not only clever but a good listener as well," interjected Rachel.

"The orphan learnt from those who knew and repeated what they did until she too crossed the river. That is one of the secrets of success in life," Moses concluded as he stood up to go for a shower.

The last day was reserved for the zoos and the aquariums. The family enjoyed seeing the marines and the animals. It was a good biology lesson that the children loved. They painted, drew pictures and researched the names of the animals and fish they saw.

Rachel enjoyed the daily evening walks on the beach. This was private time with the security a distance away. It was the most romantic time she has ever spent with Moses. They walked, played and joked. Moses enjoyed the walks too. Sneaking away from the public and the children meant they could talk freely. On one of these walks Rachel remembered her nervous breakdown, apologised for how she behaved once again and soothed her man with kisses. The lecture that followed finally brought a closure to the issue. Perfect time for healing bruised souls.

The President was much relaxed as they sat on their plane on the way to New York. He joked with the staff and requested them not to sell any embarrassing photographs. The workers at the hotel almost forgot their guest was going to be with them for a limited time. They had grown to love the man. His charm had mesmerised them. They were mostly touched when they learnt that he had sent a sympathy card to one of the workers who looked after his children but had lost her sister to cancer. The hotel manager found his conversations inspiring. But this is only half the story. The family had a full holiday enjoying themselves. For Moses, the two weeks were not a complete holiday break. Moses woke up at four in the morning every day. He was working on his programme for the next two weeks and planning for the second term in office.

President Kamawu rose from his chair as he was being introduced to the General Assembly to a standing ovation. The time had come to put Lubanda on the map. For five years he had been laying foundations for recovery. There was no doubt that the country had made the crucial baby steps. The Chinese philosopher Confucius said years ago, "A journey of a thousand steps begins with one step." Lubanda had taken so many steps that it was now being spoken of with respect and as a reference point for development in Africa.

He graciously acknowledged the welcome. He apologised for taking such a long time to address the UN in person and explained that he couldn't come earlier by quoting a traditional saying: "I was removing what was on the floor to enable me to move the things on the bed."He outlined the achievements his country had made, thanked those who were supporting progress. This was the sweetest bit. He pledged his support to the UN and made observations on areas that he thought required improving to benefit the developing countries such as

Lubanda. A lot of what he said was memorable but it was his remarks about racism that left his audience talking beyond the speech.

"Finally, ladies and gentlemen, a developing country in Africa, like those across the globe, has unique challenges. The shadow of the legacies of slavery and colonialism continue to hold us down. Africa remained behind during the ages of industrialisation and other advances. Distance kept us away from the centres of modernisation that European countries were benefiting from. The Europeans developed means of travel that helped them import early technologies from elsewhere enriched by their own innovations and shared among the nations. For centuries, the doctrines of slavery kept and continue to keep the black people from mastering systems of wealth and power. He who has power controls everything, including the way people think and act. The difference between Lubandans and their counterparts in developed countries is not that they are less intelligent and a sub species but simply a question of culture. But this is not what I want to talk to you about today."

"Following the killing of two Lubandan students in Europe recently because they were black, and the strong rise of hate and discrimination based on colour; allow me to talk to you about one danger that we in Lubanda fear will not only undermine our development but may lead to catastrophic consequences for mankind, the religion of RACISM."

"Ladies and gentlemen, racism is a religion, it has its own belief systems, and it has its own priests and monks. There are no buildings of worship because it is so common. There are systems in place to spread evil. It is preached and practised in homes, in offices, in schools, in shops, the media and everywhere. The myths are believed as truths. The result, ladies and gentlemen, is that it is very hard for a Lubandan to be treated equally and accorded due respect. There are things we are doing ourselves to emancipate ourselves from the degradation of this religion but there are things the UN can do to help all the so-called black people. We do not want sympathy, we demand respect. We know that there are forms of racism which still make money for some people just like slavery did many years ago."

"As you may know in South Africa this religion was validated and given a spiritual name, *apartheid*. We know the consequences; thanks to the Great Mandela, more bloodshed was averted. As we come to the end of this century, the religion is gathering momentum. The ridicule in the media, comments from prominent politicians and apartheid in employment and even schools is sending us down to the dark ages of slavery. What is more worrying is that the religion of racism has developed a strong thread of scientific validation through racial research. The result is going to be worse than Hitler's gas chambers."

"This religion has become a phenomenon in Europe and America yet again. We are already feeling its effects far afield in Africa. My government will not come to anyone to beg for mercy but we want our goods and services to be received without prejudice; we want our people to be able to travel freely. We invite the non-believers in the religion of racism to stand with us to fight this evil again."

"There were more right wing governments represented in the UN than at any other time in the 21st Century. Some thought the President's comments on slavery were opening up old wounds about slavery; a sin committed by their forefathers should not be burdened on those so distant from it. Yet they could not deny there was a rise in the enslavement of blacks as cheap labour in Europe. The few black people who have remained are doing the worst jobs. As the last decade of the 21st century came to a close, there was sufficient evidence that commercial activities were being influenced by racism. Travel for black businessmen and women were becoming difficult and there was open preaching of fascism in the name of free speech."

The debate as to whether racism was a religion had opened up a new frontier of philosophical debate. Is religion only classified as a religion because of a belief in a deity? Can a belief in a construct be classified as a religion? Is the absence of places of worship a disqualification basis? What is true is that there is a distinct belief system called racism which regulates people's behaviour and thinking.

After the speech to the United Nations General Assembly, President Kamawu had become well known. This once unknown businessman in Lubanda, once unknown President from a small country in Africa, had burst onto the international scene with great force. What captivated the people was not so much that he said new things, although he did say things that have never been heard in a speech to the General Assembly, but the way he said them; with convincing eloquence, originality and clarity.

The CNN news channel was the first to line up an interview with this star from Africa. There were several adverts for this interview. This was going to be his first engagement in the US as a President other than the UN.

Delilah was having breakfast with her son when the telephone rang.

"Hullo, Stephen."
"Good morning, it is me, Stephen."
"I know, how are you, is everything okay with you?"
"Yes, I'm fine, thanks."
"How is the boy?"

"He is fine – he is sitting right here. Do you want to talk to him?"

"Not just now, but please hug him for me. I shall call to talk to him later but I have a question to ask you."

"Come on, go ahead."

"Have you heard the President is going to be interviewed on CNN today?"

"Yes, I'm aware of it. He didn't tell me but of course we know."

"Good. Do you think he knows I am the father of Moses?"

"I don't know, to be honest. He has never asked me about it. He considers such matters to be too private to discuss. He is a very principled man, you know. Why do you ask?

"I have been assigned to interview him."

"Just ask sensible questions, you will be fine."

"I am nervous that if he knows our relationship, he may not be happy with me. The pregnancy caused him plenty of grief."

"He will make you feel at ease, don't worry. He knows a lot about the media mentality. I am looking forward to watching it live. Good luck."

"Thank you, sweetie."

Of course everyone knew that Delilah had a boyfriend who lived in the United States and worked for the CNN. They first met when they were both covering elections in South Africa ten years ago. They fell in love but did not quite strike a matrimonial commitment. They used to see each other more often when Stephen was in Southern Africa but since his promotion and recall, they never saw each other until Delilah led a delegation to America as Vice President. Delilah had gone on tour of a number of selected countries to study political systems that were working well and delivering stability to help inform the process of amending the Lubandan constitution. Old feelings ignited and they met at a hotel, resulting in the birth of Delilah's much talked about son. Few people knew what Delilah's boyfriend looked like.

"Good morning, Mr. President."

"Good morning, Stephen. I used to like your articles when you were in South Africa."

"Thank you, Sir. I enjoyed my time in the region. The people are nice, very warm, trusting and welcoming."

"Yes, they are but it is our strength and weakness. We can leave that for another day."

"Do you have family in Africa?"

"Most of my family is in the US, Sir."

"The story of Lubanda in the past five years can be described as a miracle, much of it is down to you. What do you think are the reasons for such phenomenal success?"

"Firstly, whatever has been achieved is not down to me alone, it is down to the people of Lubanda. Secondly, we are not yet successful; we shall be successful when we join the elite club of developed countries. That is a long way off and possibly not in my lifetime. But I believe one day it shall happen if we lay down solid foundations. The answer to your question is simple; the resilience, hard work and dedication of the Lubandans has been the key to the steps of progress we have made. The most important thing we did was to look at successful countries, found a formula that works and we adapted it intelligently to suit our context and started implementing it. We decided to learn from those who had done what we wanted to do and learn from them. Our deliberate policy is that we learn from the winners, not the losers. We learn from their mistakes and adapt what they do well. Being bedfellows with failed states ultimately will make you a failed state."

"At one time Lubanda like the majority of Africa was riddled with tribal conflicts. How have you managed to unify your country?"

"Belonging to a tribe is important and we should all be proud of it. The tribe gives people an identity and as you know, human beings are social animals so a group identity is important. They often find something that binds them together. Tribal diversity enriches the country but it has been part of our downfall as well. You and your listeners should be aware of a couple of things. In pre-colonial Africa, the state was defined by the portion of land occupied by the tribe ruled by Chiefs, in some cases with a paramount chief who the queens and kings of England did not want to recognise as kings lest they share the honour. They defended their tribal territories against any aggression. Tribal wars became intense during the slavery period as tribes attacked each other to capture slaves. The only government they knew was the chief's. So these tribal units were stronger units for identity, security and survival. Colonialism exploited this with that evil philosophy of divide and rule. For hundreds of years, a culture of mistrust and suspicion evolved perpetuated by the divide-and-rule of the colonialists. That is why you find Africans and those of the African diaspora are more comfortable trusting anyone other than those of their skin; a form of self-rejection. You need deliberate policies to break the legacies of division. These are some of the reasons that led to the fractured communities after political independence in Africa."

"In Lubanda we have put deliberate emphasis on making a proper transition from the tribal mind-set and colonial principles of organising the nation state to tested and workable principles of building a nation state. In a nation state everyone is included so we have representation from every major tribal grouping; we have strengthened political and government systems so the president, ministers and other leaders are accountable to the people. I believe that at the time of securing political independence, African countries did not make the right transitions to principles of nation states."

"Mr President, I am sure you were expecting me to ask you this – do you really believe racism is a religion?"

"Yes, I do. What is a religion? It is a set of beliefs either in a deity or idea. It has believers who propagate it. Often these people believe that their religious values are the best and even worth dying for or killing for. They build organisations and processes to propagate their beliefs. Racism has a set of beliefs, that certain skin pigmentation is superior. Why we have these skin differences, we shall wait to ask God when the time is fulfilled. Although the differences you have between peoples are predominantly cultural, more of nurture than nature, I am sure there are racists who believe they have their own God. It is the most deadly religion on earth. As an African's point of view, it is responsible for stealing the dignity of the African, stealing millions of Africans and selling them abroad into slavery and mentally destroying millions of African people in the Americas, Europe and all over the world. It is also responsible for excluding millions of black people from systems that create wealth, perpetuating poverty and indignity. Yes, I do believe it is a religion."

"Sir, you have already achieved a lot in your first term; what do you intend to do in your second term?"

"First, fight for the elections; I do not take people for granted. Obviously you do not expect me to outline my manifesto for an election two years away. I believe we need to build and consolidate what we have already achieved. If I am elected for a second term, we shall pursue programmes that put Lubanda firmly on the road to development. Building institutions that protect good governance, creating wealth for all and inspiring innovation and the pursuit of scientific knowledge."

"Sir, why did you change the term of office from five to seven years?"

"To stop people asking for more time! Life presidents are disastrous to any nation. Fourteen years with a flexibility to call for an election in the last two years of the term if you feel tired will remove the excuse of asking for more time to finish the unfinished business that will never be finished. If you cannot make change in ten to fifteen years then you will never do it in fifty years."

"Why do you think there are more failed states in Africa than any other part of the world?"

"Leadership."

"Can you elaborate, Sir?"

"There is not much to elaborate. For any society to prosper it needs to be well led. Bad governance may be a cliché in the African context but it is true. There are countries in Africa who are failed states because their economies have spectacularly collapsed. Their currencies have become so valueless they are only circulated as historical sentimental ornaments. Some countries have failed because there are no political systems and institutions. Tribal militias and war lords have fragmented the country and divided it among interest groups. Some have failed because all political, social and economic structures have collapsed. All causes point to leadership. Incompetent leadership. It pains me to see that a few years from the 22nd century; Africans are still stuck at Maslow's first level on his triangle of needs.

"That brings us to the question of democracy. Democracy in Africa is a failed experiment. It is not working perfectly. Why don't Africans understand democracy? Why do you think democracy has not taken hold and has been floundering since the wind of political change started blowing across Africa in the early 1960s? It has been over 100 years, is that not enough time?

"Stephen, where do you think democracy has worked perfectly?"

"Europe and America."

"I disagree. I don't think there is a nation with the perfect democratic practice. We need to be careful with the notion that there is one perfect package of democracy that each country can acquire and roll out to a nation. The foundations of American, Canadian and Australian democracies lie in the histories of Britain and some of the nations in Europe. The history of democracy in Europe was in no way a smooth transition. It evolved out of feudalism and totalitarian regimes over time. After several experimentations particularly after the industrial and French revolutions, Europe evolved political systems that worked better. Emigrants to the USA, Canada and Australia migrated these systems, skills, cultures that helped them to evolve their own modified systems to build these countries. Africa, partly because of the distance and mainly because of oppression and resentment, was unable to benefit from the exchange of the positive results of these political systems including technologies and trade."

"That's interesting Mr President. What hope do you think is left for Africa?"

"Not colonialism. Democracy and leadership. Democratic principles are still the best ideas for organising a nation state and creating a fairer society. Democratic principles by themselves are useless until they are practiced in the right context. In Africa that environment has been shaky."

"Sir, as you know a democratic government has been defined as the government of the people by the people for the people. This surely is simple enough for all to understand."

"I'm not sure I agree with you that it is that simple. The definition describes the ideal democratic practice – that is why I believe it is the best idea for organising a society. Every society, including those in a traditional African context, had elements of democracy. However, in practice, it is hard. All across the world you will find variations: a government of the people by the people for the few; a government of the few by the people for the few; a government of the few by the few for the few and a government of the rich by the media for the privileged. In Africa there have been too many governments of the president, by the president for the president. In America, there are several governments: the state governments, the federal government which may comprise two governments; one run by the president and the party that controls the Senate and the House of Representatives. You end up with shutdowns of governments. Establishing true democracy is a work in progress and harder than most people think."

"What would a government of the people by the people and for the people look like them?"

"A government chosen as a result of a fair majority vote, ruling in the interest of and for the benefit of the majority of the people. Quite often the majority are manipulated to vote against their interests. In some countries you find chaocracy, democratic principles without pillar institutions of democracy. I would call what you have in America a multiplecracy. That is why in Lubanda, we are working hard to build our own democratic society."

"From the explanations you have given, Sir, it appears it is hard to achieve a true democratic society. What hope is left for Africa?"

"You may not achieve the ideal democracy but the closer you get to it the more stable the society will become. For example, the American democracy which at times is dysfunctional still works better than a tyrannical system. That is what you are seeing in the countries you listed at the start of this discussion. We should all aspire for the ideal."

"Can you give us some of the pillars?"

"The core of democratic principles is compromise and rules. People agree on how to elect their representatives, to run their government and how to relate to each other. Then these agreements are put into laws and rules. The society then agrees to obey these rules and laws. This is where the rule of law comes in. To develop the rule of law you need institutions to implement them fairly and to the letter. Chaocracy starts and ends with loose agreements of casting a vote, often in unfair conditions. There are no other rules or where these exist, they are willfully flouted. This is why you have failed states in Africa. In a multiplecracy you have battlegrounds of ideological, egotistical and commercial interests that obstruct smooth practice of a government of the people, for the people by the people. There are two historical observations we should make here; the feudal systems and rule of the kings in Europe, as symbolized in the Tower of London, had evolved a culture of institutional obedience. This obedience helped establish satisfactory environments in which some of the aspects of democracy work reasonably well because the people are institutionalized. In Africa the colonial institutions were perceived as instruments of oppression so they did not help to evolve the rule of law but instead evolved systems of rebellion.

"We don't have to bring kings and queens to establish order and democracy, you need leaders who will nurture consensus, compromise and build systems which are respected by all. This means inclusivity and opportunities open to all citizens. We need systems that will challenge the president when in the wrong and remove him or her from power if he or she is found not to act in the interest of the nation or violates the constitution. In most countries there is more than one system of power. In the Middle East you have the religious systems and powers alongside civil governments; in the UK you have the royal system and the elected government, and in America you have state powers, federal government, Senate and House of

Representatives. Democracy functions well when these institutions operate honestly and adhere to agreements and compromises. In Africa you have tribes. The leader should facilitate negotiations and compromises to make agreements, subject these agreements to law and enforce them in the interest of the nation state. Therefore, the democracy evolving out of Africa or the Middle East may not be a replica of the western democracies but must be built around individual human consensus, rights and freedoms."

"Thank you very much for your time; we hope we shall have more opportunities to talk to you in future. I have been told you are going to receive an honorary PhD in government and public administration from the University of Harvard this week. Congratulations!"

"Thank you. I have been associated with that institution for years since I graduated. It is an honour. I hope we shall see you in Lubanda, visiting family soon."

"Thank you Mr President. It was a pleasure talking to you."

"Ladies and gentlemen, the President of the Republic of Lubanda!"

Chapter Twenty-Two

PRESIDENT KAMAWU arrived in Boston four days before the graduation ceremony at which he would receive the honorary doctorate in government and public administration. Coming back to Boston reminded him of the years he spent studying. He felt like a student once again as he went around meeting up with his former lecturers, only this time he had a bodyguard.

Life as a student in Boston and being a Harvard University student was initially not easy. He did not know anyone when he first arrived. On the day he arrived he booked into a hotel near Boston airport to wait for further instructions from his father. He was lonely and angry at the loss of his brother of whom he spent long hours thinking about and sometimes crying.

Memories for the ten years he spent in Boston came flooding to his mind. After opening a bank account, he received more money. He decided to rent a room he saw advertised in the newspapers. This cost him less than a third of what he was paying in the hotel. The added advantage was that he had people to talk to and to learn about the American life. Being a studious person, he read about the history of the city, the university and studied the maps of the areas in and around the university. The forced early arrival granted him an opportunity to prepare well for the first semester.

He was however worried about his family, especially his father. He had been blacklisted so he could not find a job. His health was not good. The first letter Moses got from home made him sad. Life without the boys made his father miserable.

He spent more time reading the Bible and was often seen sitting alone in the garden or his study crying. He lived on rent from his assets which Chimwanga did not know. Mum was much stronger. She realized her husband was depressed and she had to be strong for him and the two surviving children. She became the breadwinner in the day and at night she was a counsellor for her husband.

Moses realized that he had more than a degree fight on his hands. Like everything he was doing now, he resolved to succeed at university for Abel's sake. He had come to a realization that being bitter and miserable was rewarding Chimwanga all the more. He vowed to join politics to revenge the killing of his brother. Finally, he decided to find a source of income to help mum and dad. He knew that all the money his father had was the money he was given. His father had sent him abroad to protect him. He had sufficient money for his tuition and upkeep but he decided to take a part-time job at university to raise money to assist the family, in particular, to pay for his sister's private education.

As days went by, the pain of losing Abel eased for both his father and himself. The undergraduate tutoring part-time job paid him enough to pay his sister's fees and left him with extra income which he saved and sometimes sent home.

He had not come early to reminisce about his old days or because he was eager to receive a doctorate; he had come early for a different agenda. Upon arrival he met Peter and his team who had already arrived in Boston, flown in to join the President. They had planned to spend five days reading about the history of Harvard University from its founding to its present times. They met for half a day to discuss their individual research. For one and a half days, Moses had arranged visits to the various departments; they went to observe lectures and to talk to the heads of faculties. While Peter and his team were visiting departments, the President was holding a series of meetings with renowned and leading lecturers, present and retired scholars, as long as they were experts in their areas. Peter and his team spent the following day interviewing students. This part of the programme ended with a team meeting reflecting and discussing key findings.

The last event was the graduation ceremony. The team was invited as guests. They gathered brochures, videos and books to take back to Lubanda. Of course the highlight of the ceremony was the President receiving his degree. He gave a brilliant speech about the university and its influence on him. The university compiled all articles he had written for the university over the years in a book which they gave him as part of a present. The audience was surprised to learn that he had been contributing academic articles every year since his graduation. The graduates were given priceless advice. He finished off by inviting both lecturers and students to visit and work in Lubanda.

At the party that followed, he was introduced to many leading academicians, some of whom he recruited for his project. He left Harvard with a list of willing partners. Peter and his team had learnt quickly that he brought them to Harvard because he wanted to build a small Harvard for Lubanda. True to his philosophy of learning from the winners, this was certainly one of the vanity projects of his second term. He was gathering information to help design the university. They all went back motivated and energised to make the project a reality. The President wanted detailed plans for everything, from the physical buildings down to the number of students and lecturers. They had two years to deliver the plans.

From Boston, the President travelled back to Washington DC where he met the caucus of black leaders. This meeting discussed matters of mutual interest, and agreed on protocols of support and commitment to enhancing the lives of Africans and African Americans. Much of the discussions were held in private and whatever was discussed, the participants came out thrilled.

The last leg of this tour took him to Europe via London where he met leading figures of the financial sector, and Germany where he had lengthy meetings with the manufacturers' association. The last stop was in France; he was a longtime admirer of their aero industry. In every county he visited, he was invited to make a state visit. This particular trip was a private visit because he wanted to interact with many of the key leaders of industries. However, the private visits were all but in name because he was received with official ceremonies minus a red carpet.

The journey back home was relaxed. The President was visibly happy to be going back but happier with the visits he had made. Rachel who was busy looking after the children and touring while her husband was busy with his programmes was the most relaxed. To them it was a month's holiday. The children had many stories to tell Nkaka when they got back home. The twelve hours of flight were shortened by the stories everyone was telling about their visits. They shared selfies, diary entries and experiences.

Although the President had been away for a month, he was very much in touch with what was going on at home. This was the longest time he had been out of the country. He was surprised to emerge from the plane to be greeted by a multitude of supporters who had come to meet him. A brief speech, handshakes and waves were enough to satisfy the waiting party. He opted to drive the ten miles to the presidential palace than to be airlifted in order to meet with people along the way. He smiled broadly all the way down to his house. This was different from the serious tense man who left Lubanda exactly a month ago.

Lubanda, like its neighbouring countries, was rich in natural resources that included minerals, fertile farmland and wildlife. For centuries this was more of a curse than a blessing. The countries in the region had been exploited for hundreds of years. Foreign companies, legal and illegal, extracted minerals, poured in guns, sponsored war lords with no economic benefit to the local people. The western countries were hated and resented for this record.

President Kamawu was determined to change this situation. It was simply a question of numbers. There was no benefit accruing to the country from some of the economic activities. Local areas where mines were located were not advancing, and the equation of what was going abroad and what Lubandans were receiving did not balance. The largest beneficiaries were the mine owners who enjoyed more profit. If the country would give wealth to other people in the name of investment, what chance did a Lubandan have to develop? Profits were going to benefit other countries. He passed laws and negotiated to buy forty-nine percent of the companies. This was not nationalisation but he called it restructuring ownership. Being a businessman, he understood the need to share profits. Most companies agreed to sell shares. Ten percent of the shares purchased by the government went to the local area where the mines were based. Trusts were set up to manage this income. Twenty percent was sold to citizens and the government kept twenty-nine percent to be sold to the citizens in due course. This was able to bring in income. Corporate tax tariffs were renegotiated to address the anomalies created by the previous governments that handed resources to foreign investors on a silver platter.

With all the economic activities, the government generated a steady flow of income and the economy grew exponentially. However, there was still a problem of skilled manpower to ensure full participation of all Lubandans in the economy.

Every citizen was experiencing some form of economic growth. So when the President returned from his holidays and foreign trips, he decided to prioritise the second stage of upskilling the nation. Much had been done in five years but development would be accelerated if the skills gaps were filled. He decided to bring forward one of his initiatives, increase workforce skills. This would come to define the last two years of his first term.

When the President came back from holidays, he was full of energy and looking fresh. The energy could be felt in his speeches and body language. The following state of the nation address which was dominated by a report of his time away still had surprises. He thanked the people for their support during his absence especially for arresting Absalom. Delilah was beaming with pride as the President praised her for leading the people. Then came a declaration:

"Ladies and gentlemen, I am proud of what we have done and what we are doing. However, the pace of our development is being hampered by lack of skills. I am announcing an intensification of the skills programme. We have sufficient funding in our citizen bonds schemes. Our friends and well-wishers have donated and given grants that have boosted our development account."

The President never asked anybody for money but received grants offered by those who valued his efforts in raising the standard of living of his people. He received sufficient funds to build his university and school academy. The surplus was put into the development fund to go towards developing skills.

Much had been done with earlier initiatives to raise the skills level but the President wanted a strong skills base. By a presidential decree, both the public and private sector were asked to audit skills and to set aside one day a week as a work force skills day. Every worker from the cleaner to company directors had to do courses in their area of specialisation.

Companies large and small were expected to offer training to their employees. Emphasis was placed on using technologies to improve efficiency. There was a wide technological gap that needed to be closed. Workers were encouraged to learn new skills.

The rural areas were not forgotten, there were mobile training vans for training for rural skills. Men and women were asked to enroll for courses in the next two years. There were courses for carpenters, farmers, plumbers and many more. There were vans and trucks converted into classrooms and learning units moving from one area to another in every constituency. High standards were demanded from trainers. The government continued its policy of using local and foreign experts to deliver skills. For specialised courses not offered in the country people were sent abroad. Many doctors and scientists were sent on these for cutting age technologies. Schoolchildren were not spared either. Every child was enrolled on a financial literacy course specifically designed for their age. Different courses were designed for pre-schools and those higher up in the education system.

The most interesting batch of people were the politicians. The days of simply opening your mouth and cajoling your way to parliament were gone. Parliament was asked to design courses for serving MPs and aspiring MPs. Courses on good governance and nation state democracy. It was agreed by consensus that to stand in the next election you had to produce a certificate. Party leaders were obliged to undergo their own tailored course.

For once, everyone was learning. On the move, in the homes, in schools and colleges there was learning; at least everyone learnt one skill.

As the two years came to a close, it was clear that Lubanda and Lubandans were ready to take off on the way to true development. The levels of optimism, hope and ambition were unprecedented in Africa. People were calmer, crime levels drastically reduced and personal respect, respect for property and systems, had evolved a culture of patriotism, responsibility and true nation state unity. The closing event of the seven years of President Kamawu was the opening of the new state palace.

It was a typical tropical day, bright, clear blue sky and leafy tropical canopies providing cooling cover for the tired walkers. Thousands trouped to the grounds of the new palace. This was a seven-year project that cost a fortune.

The event was like opening parliament. A marque had been pitched on the grounds to shield the invited guests from the sun. The soldiers marched past the buildings in their new colourful ceremonial uniforms. All the forces matched past in redesigned uniforms in Lubandan colours. Since the opening of a clothes manufacturing company, all military clothing was manufactured locally, be it under very strict supervision. They all looked immaculate. So this was not only opening a house but unveiling other things as well.

The builders who took part marched past in their overalls and helmets with picks and mattocks. They too received loud applause. As all those involved went past, behind came a scruffy looking fellow, walking shyly in a group of five. The announcer introduced him as the architect of the building. He possibly drew the biggest applause. The first Lubandan to design a building of its quality was himself unveiling the talent the country had.

The building itself was in a class of its own. The first real attraction to the city. Nicknamed 'Vanity,' it was magnificent in every sense. A combination of modern and traditional architecture with the seven wonders of the country was evident in the design. You would not recognise the old part. The President did not want to knock the old building down but to build round it. It had been a challenge to the architects, which they seemed to have overcome with great success.

The wings named after every region were nicely blended with the surrounding trees, woods that had been preserved since colonial days. At exactly 1:30, the keys were handed to the President who opened the front door. They knew he was not moving house until after the elections but he *was* moving office. The guests were given a tour; no cameras were allowed beyond the first wing. The offices were outrageously big with furniture made from local wood, again designed and built by the local company. The entrance lobby was like a museum, complete with artefacts from all regions and pictures of the country's flora and fauna.

The passage leading to the President's new office was a hall of fame with portraits of former presidents, including Chimwanga. This opened into the reception room which used to be the old president's office. The current office was specially designed to fit Moses' tastes. There were stories that the building had three floors: floor one was underground, floor two was the ground floor and the floor above that was the third. However, from the outside, there were only two floors, the ground floor and the first floor. The first floor housed the presidential offices and the ground floor was the living quarters with guest wings for VIPs. So who would occupy the underground floor? Where was the entrance to the underground?

The gardens in the background were all natural flowers from Lubanda. The landscaping was done with precision, giving a calming atmosphere. One could tell Rachel had a hand in the colour scheme. The guardroom was too comfortable for the guards; hopefully they would not to be sleeping instead of watching!

People were not bothered about the details, they were happy to see such a building in their own country, fully paid for. They enjoyed the celebrations and went home satisfied. It was indeed a symbol of power and beauty with a Lubandan character.

Chapter Twenty-Three

THE LAST THREE MONTHS to Moses' second election were busy and exciting. They were the first elections under the new constitution. They were elections for the new House of Indunas, MPs and the President. The systems were working better than they had ever been in Lubanda's history. Three years after the election of President Kamawu, the second most important house in the land was elected. The two houses, Parliament and the House of Indunas, were working very well. Laws had to be passed by both houses. Under Kamawu, the powers of the president were clearly defined. He was not fixing prices for staple food or meddling in the affairs of established bodies. All bodies were functioning as they were meant to. Apart from necessary organisational and state secrets, the government was transparent and accountable.

Many changes had been made to the democratic institutions and practice. The law was strengthened to weed out political violence. Any politically motivated violence received a penalty of not less than ten years in prison with hard labour. Politicians advocating violence were banned from taking part in elections. All parties signed a code of conduct that prevented the insulting of opponents. Anyone found breaking the code was given a heavy fine. It was made clear in the law that policemen and policewomen not acting in the face of political violence would be fired. Rigging of elections had become a criminal offence liable to a long term in jail.

The President strongly believed that a nation state existed as an agreement of all the people within its borders. Violation of this agreement undermined the bond of unity. It was therefore important to strengthen the democratic processes and institutions to help establish a strong society where no part of the country felt alienated.

The campaigns were held in a much civilised atmosphere. A few incidents of old mentality were quickly dealt with and order established. People appeared to have learnt that elections were important because they mattered; they had learned that the difference between poverty and good living was determined by their vote.

Although the outcome of the elections was again not in any doubt, President Kamawu campaigned with full energy and vigour. Many people were convinced that the President would come through with a big majority but that did not make him complacent. He visited all regions drawing huge crowds and explaining his manifesto and thanking the people for their cooperation with all the changes and for embracing change. The main opposition came from Matthew Kapoya.

Matthew Kapoya was the most loyal party member of Chimwanga's party. He hoped he could revive the party and rule again. He decided to stand as President. He had to be persuaded to do the basic course in democracy that everyone intending to be elected was required to take and pass.

It had been agreed that many people were joining politics without understanding how democracy operated. President Kamawu had introduced several courses to help people to understand democracy and how it worked. Kapoya thought it was a waste of time for politicians to go to schools. "You don't need qualifications to talk. Chimwanga was a president but did not go to school. He taught himself how to read and write. He knew how to speak and he became president. So these courses are not for me." As the deadline for nominations was coming close, his family told him that if he wanted to stand, he had no choice, times had changed.

During the campaigns, it was clear to everyone that the ruling party of President Kamawu was in complete control. Their rallies were well attended as usual. The President himself campaigned without relenting. He was more interested in the purity of the process than the actual results. He could have been re-elected without attending a single rally but he did not want to set a complacency syndrome.

Matthew Kapoya decided to use the old tricks. He turned up at the house of the returning officer at night to ask for his help. He offered him an envelope full of notes. The stunned officer took his telephone and called the police. Kapoya did not wait for the conversation to end. He grabbed the envelope and sprinted down the village.

Lubanda was a different country now. You could not corrupt anyone and get away with it. The population had been well educated into the ills of corruption and how it destroyed the country. In the early years of Moses' term in office, several businessmen and government officials had been jailed, shamed or lost trading licences for trying to corrupt someone. The police had been cleaned. They were not only paid well but their training now involved education in corruption. Anyone caught or reported was summarily dismissed.

Kapoya was a stubborn man. At one of his poorly attended meetings he told the few who dared to listen to him out of curiosity that he and Absalom would be a political force soon. The mention of Absalom invited the wrath of his audience and the police had to come and rescue him. He decided to use the tactics that worked so well for Chimawanga. Find unemployed street youths, buy them drugs and give them money then use them to terrorise the people into submission. He worked hard to disrupt his opponent's rally. The trouble was that there were not many street boys who needed money. Many had left the streets working or engaged in sensible activities. A few drug addicts would be his best bait. He hired fifteen of them and gave them drugs and machetes. Before the rally started, word had gone round the village that Kapoya had hired criminals to disrupt the rally. Half way through the rally, Kapoya's group struck. The police and the people beat them back and arrested them, several of them injured and bleeding. They did not have to wait to go to the priest to confess. Kapoya was arrested for distribution and possession of drugs, political violence and abusing vulnerable individuals. Political violence had been banned and the law had been strengthened to stamp out the violent behaviour that existed in Chimwanga's days. It was found to be counterproductive and not civil for a political democracy. His next stop was a cell in prison; he didn't even realise that his next door neighbour was Absalom.

When the results were formally announced that the President had secured another term in office with an unprecedented majority, there was an excuse for more euphoric celebrations, only this time it was a little sweeter. The country was ready and looking forward to many more good days to come.

Part IV

Chapter Twenty-Four

PRESIDENT KAMAWU'S second term passed quickly. He ran away with the second election winning by over ninety percent. The opposition, remnants of the Chimwanga party, got less than two percent of the votes. In fact, the erroneously spoiled votes were more than the votes cast for the opposition. Over the past fourteen years Lubanda had been transformed at every level. Although the third election was more competitive, DPPL candidates did very well. President Kamawu overlooked the process that observers concluded the fairest elections Africa had ever seen.

The second term of Moses' presidency was as memorable as the first for many reasons and there were many defining achievements. His most cherished project was the new Lubanda Academy of Scholars and Lubanda Scholars University. Projects long in the making but now complete and popularly named the seventh wonder of Lubanda. Credit for this spectacular institution went as much to President Kamawu as it went to Peter Sambondu.

Soon after his promotion to the board of Philips, the managing director suffered a stroke that left him incapacitated. Peter was immediately appointed to act as CEO. He remembered the tough conversation with the President when he rang to tell him he could not do two jobs.

"Good morning Mr President?"

"Good morning Mr Sambondu. Congratulations on your appointment, I'm pleased to learn of it."

"Thank you, Sir. That is the reason I am calling..."

"To tell me you cannot do my job?"

"Not exactly, Sir. That it will be difficult to do two jobs."

"What is your suggestion Mr Sambondu?"

"It is a tough decision, Sir."

"Mr Sambondu, there is no need to worry. I chose you because I wanted someone with corporate experience, an intelligent self-starter with passion for moving Lubanda forward. I suggest you continue chairing the group. I will add someone else to the team. I still believe you are the right man for this project. Becoming the managing director is a blessing because when you move to head the university you will be better equipped. We shall pay for all your expenses and I will write to your board chairman about this arrangement. If they want us to pay them we shall. Is it acceptable, Mr Sambondu?"

"Yes, Sir. Thank you for putting trust in me, I will not disappoint you."

Sambondu was not sure whether it was the President who engineered the promotion or whether he was simply taking advantage of him. But after nearly two years of countless meetings with the President, he had grown to know him and respected his judgement without question. The Phillips Board were happy to be associated with the project but would also benefit from the goodwill which soon paid off. Six months into the post Peter won a tender for electrical fittings and upgrading technology to the new Presidential palace. The only company to be allowed access to all the rooms in the palace. There was no evidence President Kamawu had anything to do with it although people were suspicious, but knowing how he did his business, he wouldn't be involved in such deals.

Only Rachel seemed to be aware of Peter's choice and why the President was so loyal to him. He once said he thought the man had integrity, intelligence and passion to one day lead this country, with good training. Although this conversation had never come up again, Rachel was convinced her husband had identified him and was training him through the university project.

After three years as the CEO of Phillips Peter resigned to concentrate on the project. The major milestone for the project was the completion of the plans and the model. On his 40th birthday, he flew home with a model of the new school and university completed. Peter was sitting by the window as the plane taxied to a stop. He was longing to be home and see his children. This was at least the tenth or twelfth time he had been to Boston in the last two years of President Kamawu's term of office. And for sure, it was not the last. This was after all the President's vanity project. Every bit of the plan had to be designed to his liking. Before the plans were unveiled the following week Peter had at least two days to catch up with work and celebrate his birthday with his family.

The model was taken straight to the Cabinet office and placed in a protected glass casing. Next to it was a screen for comments and a camera for remote viewing. Peter went to the office – not much was missed these days. He had evolved a way of handling both responsibilities. He carried special equipment for briefing from his office when he was abroad. He could even sign documents away from the office. But he still needed to brush with flesh to give his people assurance. He spent two hours going round the company each time he had been away for more than ten days.

By the time he got home he was shattered, but fortunately he came in early and slept before the children came back from school. After the now traditional kisses and gifts, he showed them pictures of the university model. He also showed them a big file with all the detailed plans of the new university as if to prove to them he was doing a job for the good of all.

He spent the day receiving good wishes and relaxing with children at home. Joyce told him that they were going out for a meal at one of the best hotels. They got prepared, jumped in their new Mercedes Benz with Joyce driving. Upon arrival, he realised it was not a meal but a huge party. The best kept secret had eluded the sharp thinking Peter. Even the children all colluded in keeping things from sight and memory.

Soon the jiving and eating started and the evening was filled with live bands and excited revellers. He actually learnt later it was a joint arrangement by the company, think tank and the family.

"Dad, tell us about the new university?"

"Yes, yes!" shouted the people, drunk and sober alike."

"I will show you a bit of it only. As you know I am in charge of the President's second vanity project. He wants to build Lubanda University of Excellence. Linked to it on another site will be a school for the super gifted. The school will enrol gifted children from all the primary schools. They will be given special selection tests and examinations. Those who get ninety and above percent will be selected and the state will be responsible for all their fees and needs. Although the school will have a capacity for three hundred children, its intake will depend on those qualifying. If in a year only five children qualify, that will be it. The entry requirements will never be altered."

"That is a waste of resources," someone shouted.

"No, it is intended to drive standards. Eventually he wants every secondary school to be a high achieving school."

"And the university," another half drunken deep voice echoed.

"Before I show you the pictures of the university, here are the pictures of the secondary school, what it will look like."

"Will I go there Dad?" Moses asked.

"I don't know sonny, you have to pass very well."

"I will pass very well."

Discussions broke out among the party revellers talking about the school. Parents were already planning for extra lessons for their children to aspire to this school.

"The university will be much like the school except bigger. All children shall be eligible to apply but again you have to pass with exceptional grades to qualify. It will specialise in engineering, maths, science and economic disciplines. He wants to nurture top class citizens in these fields. As of Monday you can view the proposed plans and the models. I cannot say much because the President himself will unveil it tomorrow."

"Well done Peter," shouted his friend across the room. "Will you be the chancellor?" he added before any response.

"Thank you very much, there is more food and drinks; please help yourselves. Remember this is my party, not the party for the vanity project!" Peter retorted as he went to help himself to the steaming chicken.

It took nearly five years to complete the buildings. Several Lubandan companies took part in the construction. It was a complicated building but the planning was excellent. The president himself was like a site engineer. He was often seen at the site in the evenings inspecting the work. At the time the construction was underway, Peter and his team recruited and trained teachers and lecturers and developed all entry examinations and tests. After leaving the company Peter was also appointed Champion of Business development, an advisory role in the office of the Vice President.

The opening of the university was a significant event attended by all who had input into the project. It was one of the largest gatherings of academicians in Lubanda. Both the school and the university were futuristic projects. The project underscored Moses' vision for Lubanda. He often talked about the technology, education and skill gaps between Lubanda and the developed countries. He decried the low standards on offer in most of the institutions. During his tenure, he had forced bogus and poor quality universities to close and put more money in all the state sponsored schools and universities. But he wanted one leading university that would be a beacon of standards. Whilst other presidents spent time building vanity projects for themselves, Moses put the country and people first. In fact, the university was one of three wonders of President Kamawu's reign; the other two being the State Palace and the Parliament.

They were all spectacular buildings with Unique Lubandan characteristics. The Parliament was upgraded with technology that enabled parliamentarians taking part in discussions if they were not physically in the house. The public would monitor their representatives by tuning in remotely to the online public gallery. There was no room to hide incompetence. This building, with a separate wing for the House of Indunas, was as good as you would find anywhere in the world. What was most astonishing was that all the projects were built on budget and without debt. Moses never embarked on any project without money. Every project big or small was costed and sources of funding identified. Only then would he start the project.

Kamawu's most loved pride was the University of Excellence. It took two years to plan and five years to build. In the last four years, it had become a world class institution. The secondary school became so popular that middle class parents were spending fortunes to train their children to qualify. Standards in all schools and universities in the country were rising. In two years, there had been three groundbreaking researches. It was observed that if the President was not in his office, he was probably at the university. If he was dozing and you asked him what the best achievement of his presidency was, he would say the university.

The research institutions were world class. This is what he loved best about his university. The laboratory for treatment of tropical diseases had already found a possible alternative cure for malaria. He even had grand plans for a space institute. He believed one day Lubandans would go into space. Lecturers had to pass tough examinations. Lubandan students were sponsored by the university and received free education. Only five percent of the places had been opened up to foreign students. An admission criterion was strictly followed. It was an elite institution for all Lubandans. Nobody would buy a place no matter how rich you were. It specialised in engineering, business and economics, science, and mathematics. The quality of students, personnel, and the facilities made it one of the leading institutions in the world.

Other important achievements of the second term of President Kamawu, were the new cultures and systems that had emerged. Given his proven record in his first term, it was not hard to convince the people to support his vision. Corruption had become a shameful and distasteful practice. Those found guilty served long sentences. Faith in the key institutions was gradually restored. The judiciary was held in good stead. Perhaps the greatest achievement was the migration of the minds of the police, intelligence services and armed forces from serving the party in government to serving the nation. Grey areas once abused by the previous governments had been clarified. In less than five years, the forces had become true professionals. The presidency was immensely respected. President Kamawu was never heard uttering insolent words at his opponents, not even at times of extreme provocation. A refreshing atmosphere compared to the times when Chimwanga would insult his opponents each time he opened his mouth. It was well known that under Moses ministers and civil servants were most in awe of the president because abuse of power, violation of the law or the constitution was ruthlessly punished, whether openly or behind closed doors.

A story is told of what happened to Permanent Secretary Kabusha, in the ministry of lands. The President wanted a piece of land for his cattle. He filled in the forms himself and sent them to the Ministry of Lands. This amused the office because no President had ever done that. They often identified a piece of land they wanted and the rest was done for them. Kabusha saw this as an opportunity to be in good standing with the President. He went to the land applied for, extended the boundary and forcibly removed the villagers. Six weeks later, the President went to see his land. He was horrified when he saw houses recently vacated.

"Mr. Kabusha, who lived here before you gave me the land?"

"The Kuunda village, Sir."

"Where are they, when did they move? Why did they move? How did they move?"

"When we gave you the land, Sir."

"Because you wanted to give me the land?"

"Yes, Sir."

"You did this in my name?"

"Yes Sir."

"Where are they?"

"Five miles down the stream."

He jumped into the car, drove off leaving the chauffer stranded and protesting.

The security and the rest of the people who were with him drove behind in silence. At the village he interviewed the surprised villagers. They told him that it was their ancestral village. They were sleeping in temporary grass shelters and had not been compensated. He told them to pack their belongings; he was going to send transport to take them back.

The next three days workers were sent to restore all the houses. On the fifth day all the villagers were returned to their land and given money and food. Kabusha did not only lose his job but he also paid the bill for repairing the houses. "We do not grab land from the people in the new Lubanda," he was told in no uncertain terms.

Strengthening democratic institutions and government organisations was an ongoing theme. He made sure that the codes of conduct for every office were being followed. There were no arbitrary decisions by government officials or the politicians. The next seven-year plan was the guiding blueprint. Every government institution had targets to achieve every year for the next seven years. Schools, hospitals, and all other service sectors had targets too. The overall target was excellence of provision. There was a defined description of excellence and steps to achieve excellence. Every office had a SWOT chart on the wall next to its plan of action. There was no mistaking that the civil service under Moses was professional and efficient.

All citizens were taught their roles of building and preserving a strong nation. They were told the ideal conditions for strong nation states, the dangers and how they all contributed. This was a painstaking exercise but necessary. Government and public property were respected and protected. There was a strong sense of patriotism.

Moses' vision was built on what came to be known as the 3Ds. He told his people that development comes with learning. People should learn new skills and increase their knowledge. Thinking within the confines of your physical experience limits your imagination. Until recently, people in Lubandan had very little knowledge of experiences of other people abroad. Much of what they knew was through films and television. These, according to Moses, were superficial sources of knowledge because it was constructed knowledge. Lubandan had to become a learning nation; this was the first of the 3Ds, D-Learn.

The second D was his philosophy that development came about when people earned. "You cannot change your life circumstances for the better if you have no money," he would say. This involved enhancing the people's ability to earn; good jobs, growing businesses, entrepreneurship and innovation. D-Earn.

The third D was that development required changing the mind-set. The mind-set of inferiority complex, self-rejection and poverty conditions the mind to stagnation. Lubandans needed a change in their mind-set, D-Mind. For each of these areas, there was a champion to lead on it.

Delilah had grown in her post as Vice President and potential President. The president liked her because she was hard working and understood the vision of the president. As far as her work was concerned, she was impeccable and a worthwhile understudy. However, the nation had grown concerned about her as a cultural symbol of the nation. There was a wide difference between her and Rachel. Rachel was regarded as a model because she projected traditional values. Delilah did not command this admiration. They did not like the way she dressed which they said did not reflect Lubandan decency. She was also too social, sometimes being found in places demeaning her position. Rumour had it that she often disguised herself and attended night clubs. There were so many rumours about her that nobody cared to prove them.

However, the President was still loyal to her. He defended her publicly and though privately it was widely believed that she was often rebuked. When her second pregnancy became public knowledge, it was met with great disapproval. The future president should not be having children out of wedlock. There were cries for her to be dropped from her post. The President was becoming embroiled in the issues. Although his ratings remained very high, people were questioning his loyalty and judgement to his VP. Thoughts of a romantic relationship were long banished and unthinkable but people were worried it might not be long before Delilah brought down the government.

Her maternity leave early in the second term was a necessary reprieve for both. Peter was drafted in to help and he was assigned various responsibilities in the office of the Vice President. Although Peter lacked the charm of Delilah, he was a very hard worker and intelligent man. He assumed the responsibilities of overseeing some aspects of the Emancipation Programme.

By the time Peter left to open and head the university, he had become the third well known individual other than Moses and Delilah. Moses had even persuaded him to set up an innovation centre in the school of economics at the new university: a centre for providing information to entrepreneurs; a department for developing innovative ideas and a department for trialling new ideas – a responsibility that would keep Peter in the limelight.

The Emancipation programme had worked remarkably well. When it was launched, the IMF and the World Bank criticised it as being irresponsible. According to them, austerity was the only answer. The governments before Chimwanga had tried the IMF and the World Bank treatment but it did not work. To stop a government from providing essential services only the government can provide is irresponsible. The socio-economic consequences resulted in poor health and deepened poverty. Chimwanga's mismanagement made the situation almost irretrievable.

Some economists criticised President Kamawu for providing capital either by cash or guarantee as a recipe for economic failure because governments are not good at running businesses. They are better off confining themselves to policy making. There was fear of inflation as well.

President Kamawu was not dissuaded by these arguments. He believed that the circumstances of Lubanda required a different approach. He would try it and if it failed, he would have to think of other alternatives. This is the reason he did not get any loans from the IMF or the World Bank, fundamental economic differences. He believed in trying something new. He also believed appropriate leadership was essential for any strategy to be successful.

Several years on President Kamawu was right. The Lubandan economy was not only bucking the trend but registering real term growth. The economy was not driven by trickledown economics, the economic myth used to perpetuate privilege as Delilah described it, but it was growth marshalled by all citizens and sectors. The government was bringing in a lot of revenue from taxes and dividends. The President praised Vice President Delilah for much of the success in implementing the programmes. She had an incredible ability to explain complex concepts to the ordinary people. Once she understood what Moses was trying to do, she wholeheartedly embraced it and explained it to the people. She could easily operate at the level of ordinary people. Like the President, everything they did was a mission. It was not all smooth sailing but it was working. This is one reason the President held on to Delilah. He always defended her, maintaining that she was not a traditional high priest, a position he would not consider her for because her CV would fall short.

The family loans programme had taken off equally well. Peter's first task was to consolidate this programme which took him to every corner of the country. There were small, medium and a few large businesses. The next step was to develop strong associations for similar industries. The associations would help not only in marketing the products and services but help to compete with similar businesses overseas. They maintained standards and continued to train their members. Like all other initiatives started by Moses' government, there had been thorough research and the right people trained and deployed. This was the next stage of development. Although a few businesses had been taken over by the government, thousands of these worked extremely well and had become a serious sector of growth. There were associations for every sector, retail, manufacturing, training and many more.

The President formed a new autonomous department to manage and oversee the Emancipation programme and government investments. This department was like a parastatal organisation with a difference. All its activities were enshrined in law, for fear of misuse by successive governments. The powers of the government were spelt out and precisely defined.

At the time Moses took over power, Lubanda did not lack entrepreneurs. For their survival many Lubandans were involved in one form of business or another. However, these were all small ventures with overpriced goods. Many of the goods they sold came from abroad. The President tapped into this industrious culture and encouraged local businessmen to go into manufacturing. In some parts of the country, small businesses formed cooperatives. The government provided machinery and management in return for some shares. In his fourteenth year, manufacturing had become another important sector of the economy. Peter's job was to sell the government shares to the public. His aim was to make the economy truly owned by Lubandans. Overseas investors were welcome but the only catch was that part of their investment was owned by the locals. No foreign investor owned more than fifty-one percent. This arrangement benefited the country as skills were transferred to Lubandans. Again contrary to what some economists had argued that investors would not come to Lubanda, it became the choice country for investment.

The President had come up with many clever ideas to help the economy. As a firm believer in fifty-fifty benefits, he wooed investment from Black Americans. They were given the same incentives as the Lubandan diaspora returning to the country. Of course this was not all about economics; it lay in his belief of building bonds with black people globally. "The English had special relationships with the Australians so why can't the Lubandans?" he would challenge his critics.

Another smart move was the establishment of trade alliances and cultural exchange with the Caribbean countries. After his visit, they agreed to form an Afro-Caribbean Union. A number of African countries joined in and in the past two years they changed the name to Union of Black countries. Trade between these countries had soared, to mutual benefits. There was now growing political influence from this cooperation. A few countries who had taken advantage of both regions in the past were starting to play their usual card of divide and rule. For now, this was not likely to succeed.

While the first term had laid the foundations of prosperity the second term saw the boom of prosperity. Many Lubandans were running away with the wave of prosperity but there were some who remained behind. President Kamawu had an ambitious target, to offer opportunity for lifting every single Lubandan out of poverty. Lifting people out of poverty involved freeing them from constant worries of basic needs: food, shelter and clothing. At least every Lubandan was dressed. Parents with more children who could not afford to meet the clothing needs of the family were given help. This the president ticked off his list.

He never stopped telling the Lubandans that there were three layers of involvement that would bring development to the people. Firstly, there were things the people would do for themselves such as acquiring new skills and starting businesses. In the past citizens had been made to believe the government would do everything for them. The second agency of development according to Moses was the regional government. There were things the people could not do for themselves such as providing amenities and security. Thirdly there were things the central government could do; providing infrastructure such as roads and policies that helped the economy to grow. The reason they were not progressing in the past was that the three layers were not functioning. Every Lubandan, assisted by the government, was advised to write a plan of what it meant to them to progress and steps of how to move forward. Moses strongly believed that the traditional institutions of villages, chiefs and village headmen was an asset that needed to be revitalised and used to achieve development. Each of these layers was obliged to draw plans for progress. These institutions and government functions were harmonised and complementary but with clear lines of operation. He offered the headmen an allowance in return for monitoring and championing development. "Use the people that are trusted by the community and they will deliver if properly managed."

The family loans had boosted food production. The initiative to build food silos in every constituency with smaller ones in various wards guaranteed food security. Farmers would sell their surplus to the agricultural boards who stored it locally. This helped stem food shortages. There was a drive to provide clean piped water. The government undertook to fund this but asked those who were able to contribute by paying for the water.

Shelter was the biggest problem but even this was achievable. The special bond established in the first term had accumulated sufficient resources to provide decent shelter to all Lubandans who needed it. Many citizens had built their own houses. A scheme was initiated to help the most needy people.

The strands of the Moses' Emancipation plan were fully embedded in the community with accountability structures. Retired civil servants who were unable to work were encouraged to offer their skills to the local community. "All I have to do is unleash the power of the people," Moses would often be heard saying at meetings. The skill base had been strongly widened with people feeling independent and empowered. Much of the state borrowing to enhance citizen skills and development was on target with excellent recovery rate. The Moses Plan, code-named the 'Lubandan Marshall Plan', had captured the imagination of not only the Lubandans but the region as well.

The economy was creating enough jobs for everyone. The discovery of new minerals that were used to manufacture safe identity chips to be embedded in people had boosted the economy. There had also been a boom in agriculture as a result of the climate changes. Lubanda was fortunate to be getting a fair amount of water for agriculture while many countries suffered serious droughts. These trends helped President Kamawu to advance his agenda. It was a miraculous economic boom. The prudence of the management of the public funds enabled the country to develop and build up a health reserve.

There were several vanity projects by the private sector. The government gave tax breaks to companies and organisations who wanted to put up a project that would add value to Lubanda PlC. By the time President Kamawu was exiting the presidency, the landscape of Lubanda was changed permanently.

President Kamawu had a secret agenda, or was it just unfounded fear? He strongly believed that he had a mission to save the generations unborn. He came to this theme regularly, more so in his last term. He said history was going to repeat itself and that there would be a threat to enslave the black people. He said, "Ideas don't die, they run out of steam until the next incubating conditions." He therefore feared that the young and unborn Lubandans might be enslaved, recolonized or even mass slaughtered like the Jews were under Hitler. He ordered that history of slavery be taught more effectively to help the young people understand this danger. Lessons taught not only the history of slavery and colonialism but the Jewish holocaust. Teachers were asked deliberately to teach children resilience strategies. The other component of this strategy was teaching a curriculum that raised awareness of the dangers that lie beyond the borders.

At the Think Tank leadership conference, he spoke scathingly of the African Leaders' inept attitude and for wasting time in office instead of raising awareness and building resilience for the black people. He was convinced the Black led governments did not use their time wisely to prevent a black holocaust. They were complacent after the emancipation of slavery acts and acquisition of political independence in Africa. Bad people did not die with Hitler; racism was an ever present danger to a black person.

He established a secret unit at the new university that researched and published a digest of social, scientific and political trends across the world, especially those relating to the Religion of Race and which may have implications to be used as racial weapons. Code named *Invisible Threat Team*, its publications were secretly distributed. The second strand was building up a capable military defence. Government land and mineral policies always carried impact assessment to ensure that no decisions were being made which in future would disadvantage the Lubandan. His fears became a reality when the United Nations suddenly collapsed.

The President was working on the last draft of his speech to the United Nations in three days' time. He was scheduled to leave that evening. The Director of the Invisible Team walked into his office.

"Good afternoon, Sir, I am sorry to come without an appointment."

"That's fine, please sit down. I expect you have something important to say."

"Sir, we think you should not fly tonight."

"Why? I'm just finishing my speech."

"Sir, we think the UN will collapse. As you may well know, Sir, the Eastern Power has threatened to take more countries by marching its armies into five of their bordering countries. The United States of America tabled a resolution to suspend the Eastern Power from the UN but this was blocked by many nations. The new US President has therefore unilaterally suspended its membership of the UN. He felt that the USA had done a lot for the world but it is not appreciated. He has ordered his forces serving in non-strategic parts of the world to return home. They have changed their strategy to defending the mainland instead of the world. 'The rest of the world will look after themselves,' he said as he ended his state of the union speech. As you would expect, their closest allies have equally suspended their membership. In the news an hour ago, the U.S.A has asked the UN secretary general to seek an alternative country to host the UN."

"Is this an overreaction?"

"It has been coming, Sir. We published an article a year ago in which we stated that there were strong voices in the USA questioning the ungrateful world they have helped to save since 1945. Meanwhile the Eastern Superpower has been building up its defence capabilities and increasing its hostility."

"Thank you very much Director."

Moses immediately constituted a special team and tasked them with analysing the implications of this unprecedented development. They spent days looking at the world order before the second world war, the losers and winners and what Lubanda must do to defend itself. Much more, which side should Lubanda support? After many late nights, they finalised a strategy: *The Defence of Lubanda* – a document, the content of which was a state secret, that would potentially save Lubanda deep into the twenty second century.

Not long after the collapse of the UN, the Eastern superpower had colluded in the overthrow and destabilisation of a neighbouring country south of Lubanda. It was a state smaller than Lubanda that had for many years embraced citizens from the Eastern superpower to the exclusion of black Africans. The migrants bought large chunks of land and they were now in charge of sixty percent of the economy. The overthrown president tried to prevent the remaining forty percent from being owned by these people. He realised rather too late that without land available to the Southern state, people will struggle and possibly perish. The indigenous people were already being squeezed, economically, politically and on the land. The settlers had more representation in the parliament than at any time in their history. The Eastern Superpower marched in and overthrew the government of the people. It was an open bullying of a state by another. There was no UN to turn to and what the region thought was a distant problem was now right on their doorstep. After all, most of these countries backed the Eastern Power during the General Assembly vote. Was this the beginning of the next official scramble for Africa?

President Kamawu was alarmed at this prospect, but prepared. The country would not stand for many days if attacked by the Eastern Superpower but he had a strategy to put up a formidable fight. The invasion of the southern state would occupy Moses' remaining time in office and possibly define his future. In his last days, he was confident Lubanda would be safe. However, this was not true regarding the other countries. Many of them, because of greed and ignorance, had not seen the danger coming. There had also been tensions in the region following the chasing away of black people from some of the countries while embracing non-black foreigners who were now turning on them.

Moses and his *think tanks* had studied how the white people colonised Africa. It started with one or two coming, offering gifts to the chiefs and asking for land. Usually a missionary with a bible in one hand. With the backing of their home countries with whom they shared their spoils as taxes or shares in their companies, they increased in number and influence to the point when they declared themselves administrators. Armed with superior weapons, they conquered, occupied and plundered. This pattern was repeated at the beginning of the 21st century and would end up in the same way, occupation and possible annihilation of the so-called black race. He spent the last year in office trying to work with some of the countries to increase awareness and build defences. He risked being singled out by those who saw him as a threat and risked being betrayed by the sheepish leaders but it was a risk worth taking. In addition, he needed powerful allies in the absence of the UN. He studied the situations carefully and decided on whom to build alliances with. He worked so hard convincing the other leaders that by the time he was leaving office, there was a realisation that African leaders should look beyond their time to prevent aliens occupying the continent and driving every African into the oceans.

Chapter Twenty-Five

"**SO HELP ME GOD.**" President Moses Kamawu offered his hand to the new President and said, "Congratulations," then turned round and waved to the subdued crowd. The people broke into sobs and cheers. He waved with both hands, bowed to the crowd and walked slowly down the podium. Rachel spotted a tear down his cheek which was quickly wiped; it was the second time since becoming a president that the man cried. "How he loves his people," she whispered as she hurried down to join the exit salute.

The first day of the 21st Century was a unique and memorable year for Lubanda in more ways than one. It was the first turn of the new century so there were celebrations. It was also the day the new Lubandan President would be sworn in but most importantly, it was the day President Kamawu was handing over power. This was the most important of all the events taking place simultaneously.

The last month in office was very busy for President Kamawu. He was expected to go round the country thanking people and to make sure the elections run smoothly. He had invested much in the political process so he wanted it to run well. His reputation hinged on these elections. There was energetic political activity in the country with new parties wishing to challenge the DPPL candidate. Moses saw his role as a statesman who should preside over a fair election. He was more concerned with the process and not necessarily the outcome. He knew his candidate would win but it ought to be a clean franchise.

He travelled all over the country commissioning new projects and bidding the people a farewell. They would have loved him to continue but they dared not say it to him. He had told the nation in no uncertain terms that "Great nations are not built by an individual leader. They are built by the cumulative impact of good leadership and new ideas. The longer you hang around in power the more likely you are to become complacent and possibly corrupt as you seek to defend your mistakes. It is good for the country for a long-lasting president to leave."

The tours had taken him to every corner of the land. His last visits were to Lubanda Central hospital and a primary school in the once most deprived part of the city. The hospital was almost in ruins when he took office. It was the last hospital to be rehabilitated and refurbished. Much of it required rebuilding. Joyce who was now an undisputed guru of turning around failing hospitals in the country, had been promoted to a key position at the Ministry of Health and took upon herself the responsibility of reshaping this institution. Now that it was complete and all the staff retrained, it was fitting to be the last hospital to be commissioned by the outgoing president.

All hospitals in the country had new beds, bedding and additional facilities. Standards were high all round. But the Central Hospital had a different status. Not quite a vanity project but not far from it. As the president went round the wards, sitting on beds, greeting patients and talking to staff, it had become the symbol of health care and political will. In Chimwanga's days, it was a dirty, smelly building where you walked in with tissue to spit on. Going to this hospital was a death warrant. Now the President could sit on the bed and drink tea with patients. The staff from the cleaners to the doctors were smartly dressed and professional. Many patients who had deserted to go to the private clinics were coming back. It was not only physical change but a cultural shift as well. The patients and the staff saw it as their hospital. Of course they said their President built it as well. It was a cherry on top of the healthcare transformation. As Moses left, patients who could manage to leave their beds, some with intravenous bags hanging from supports, stood together with the staff to present a guard of honour for the man they called the real president. "There was one Mandela, there will always be one Kamawu. Great leaders do not come easily," said the Chief Medical Officer as she waved her hand to the departing presidential motorcade.

The last afternoon in office was spent in a primary school in what used to be the worst part of the city where nobody wanted to visit either as a professional or a relative. In this part of the city you dodged bullets and people on the road. Human excrement was flowing in the streets. It was indeed a slum – and yet it became the measure of the success of the government. In here, anyone who was going to change it, even a little, would be remembered as a hero for life.

Over the past fourteen years, Moses took on this challenge. First he tackled the sewage system to generate belief. After persuading companies and mobilising the local people, the sewage system was improved. Once the people saw this change, they became the most committed and complying citizens. At last they were being treated as human beings. The government redesigned the area and built decent accommodation. Using all the different initiatives available the houses were completed in the tenth year. The last project in the development plan for this area was this school. The president had piloted schools that comprised a nursery, the primary and secondary school built next to each other and feeding each other. Many of these schools were popular and ideal for this location. Considering the population density, they needed five of these schools in this area. The President spent the afternoon talking to children and staff. Parents and well-wishers came in full support to thank him. He did not have to tell them to look after their school because as he was going past one classroom in the secondary school, he heard one boy telling off the other for graffiti on the table. "This is my property, it is your property and it is your child's property, look after it well. Remove the graffiti now!" The Headteacher explained to the President who stopped to eavesdrop that the students and parents were proud of their school and in a way policed it themselves.

The beaming President called the girl, thanked her and told her that one day she should be a minister of education. Thousands of residents gathered to bid him farewell. He praised and thanked them for their patience, co-operation and hard work. "This," he declared, "is the symbol of my time as President."

The local MP who could not contain his joy stood up after the President. "Ladies and gentlemen, what should we call this school?" he asked. In unison the reply came: "Moses Kamawu School!" This part was so spontaneous that it took everyone including the President by surprise. "Any opposition to the name?" he asked.

"No," came the answer. It was the first school to be named after President Kamawu by the people, not the council; and the first and last to be named after the President while still in office. He resisted such overtures while he was in government but this one he had no occasion to turn it down.

As the motorcade left the school, the residents and the children lined the streets and sang: "Moses, Mosses, Moses!" The chanting could be heard in the distance.

Moses' last press conference as President was held in the room where he held the first one. He actually moved back to his house six months before the final day. Fewer journalists who attended his first press conference were present. Many had retired or moved on.

After fourteen years of hard work, Lubanda was standing tall among many nations. With the politics sorted, the economy literally built from scratch, Lubanda was on course for real development. As Moses wound down his second term in office, he was full of pride for the work he had done while the people were sad he was going but thankful for putting them on a purposeful journey. This was the mood in the room, a mix of celebration and sadness.

When he entered the room, there was no one sitting down. They clapped and clapped while Moses nodded to acknowledge the gesture. After the usual national anthem and introductions, President Kamawu took the stage. He was relaxed, jovial and jokey. He thanked them all for their good work for representing him and misrepresenting him sometimes. One could not mistake the respectful atmosphere in the room. It was a blessing to be in the presence of greatness. Everyone in the room had benefited from the ideas and actions of this man. As for what he did to Lubanda, the living, the dead as well as the unborn would forever be grateful. His influence and the influence of Lubanda had gone far beyond its borders. Delegations were arriving and leaving every week to see for themselves and to learn from this country.

Like most great men and women, pride of achievements was differentiated from the lust of the heart. He was humble in admitting his great gifts. When he tuned into his thinking mode and began talking to you, you appreciated the power of harnessed intelligence and wisdom. His ability to engage with the common man as well as university professors, national leaders and friends alike, in a way that showed them respect yet unobtrusively pointed out their faults and shortcomings when necessary, was unique. After the failed coup attempt he addressed the leaders of the region with the leader of the southern state present. It is believed that he attended against the wishes of all the other leaders. In fact it was Moses who convinced the other leaders not to walk away from the meeting because of his presence.

He stood up and praised the achievements of the leader of the southern state who felt good and began nodding. Having said this, he turned to the consequences of each of the achievements and as he drew his chair to sit down, the leader of the southern state had no idea what had hit him, being too ashamed to raise his head, and yet too angry to have been led into this trap. His reputation and achievements had crumbled before his eyes. He was too afraid to confront this young eloquent leader, for any such attempts would have been suicidal of course – because Moses rarely lost arguments or debates.

One of the lines of attack on him was his claim to a status of a statesman. President Kamawu started by praising statesmen in the region since the leader of the southern state wanted to be called a statesman. Then he broke loose: "A statesman who denies his people freedom is no statesman but a prison warder. A statesman whose people are worse off than they were under the colonial settlers is no statesman but an illusionist. A statesman who sends troupes into another country without provocation is an angel of death, a danger to the region who needs to be moved out of office." Then he turned round and faced him squarely: "Old man, you will never be a statesman. If that is your dream, it is fantasy. I have enough forces to attack you but since no Lubandan died, I hold my fire. However, never ever meddle in the affairs of Lubanda at night, during the day or in your remaining time in office." It is believed that this humiliating address coupled with the evidence Moses provided for the other leaders weakened him and ignited the flames of the opposition that eventually pushed him out of power unceremoniously.

So the journalists knew the power beyond the humility. Besides, this was not the time to rough the edges; it was a time for appreciation and celebration. Like many of the citizens they felt that another term in office for him was acceptable. He could have easily extended his reign with their approval but he had convinced them to accept his will. It is true some leaders are born, others are made. Surely, Moses belonged to the former. Lubanda was fortunate he was born Lubandan.

"Mr President, which of your achievements would you regard the greatest?"

"The University of Excellence."

"Why?"

"It will provide knowledge and produce future leaders for Lubanda."

"What does one need to be a successful leader?"

"Brains, conviction and wisdom."

"Mr President, you are leaving power now even when you can still go on. What advice do you have for those leaders who want to be leaders for life?"

"Leave now. You are not indispensable."

"Why do you think they don't want to go?"

"They are scared of shadows of incompetence."

"What are you going to do after leaving office?"

"Do you want to give me a job? I am going to rest, tender my orchard and spend time with my family. And perhaps lecture at the University of Excellence for a day if my CV will meet their standards."

"What are the political threats for Lubanda?"

"There are many potential threats from within and without. A country like Lubanda should always be ready to defend itself. Racism and the power of the East are undoubtedly the greatest threats."

"How about the West, Sir?"

"They are more predictable so it is easier to plan. Their institutions and values help to bring about this understanding. The Eastern power is shrouded in secrecy and they choose when the rule of law becomes relevant."

"What are the chances that Lubanda will not slip back?"

"There is always a possibility of stumbles along the way. That is why we have strengthened the systems, changed the mind-set of the nation and trained Lubandans to be the custodians of their nation. We have realigned our traditional values with a modern society. I am confident the foundations will hold strong in many more years to come. You might wish to know that we have plans until 2150. If future leaders stick to the plans, there will be fewer problems."

"How would you like to be remembered?"

"A Lubandan who helped lay down the foundation of progress and prosperity."

"What is Abel intending to do?"

"I want him to be a successful Lubandan but he wants to be president one day. That is for him and Lubandans."

"And the girls?"

"I have no idea; I think they are more ambitious than Abel!"

"Ladies and gentlemen, I invite you to a photograph for my wall. Thank you very much and I wish you and Lubanda all the best hereafter."

All journalistic hats on the floor, they gave him a long standing ovation.

"We shall miss him," said one journalist who had attended every single press conference of President Kamawu. She wiped away a tear and rushed out to try and sit next to him for the photograph.

Now it was time to exit. As Moses descended from the stage, the new President who was equally fighting emotions of joy and sorrow shouted to the crowd: "Ladies and gentlemen, fellow Lubandans, there goes the Real President! There goes the true statesman!"

End